"*What a delight to escape into the world of the irrepressible Poppy Denby in this cleverly-plotted debut.*"
Ruth Downie, author of the *Medicus* series

"*A delightful period romp, neatly sprinkled with the choicest historical detail.*"
D.J. Taylor, author of *Bright Young People*

"*An intriguing mystery, fizzing with energy.*"
C.F. Dunn, author of *Mortal Fire*

THE
JAZZ FILES

POPPY DENBY
INVESTIGATES

Fiona Veitch Smith

LION FICTION

Published by Lion Fiction
an imprint of
Lion Hudson plc
Wilkinson House, Jordan Hill Road
Oxford OX2 8DR, England
www.lionhudson.com/fiction

ISBN 978 1 78264 175 9
e-ISBN 978 1 78264 176 6

First edition 2015

Acknowledgments
Extract pp. 151–152 taken from *Wilfred Owen: The War Poems* (Chatto & Windus, 1994) ed. Jon Stallworthy, copyright © Wilfred Owen. Used by permission.

A catalogue record for this book is available from the British Library

Printed and bound in the UK, August 2015, LH26

For my mam, Elizabeth Veitch.

I miss you.

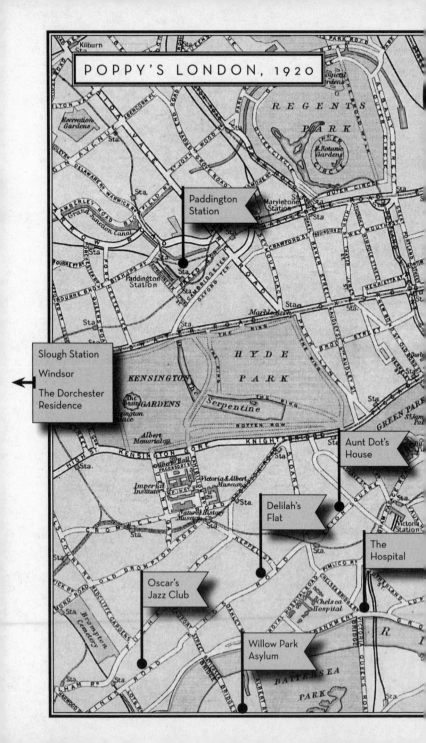

POPPY'S LONDON, 1920

Paddington Station

Slough Station

Windsor

The Dorchester Residence

Aunt Dot's House

Delilah's Flat

The Hospital

Oscar's Jazz Club

Willow Park Asylum

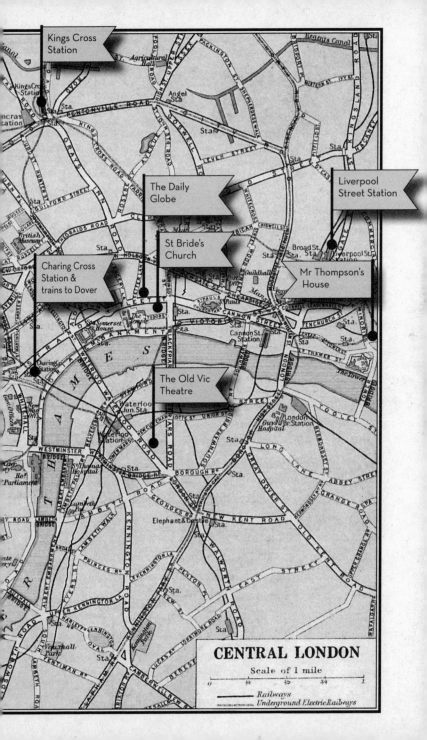

Kings Cross
Station

The Daily
Globe

Liverpool
Street Station

St Bride's
Church

Charing Cross
Station &
trains to Dover

Mr Thompson's
House

The Old Vic
Theatre

CENTRAL LONDON

Scale of 1 mile

0   ¼   ½   ¾   1

—————— Railways
Underground Electric Railways

Acknowledgments

Thank you to Tony Collins, who has believed in me as a writer for over eight years and guided me to write the kind of book I really needed to write. Thank you too to Jess Tinker of Lion Fiction, who caught the spirit of Poppy Denby from very early on – you truly are a flapper at heart.

Thank you to my fellow Lion Fiction authors, Elizabeth Flynn and Claire (CF) Dunn, who have supported me through the waiting times. As a fellow pride member of the Lioness Club, I can't wait for our next "hunt".

Speaking of all things feline, my thanks go (posthumously) to Denby the cat, much loved and missed moggie of my friends Trevor and Caroline Flint, from whom I took Poppy's surname. Her first name was suggested by Elizabeth Flynn. Thanks, Fizz!

I am also grateful for the prayers and support of the un-reverend Aaron Parsons, who – for reasons known only to himself – was desperate that I include a ninja cat in my story. Sorry, there is no cat, but I wouldn't have been surprised if dear Denby had turned into a ninja at night.

A hearty big thank you is also due to my editor Julie Frederick, who brought a great deal of spit and polish to the manuscript and somehow knew how to turn those pesky "close quotation marks" the right way round. And while I'm tossing bouquets, can Jess Scott, Simon Cox and Rachel Ashley-Pain line up too?

Thanks too to CSI Paul Trembling, who advised me on the drying times of blood and ink. Without him I would still be experimenting with pin pricks and a stop watch in the kitchen. And finally, to my wonderful family, Rodney and Megan, who since they first heard the name Poppy Denby in that Rothbury cottage, have made room for her in their hearts and in our home.

Characters

Fictional characters

Poppy Denby – cub reporter on *The Daily Globe*.

Dot Denby – Poppy's aunt. A former West End leading lady and infamous suffragette.

Grace Wilson – Aunt Dot's companion. An accountant and former suffragette.

Frank Wilson – Grace Wilson's estranged husband. Former women's suffrage activist.

Delilah Marconi – nightclub dancer, socialite flapper and up-and-coming actress.

Gloria Marconi – Delilah's mother, suffragette and former actress.

Elizabeth Dorchester – former suffragette.

Lord Melvyn Dorchester – Elizabeth's father, Tory peer and leading industrialist.

Viscount Alfie Dorchester – Elizabeth's brother, Bright Young Person, recipient of the Victoria Cross.

Lady Maud Dorchester – Elizabeth's mother and a suffragette.

Sophie Blackburn – researcher at the Radium Institute, Paris, former nurse and suffragette.

Marjorie Reynolds – leading female MP.

Oscar Reynolds – Marjorie's son, owner of Oscars' Jazz Club.

Mr Thompson – a window cleaner.

Mrs Thompson – Mr Thompson's wife.

Vicky Thompson – Mr Thompson's daughter.

Billy Thompson – Mr Thompson's son.

DCI Richard Easling – detective chief inspector with Scotland Yard, Metropolitan Police.

Rollo Rolandson – editor of *The Daily Globe*, originally from New York.

Daniel Rokeby – photographer at *The Daily Globe*.

Bert Isaacs – political editor at *The Daily Globe*.

Lionel Saunders – arts editor at *The Daily Globe*.

Mavis Bradshaw – receptionist at *The Daily Globe*.

Ivan Molanov – archivist at *The Daily Globe*.

Miss Swan – member of Thomas Cook touring party to Paris.

Henri – receptionist at The Radium Institute, Paris.

HISTORICAL CHARACTERS

Marie Curie – head scientist and founder of The Radium Institute, Paris. Joint Nobel laureate for the discovery of radium.

Lilian Baylis – founder of The Old Vic Theatre, London. Later to found the National Theatre, Opera and Ballet.

Robert Atkins – leading West End actor and director. Director of Shakespeare at The Old Vic.

Charlie Chaplin – Hollywood film star, writer, director and producer. Originally from London.

Coming

By Charlotte Perkins Gilman

Because the time is ripe, the age is ready,
Because the world her woman's help demands,
Out of the long subjection and seclusion
Come to our field of warfare and confusion
The mother's heart and hands.

Long has she stood aside, endured and waited,
While man swung forward, toiling on alone;
Now, for the weary man, so long ill-mated,
Now, for the world for which she was created,
Comes woman to her own.

Not for herself! though sweet the air of freedom;
Not for herself, though dear the new-born power;
But for the child, who needs a nobler mother,
For the whole people, needing one another,
Comes woman to her hour.

*From: **Suffrage Songs and Verses** by Charlotte Perkins Gilman
(1860–1935). New York: The Charlton Company, 1911.*

Chapter 1

5 November 1913

A scattering of snow lay across the railway yard, transforming the industrial clutter into a picture postcard: a work of art that could be hung for a night but removed when light and sanity returned. A woman, whose skeletal frame was wrapped in a coat that had once been worn to Royal Ascot and a silk scarf that had graced the owner's neck at a reception at Windsor Castle, picked her way from sleeper to sleeper. She hoped to reach the commuter station at Slough before the snow soaked through her kidskin shoes and her frozen fingers lost all feeling.

A whiz, squeal, bang caught her attention and she watched as green, blue, and red flares lit up the sky above the roof of the locomotive sheds. She wondered for a while what it might be, not really caring, but at least it gave her mind something to think about apart from the limb-numbing cold.

Ah, it's Guy Fawkes, she concluded, not knowing the exact date, but feeling that it must be early November. She counted back the days, the weeks, and the months to the end of July when she had been arrested and dragged to the Old Bailey to be tried. If she'd known then that she would be kept in the same clothes for the whole of her three-month sentence she would have worn something more appropriate on the day she joined her sisters to firebomb the members' stand at Lord's.

Her stomach growled. It had been days since she'd last had a proper meal – if you could call a porridge of milk and bread pumped through her nose a meal. She'd managed to scavenge some late blackberries from the hedgerow near her family estate in Windsor, and her hands were stained the colour of claret. Her face probably was too, but she had not stopped to check in one of the gilt-framed mirrors when she'd broken into her former home. She had one thing, and one thing only, in mind: to retrieve the cedarwood box from the safe. She had been surprised to see so few servants about – which made her clandestine task easier – and as another barrage of fireworks lit up the night she realized that most of them would have been attending the bonfire party held in the grounds of the manor house every year. So she had snuck in and snuck out without being noticed, with the precious cargo tucked safely away in the canvas satchel she carried slung over one shoulder.

She had just one more thing to do before she could get on the train to Paddington on the first step of her journey to freedom. She and her friend Gloria – who had also been held at Holloway prison – had agreed to meet between the railway yard and the station at Slough. The cedarwood box would be handed over and in return she would receive a one-way ticket from Southampton to New York. Gloria would then take the box to the sisters in Chelsea, who would turn it over to the authorities.

The flurry of snow was becoming a steady fall. The woman took her thick auburn plait and tucked it into the collar of her coat. *Just around the next bend,* she thought and resolutely quickened her pace.

The tracks running on either side of her began to vibrate. A train was coming. She stepped off the line and continued her journey a safe distance away from the locomotive track. She rounded the bend at the same time as the train on its return journey from Slough. In the spotlight she saw a woman: about ten years older than her with long, wild black hair under a floppy green felt hat. It was Gloria. The auburn-haired woman raised her arm in greeting, but as she did a shadowy figure ran at full pelt and launched itself at her friend. Gloria's scream was drowned by the howl of the locomotive releasing its steam and all the auburn-haired woman could see until the train chugged past was a cloud as white as the falling snow.

And then she saw Gloria, a broken rag doll on the tracks. The train screeched to an emergency stop behind her. She stumbled towards her friend, but as she did, the shadow emerged from the cloud, hands outstretched. It called her name. She ran.

10 JUNE 1920

Poppy Denby emerged from the steam of the *Flying Scotsman* onto Platform 1 of King's Cross station, hauling her trunk behind her. She looked around, hoping someone had come to meet her, and was disheartened to find she was alone. She checked the station clock to confirm that the time of arrival she had telegraphed to the people who were supposed to meet her was correct. Four o'clock in the afternoon – exactly on time. She shuffled a little further down the platform, as quickly as the weight of her trunk would allow her, to see if perhaps someone was waiting beyond the crowd of people and reporters who were gathered around a dais. But there was no one there.

Poppy, wearing her fawn coat with brown-fur trim, fawn cloche hat and brown T-bar shoes, blended in anonymously with the other commuters. The colours did nothing to enhance her pale, northern complexion, which might have been brightened if she had allowed her honey-blonde curls to escape the tightly wound chignon at the nape of her neck. And her eyes, like two bluebells on a frosty morning, would have lit up the whole platform brighter than the camera flashes, if they could be seen under the low-slung brim of her mother's choice of sensible hat.

Poppy skirted the back of the crowd surrounding the dais and heard someone giving a speech: "Untold sacrifice... eternal gratitude... sorrowful loss..." Something to do with the war. She stopped to listen, but the speech was coming to an end and there was nothing to hear but polite applause. She turned around to pick up the strap of her trunk again and bumped into one of the photographers. He was holding one of those new-fangled portable cameras, about the same size as the box that her brother had kept his gas mask in.

"Excuse me, miss. I think you've dropped something." He held the camera under one arm like the bellows of a bagpipe, while with the other he thrust something in her direction. A book. The one she had been reading on the train.

"Thank you, sir. I didn't realize."

She took it from him, raising her eyes only enough to see he was in his late twenties and wearing a bowler hat.

"That's a nice accent you've got there," he observed in his own London lilt. He sounded educated but not high society.

"What is it? Scots?"

"Northumbrian."

"North-hummmm-bree-un," he mimicked.

Unsure whether or not he was mocking her, she tried not to scowl. She failed.

"Sorry, miss. Didn't mean to offend. I think it's pretty."

She doubted that "pretty" was the right word for it, but she appreciated his effort at apology.

"No offence taken." She raised the book in his direction like a steward's flag at a boat race. "Thanks for this."

"*The Mysterious Affair at Styles*. Any good?"

"Not bad so far. It's by a new writer. A woman. Agatha Christie's her name."

"A woman mystery writer, eh? Times are a-changing!"

"Indeed they are, sir." She picked up her strap, ready to move on.

"Hold on there, miss; I'll give you a hand. That looks heavy."

"I can get a porter…"

"They're on strike."

"Really? I was wondering why there was no one around."

"And if they're not on strike, they're dead."

She looked up in surprise. "What an odd thing to say."

He nodded to the wall above the dais. As the crowd dispersed she could finally see what all the fuss was about – a memorial listing the names of hundreds of men who had previously been employed by the Great Northern Railway but had died across the sea.

"Nigh on a thousand," the photographer commented in a flat voice. "God-awful waste."

"I don't know what God has to do with it," she said, embarrassed by his blasphemy.

"Exactly." He began fussing with his camera and kit. She suddenly noticed the skin of his hands: red, angry, scarred.

"You were at the front?"

"Yes."

"My brother too. He never came back."

He finished buckling up his satchel, slung it over his shoulder, and reached out to take the strap of her trunk. "God-awful waste," he said again, then headed off, dragging her trunk behind him.

She didn't know what to do. In just a few moments he had changed from a playful young man teasing her about her accent, to an embittered ex-soldier. Was it safe to follow him? Her mother would have said absolutely not. Her father would have been appalled that he had used the Lord's name in vain – and in front of a lady too! But neither of her parents was there, and besides, the man had her trunk. She had not hauled it all the way from Morpeth to London for it to be lost in the afternoon commute.

"Hold on, sir!" she cried and ran after him in what her mother would have declared a most unladylike scamper.

She caught up with him in the station atrium, a hexagonal concourse with doors leading out onto King's Cross, Pentonville, and Euston Roads. Shops lined the sides of the hexagon, and commuters, waiting for their various trains on lines which spanned out from central London like threads on a spiderweb, bided their time shopping and browsing. He had stopped in the middle of the atrium, creating a little island of space around him as the sea of travellers parted to accommodate him and the trunk.

Poppy didn't seem to have the same effect on the crowd and she had to zig-zag her way through with apologies to left and right. When she reached him she was greeted with: "Is someone coming to meet you?"

"I thought so. My aunt and her friend. My aunt's in a wheelchair but her friend drives."

"I don't see any wheelchairs. Perhaps the friend came on his own."

"Her own."

"She drives?"

"Lots of women drive."

"So they do. Well, miss, it looks like they might have forgotten you. Did you telegraph your arrival time?"

"Of course." Poppy's voice sounded more high-pitched than she would have liked. She didn't want to give the impression she was in a panic. She wasn't. Well, not yet anyway. But it was a bother being stuck at King's Cross without anyone to meet her.

"Perhaps I could telephone."

"They have a telephone?"

Poppy raised her eyebrows at him. He took the bait and grinned. "I know, I know, lots of women have telephones."

Poppy laughed. "We don't, back in Morpeth. But they do have one at the Post Office. When Aunt Dot first had her telephone put in, she rang the Morpeth exchange and asked to be put through to us. She was most put out when they told her there was no listing for anyone called Denby. So then she sent a telegram instead – like any normal person would have done in the first place!"

He was looking at her and smiling.

"What?"

"You are very pretty when you laugh, Miss... Miss... Denby?"

Poppy flushed, embarrassed by his brazenness but delighted by the compliment. "Yes, Denby. Poppy Denby."

"From Morpeth in Northumberland."

"That's correct, sir. You seem to have learned an awful lot about me in a very short time. And I know nothing about you."

He grinned. "Sorry, it's the job. Bad habit. I start interviewing people before I even realize what I'm doing."

"And before you even introduce yourself, either. How rude!" she said in mock chastisement.

He looked chagrined and pushed out his hand. "Pardon me, Miss Denby. My name is Rokeby. Daniel Rokeby. From Hackney. I work for *The Daily Globe*."

"You're a press photographer?"

"I am."

"Oh, how exciting! I've always wanted to be a journalist."

"You have? Well, there are not too many women doing that job."

"No? Then it's time things changed."

He laughed again. She was beginning to enjoy hearing it and she would have carried on with their chit-chat if she hadn't the vexing problem of not having anyone at the station to meet her. She looked around her again: still no Aunt Dot or her friend, Grace Wilson. Grace was a tall, slim woman with grey hair – no one fitting her description was in sight. But a Post Office was.

"Do you think they will have a telephone in there?" She nodded in the general direction.

Daniel Rokeby's eyes widened. "Better than inside – there's one outside. I covered the opening back in March. Over there: that funny-looking kiosk that looks a bit like a skinny garden gazebo with a kaiser's helmet on top."

"There's a phone in there?"

"There is."

"But how do we pay for it?"

"There's a little slot you can put a penny into."

"Well I never! What a splendid idea, Mr Rokeby." And with that Poppy zigged and zagged her way back across the concourse with Daniel and her trunk in tow.

In the "gazebo" Poppy reached into her purse and found a penny. She didn't have much money left after paying for her lunch on the train – which was far more expensive than she had anticipated. She would have to go to the bank tomorrow, but for now she hoped Grace or Aunt Dot would be home. If they didn't come to fetch her she doubted she would have enough for the tram or bus fare to Chelsea. She opened the folded-up telegram and found Aunt Dot's telephone number. She put her penny into the slot and picked up the earpiece. Suddenly a voice came through: "London Exchange. Can we connect you?"

Delighted at the novelty of it all, Poppy gave the telephonist Aunt Dot's number and waited to be connected. It only took a few moments before her aunt's theatrical voice answered.

"Poppy, my darling! Whatever are you doing here? We were expecting you tomorrow."

"Tomorrow? No, it's today. I sent you a telegram."

"Indeed you did, but the date was for tomorrow."

"But it said –"

"Obviously a mixup. No harm done. Just get the bus to King's Road. Or a cab."

"Erm – Aunt Dot – can you come and fetch me? I don't have very much money."

"Well, that was very short-sighted of you, wasn't it?"

"I'm sorry. I didn't realize, I – "

"I'm teasing, Poppy, teasing! I see you have your mother's sense of humour. But there is a teensy weensy bit of a problem. We won't have the motor back until tomorrow. It's having a service, and as we weren't expecting you until tomorrow…"

Poppy sighed. There was no point reminding her that she had most definitely told her today, not tomorrow – and she had a copy of the telegram she'd sent to prove it. What was done was done and new circumstances required a new plan.

"What if I get a cab, Aunt Dot? Will you be able to lend me the cab fare when we get to your house?"

"But of course! What a marvellous idea. Tell the driver it's 137 King's Road, just opposite the Electric Cinema Theatre. And don't worry, it will be quite safe. The newspapers greatly exaggerate the dangers to women travelling alone. They're run by men, you see, and –"

"Ten seconds."

"I'd better go, Aunt Dot. I'll see you shortly. About an hour?"

"Yes, that should –" They were cut off.

Poppy came out of the booth all smiles. "Sorted," she announced. "I'm to get a cab to Chelsea."

"On your own?"

"Mr Rokeby, while I very much appreciate your concern, and your kindness – and you a virtual stranger – I have just travelled four hundred miles on my own today; a few more will not do me any harm."

Chapter 2

Elizabeth Dorchester was enjoying a most rare opportunity to take in the late afternoon sun. It wasn't very often her "hosts" – as they liked to be called – allowed her into the garden unaccompanied. They said it was for her own good – there were many dangers lurking beyond the walls of the facility, and solitude was not something she should make a habit of. But, Elizabeth countered, the fresh air would do her good; being close to nature would restore her soul – and the solitude helped her to think more clearly. She wasn't sure her hosts were convinced by the last, but they seemed to think the first two might have some credence.

She wished she could see beyond the ten-foot stone walls surrounding the garden. It had been seven years since she had seen any of the sights of London. For all she knew, she wasn't even in London any more. It could be any garden, anywhere in Europe; anywhere with roses and hydrangeas and jasmine. She had once loved the smell of jasmine. Now it was the smell of imprisonment.

Her hosts of course denied that she was in prison. They claimed she was "convalescing" in a healthcare facility for people of a fragile mental disposition and that she would be free to go as soon as she was better. But whenever she thought she'd managed to convince them she was better, *he* came; and after cloistered conversations with doctors and nurses, her hosts always came to the conclusion that she was not better after all.

He was coming again today. She had been told that he had telephoned ahead to say he was going to be a little late, as he first had to attend the unveiling of a war memorial at King's Cross station. But he would come as soon as he could. Her hosts said she could wait in the garden. So Elizabeth Dorchester turned up her face to the dying rays of afternoon sunshine, fearing it was the closest she would ever get to being free.

The window cleaner who claimed King's Road, Chelsea, as part of his patch was just finishing up for the day when the black cab pulled up in front of number 137. His horse lifted her head wearily and looked at the motorized contraption, not realizing that soon she and her kind would be completely redundant. But she had a few years left yet; business had not been going that well for her master since the influenza, and the man could not afford such a huge financial outlay. He had lost quite a few clients to the illness. He himself had caught it and was laid up for three months. But even when he recovered, it was with reduced stamina and he could not clean as many windows in one day as he once had.

The window cleaner wheezed as he lifted his ladder and bucket into the back of the cart with Thompson and Son scrawled down the side in flaking green paint. He remembered when he and his son had painted it together before the war, their hopes for the business as fresh as the paint they stroked into the wood. But the son had died in a field in Flanders and in the five years since, the father had not had the heart to repaint the wagon without him.

Now he had no one to leave his business to. Yes, he had a daughter, but unless she married and her husband wanted to go into business with his father-in-law, best he sell up and use the money for her dowry. It never crossed the father's mind that his daughter might want to run the business herself. She had got a taste for working outside the home in the munitions factory during the war and hoped that her father would see that she was worthy to take up the mantle of her dearly departed brother. But it simply wasn't the way things were done in their family. Thompson and Son had been passed down the male line for three generations and the father could not imagine a world where things were any different.

So he took his pay from the lady at number 137 – the lady, it was rumoured, who had been giving girls like his daughter ideas beyond the natural order of things – then doffed his hat, and with a "Gee-up, Bess!" trundled away down King's Road.

Grace Wilson was just about to shut the front door when she spotted a young woman step out of the black motorized cab.

"Looks like your Poppy has made it," she called down the hall behind her.

"Poppy! Darling!" came the reply.

Half an hour later Poppy had freshened up in her room, changed into something more suitable for evening wear, and was entering the parlour where Grace and Aunt Dot were waiting for her, playing a game of snap.

"Snap! Snap! Snap!" cried Dot and giggled like a schoolgirl. "Ah, there you are, Poppy! Come and give your old aunt another cuddle." Aunt Dot had always been a full-bosomed woman and Poppy had memories of being suffocated in her ample chest as a small child, fearing she would never be able to clamber out. Since Dot's accident ten years earlier, the bosom had expanded even further and it rested like a pair of giant marshmallows on layers of meringue. The whole delicious confection – clothed in voluminous peach silk – was squeezed into a wicker basket-chair on wheels.

Dot's hair was the same as it had been when she first stepped onto the West End stage in 1900 at the ripe old age of thirty:

a nest of blonde ringlets and bows. If there was any grey in the cascade of curls, it was well hidden or dyed. Poppy looked a lot like her paternal aunt – apart from her girth – and the same bluebell eyes twinkled back at her from a plump, cherubic face.

Grace Wilson, on the other hand, was as tall and slim as a teenage boy. Her grey hair was cut short in a no-nonsense style, and she wore a sensible grey serge skirt and blouse. But belying the severe schoolmarm look was a warm smile that embraced Poppy gently as she extricated herself from her aunt's arms. Grace and Dot had been friends for as long as Poppy could remember. Unlike Dot, Grace had once been married. Her husband, Frank, had been one of the few men active in the women's suffrage movement and he had been a regular visitor to 137 King's Road in the years before the war. But then something had gone wrong. Poppy did not know what, and the most she could get out of her parents was "poor Frank".

Poppy sat down and accepted a cup of tea from Grace and a slice of cake from Dot. She looked around her and took in the Edwardian parlour that had not changed much since she had last been there when she was twelve years old. She and her parents had visited Dot when she first had her accident and tried to convince her to come back to Morpeth with them to convalesce. Dot would have none of it.

"They need me here more than ever," she had declared. "They" meant her friends and colleagues in the Women's Social and Political Union of which she, Frank, and Grace were members. On the sideboard, bedecked with a purple and green runner in the colours of the WSPU, Poppy noticed a photograph of Dot when she could still walk. She was standing with a group of friends, including Emmeline Pankhurst and Emily Wilding Davison, under a WSPU banner. Dot noticed her looking at it.

"That's the only picture I have of dear Emily. And some of the others." Dot's hand shook as she passed the sugar bowl across the silver tea tray to Poppy.

"Poor Emily," said Grace quietly, and she looked out of the window across the courtyard garden, lost in thought.

"She was a heroine. They all were," said Dot fiercely, the cherubic face galvanized with a strength Poppy knew was always just under the surface. Poppy reached out and squeezed her aunt's hand. Dot patted hers in return.

"I'm all right, pet." Then she shook out her curls, brightened her smile and asked: "So how are things with the family? I'm surprised your mother let you come."

"Let's just say it took some convincing," said Poppy wryly.

Dot's eyes twinkled and she knew her aunt was imagining the scenario when Poppy took the letter to her parents in which she was being offered formal employment as a companion and nurse to her invalid relative.

"Father had to keep reminding her that I am now twenty-two, so legally I can do what I like."

Dot giggled again. The schoolgirl was back.

"And of course he couldn't help mentioning that I had so far failed at securing a husband and needed to start earning my own keep unless I was to remain living off them for the rest of my life."

Grace's mind had returned from wherever she had wandered to a moment earlier. "But weren't you helping them at the mission?" She was referring to the charity shop and food kitchen run by the Methodist church in Morpeth, of which her father was the minister.

"I was. Running the shop and doing the bookkeeping. But I was never good at figures and they both knew it couldn't last long."

"You take after me, darling. A woman of words, not figures. Thank heavens I have Grace, or His Majesty's Customs and Excise would have had me in Holloway years ago!"

"So I really am grateful to you, Aunt Dot, for offering me this job."

"Job? What job?" she giggled again. "There's no job, darling! I just wrote that so they would let you go without too much of a fuss."

Poppy had a sinking feeling in her stomach. "What do you mean, there's no job? You said you needed a companion. And you would pay for it."

"Whatever could you do for me that Grace does not do already?" She squeezed her friend's hand warmly, but Grace pulled away and stood up, glaring down at her.

"Don't be so cruel, Dorothy! I told you it was not a very good joke. And just like I predicted, no one finds it funny except you. This is so typical of you!"

Dot patted the chair beside her. "Oh, do sit down, Grace. I'll explain it all to Poppy. Like I told you – and I will tell her – it's for her own good."

Grace was only slightly mollified, but she did as she was bid.

"As you say, Poppy, you are twenty-two and not getting any younger."

"But I don't want to get married."

"I'm not talking about marriage; I'm talking about starting a career."

"A career?" Poppy could not mask the surprise in her voice.

"Oh, do stop repeating my words like a parrot; it's very annoying. Yes, a career. There aren't too many work prospects in Morpeth for a bright young woman, and Newcastle isn't much better; but London, in London you will have a chance. I just needed to get you away from your parents – good as they are –

and show you the opportunities that are available for you here. Grace, pass the paper."

Grace again did as she was bid. Dot opened the newspaper to the situations vacant section and showed Poppy a cluster of red-pencil circles. "Look here: secretary wanted, central London law firm; assistant manager, Oxford Street stationer's; editor's assistant, *The Daily Globe* –"

"*The Daily Globe*? Let me see…" Poppy took the paper from her aunt and ran her finger down the column until she came to the correct circle. "That's a newspaper, isn't it?"

"It's this newspaper," answered Dot.

"And you think I would have a chance if I applied for this job?"

"More and more women are working these days," agreed Grace. "I would be if I didn't have your aunt to look after."

"How many times have I told you, Grace? You can work if you like. We can employ someone else to help me."

Grace reached out and took her friend's hand. "But you know they wouldn't look after you like I do. And besides, no one else would put up with your nonsense."

Dot laughed in agreement. "That's true." Then she turned to her niece. "Would you like to have a career, Poppy?"

Poppy's heart was racing. A career? Earning her own money? Making decisions for herself? It was all a bit too much to take in. "I don't know, Aunt Dot. What would Mam and Dad think? They only let me come because they thought I would be working for you."

Dot sighed then raised her hand to her forehead. "Grace, I think the wrong Poppy Denby has arrived. This is not the young girl who spent her days here reading women's suffrage tracts and writing letters to newspapers." She nodded to the dresser. "Top drawer please, Grace."

Grace seemed to know exactly what Dot wanted, as she opened the drawer and pulled out a small pile of letters tied with a pink silk bow.

Poppy gasped. "You kept them?"

"Of course I kept them, darling. I was so proud of you for writing them. Only twelve years old and already seeing the injustice in the world."

"But you didn't post them."

"Only the first one. I didn't dare post the rest after your mother saw your name in *The Times*."

Grace laughed. "Oh yes, Poppy, her expression was priceless. Dot was all set to send off the rest under the nom de plume 'A twelve-year-old suffragette', but I managed to talk her out of it."

Poppy smiled, remembering the delight at seeing her name in print for the very first time. She had sworn then that she would one day be a journalist. But as the years passed and the war and her brother's death and the worthy but dull work of the Methodist Mission had taken over her life, she'd almost forgotten the dreams of her twelve-year-old self. But then, when she'd met that photographer at the station… was it possible? No, she chided herself. Her parents would be furious.

Grace's brown eyes stared intently into hers. "Don't throw your life away, Poppy. Your aunt's right. You have a chance here. Why don't you take it? I'm sure we can get your parents to agree once you've got a job. And if they don't…"

"But they will!" piped in Dot.

Poppy wasn't sure they would. But she couldn't take her eyes off the pile of letters wrapped in the pink bow.

"All right. I'll give it a go. But don't tell Mam and Dad yet please. I don't want them to worry."

"Of course not, darling. My lips are sealed." Dot zipped her lips with her thumb and forefinger, then pushed the newspaper over the table to Poppy. "It's decided then. Tomorrow you will reply to these advertisements and see if anyone calls you for an interview. And in the meantime, all this talk of work is making me hungry."

Grace smiled at her plump companion. "I can get started on dinner…"

"No, don't do that. Let's go out! We'll go to Oscar's." Then to Poppy: "It's a new restaurant at the bottom of the road. They even play jazz!"

"Jazz?" Poppy echoed.

"Oh yes, jazz! My darling, tonight your education will begin!"

CHAPTER 3

Anyone who was anyone would have given their eye teeth to get a table at Oscar's, and bookings were being taken two weeks in advance. But Aunt Dot, as a formerly famous actress and more recently infamous suffragette, had some sway. And an old friend of Dot's – one of the first elected female MPs in 1918 – was the mother of Oscar Reynolds who owned the club. So by seven o'clock, Grace, Poppy and Dot made their way to the front of the queue waiting to be seated. They were ushered to a prime table, just left of the bandstand, by an effusive Oscar. "Miss Denby! Mrs Wilson! How delightful to see you!"

"I'm sorry if we put you out at such short notice, Oscar. It's just that my niece has come to stay with me and I wanted her to taste the best food in London."

"Oh, Miss Denby, you're too kind! And may I say you are looking beautiful this evening?"

"You may and you must!"

"Thank heavens for that! You never know with these women's rights types; a fellow could get a slap across his chops for daring to be such a gentleman in this day and age."

Oscar and Dot laughed as if they were sharing a private joke. Grace did not look quite so amused. Nonetheless she allowed Oscar to pull out her chair for her and the three women made themselves comfortable as menus were handed out.

"How is Marjorie? I haven't seen her in a while. No doubt up to her gills in legislation. Your mother's done a sterling job, Oscar. You should be very proud of her."

"She wouldn't be where she is now if it weren't for you." Oscar produced a wine list with a flourish. "May I recommend the Bordeaux? Or if you're in a party mood, the champagne. A particularly good vintage…"

"Oh, definitely the bubbly; what do you say, Poppy?"

Poppy, who had never had "bubbly" in her life, was not quite sure what she was agreeing to, but she did so anyway. However, when she opened the menu she balked at the prices. There was no way she could even afford a starter. But Dot told her not to be so silly; that she and Grace were treating her. Poppy wasn't sure where Dot got all her money, but it was rumoured that when she was an actress she had been the favourite of the Prince of Wales and had been on the receiving end of extravagant gifts. She had converted them to cash and on the advice of her good friends Frank and Grace, had invested it in shares. Now it seemed Grace managed her portfolio for her. It provided a tidy income for the pair, as well as helping to bankroll WSPU campaigns.

So not only did Poppy have champagne for the first time, but oysters and sea bass too. She felt a little guilty eating so much when she knew the people at the mission in Morpeth would be having bean stew at best, but she reminded herself that Dot made substantial donations to the mission every year and that she could do the same when she started working. She was going to start working! She was going to have a career! She felt positively giddy from excitement and champagne, and whatever guilt she might have had about her parents was disappearing in a bubbly haze. And then, just when she thought the night couldn't get any better, the band struck up a tune.

So this was jazz. Poppy had never heard anything like it. Back home at the Methodist chapel her mother would plonk out old Wesley hymns on the honky-tonk piano that had lost most of its felts. And she could never do anything in F Major because the B Flat above Middle C was missing. But nothing was missing tonight. Joining the pianist was a drummer, a clarinettist, a trumpeter, a trombonist, a double bass player and a dapper chap in a pinstripe blazer playing what Poppy believed was called a banjo. Aunt Dot told her the joyful, toe-tapping tune was called "The Tiger Rag".

"If I wasn't in this wretched chair, I'd get up to dance!"

As if on cue, couples tossed down their napkins, leapt out of their chairs and began cavorting across the dance floor. "It's called the Black Bottom!" Dot clapped and laughed, and even Grace cracked a smile. As the band brought "The Tiger Rag" to a close and moved into another upbeat number, a young woman spun out of her partner's arms and started dancing alone in the middle of the floor, her arms spinning like a windmill, her knees turned inwards and her legs kicking out to the sides. The other couples formed a semi-circle around her and started clapping and cheering. Poppy was itching to get up to dance herself, but she didn't know how. But then people started forming a train behind the solo dancer and she led them around the room in a quirky little dance with legs kicking to left and right. As the train passed her table, Poppy jumped up and joined the end. The train got faster and faster as it snaked its way in and out of tables – then, at one point, over a table! – and Poppy's head started spinning. The whole room became a blur: the dancers, the music, the lights. Poppy let go of the person in front of her, lost her balance and spiralled to the floor. But the train went on, circling around and around her. Poppy pressed her forehead to the floor; the cool of the tiles was soothing. The music faded, the dancers began to clear and suddenly, above her, someone came into view. It was the solo dancer, smiling and reaching out her hand. Poppy took it and was hauled up. The young woman laughed.

"Are you all right?"

"I – I – think so."

She laughed again and led Poppy back to her table.

"Too much champagne, I think," said Grace and passed her a glass of water. Poppy drank it gratefully.

"Delilah, darling! I didn't know you were coming tonight. I would have booked a table for four!"

Poppy, feeling a little better, focused on her rescuer. She was in her early twenties, short and slightly built with a sleek black haircut in a fashionable bob, Mediterranean olive skin and dark eyes, accentuated by thick lines of charcoal. She was wearing the shortest sleeveless dress Poppy had ever seen. A shimmering gold number, covered in tassels from neck to hem, which stopped a good two inches above the knee. The woman wore a long string of pearls, knotted halfway at waist level, and matching "slave bangles" on each bicep. On her right forearm she wore another bangle, styled like a snake, winding its way up from her wrist. Poppy imagined for a moment that this was what Cleopatra would look like if she were reborn into the twentieth century.

"Delilah, this is my niece Poppy that I've been telling you about. My brother's daughter from Northumberland. Poppy, this is Delilah Marconi. Her mother, Gloria, was a dear friend of ours. Like Emily, she was a sister in arms and was taken from us too soon."

"Too soon," echoed Grace and slipped again into her faraway place.

But Delilah wasn't going anywhere. She pumped Poppy's hand up and down enthusiastically.

"I'm very pleased to meet you, Poppy Denby. If you're anything like your aunt you are going to be great fun. You look a lot like her, you know?"

"I know," answered Poppy. "Sorry about earlier. I'm not used to all of this."

Delilah looked her up and down appraisingly, but not unkindly. "I see that. Don't worry, Dot, I'll have her jazzed up in no time."

"Good raw material, eh, Delilah?"

Delilah gave a delicious little laugh and plopped down on the vacant chair between Poppy and her aunt. "Oh, definitely."

The idea of being "jazzed up" by Delilah might have worried her at another time, but tonight Poppy felt she was ready for anything. "I'm going to be applying for some jobs in the morning."

"Oh really? Where?"

"There are a couple of options in the paper. One of them's at *The Daily Globe*. I've always wanted to be a journalist. The advertisement said they were looking for an editor's assistant; I'm hoping to work my way up."

"It's the only way to do it. I'm hoping the same in my job."

"What do you do?"

"Delilah is an actress! Just like me! How did it go at the audition?"

Delilah's face lit up. Poppy had never seen someone so exotically beautiful.

"I got the part!"

"Titania?"

"No. One of her fairies. But at least it's a named part. Cobweb."

"Cobweb today, Titania tomorrow! I'll drink to that." Dot raised her glass and the other women did the same. "To bright futures for us all!"

Elizabeth Dorchester readjusted her position on the bed, trying to ease the pressure of the straps on her wrists. She would have to put up with them for at least another night – she always did after one of her "reassessments". A doctor would come and see her tomorrow and explain, yet again, why it was for her own good. If she could control herself enough and not lash out at him – as she had done at her visitor earlier – she would be spared the medication. She wanted to keep a clear mind and she needed to be free of her bonds so she could write the letter she needed to write. No one could know her plan; she had to play it cool. She had to keep on the sweet side of the person who was beginning to show some sympathy to her. At the appropriate time she would pass on the note and pray that it would be delivered to the right person out there in the world.

She could hear some music down the hall, beyond her locked door. One of the orderlies had brought in a gramophone and was playing a disc record. They played the recordings most nights and Elizabeth had memorized the piece note for note. It was a new style of music and she had heard the staff refer to it as jazz. A lot had changed in the seven years Elizabeth had been locked up. Apparently there'd been an entire world war. She wondered if she would even recognize what was left of the world when she finally got out.

CHAPTER 4

Poppy got off the bus at the bottom of Fleet Street. The bus had been full and she had been forced to sit on the top deck, open to the elements. On a sunny day she wouldn't have minded, as she would have been able to take in the sights of London between Chelsea and Blackfriars: Buckingham Palace, Pall Mall, Marble Arch, Trafalgar Square, The Royal Opera House at Covent Garden… but today was overcast and drizzly, and whatever view she would have had was blocked by a curtain of umbrellas. However, she was grateful for them and she got off the bus relatively unscathed, with both her hair and her new outfit dry and uncrumpled.

She had bought the navy blue drop-waisted dress and matching jacket with white trim on Oxford Street the previous week. It had been a compromise between Grace's suggestion for "sensible office wear" and Aunt Dot's insistence on "something with a bit of flair; something to make you stand out". The blue had been Poppy's idea: a halfway house between Grace's grey and Dot's scarlet. Grace had taken one look at Dot's proposed outfit and declared: "She's going for an interview at a newspaper, not an audition for *Carmen*!"

It had taken Poppy nearly three weeks to secure the interview. Despite Dot's declaration that finding a job would be "easy peasy", it had turned out to be far more problematic than anticipated. She had written a dozen letters in response to situations vacant, but only received replies to five of them. It had taken ten days for the first reply to reach her and she was getting very anxious that Dot's great career plans might not work out at all. She was also feeling guilty because she had to lie to her parents. They had written and asked her how her new job with Dot was going. She was as vague as possible about the specifics and just said she was learning lots of new skills and that Dot was very encouraging. Both were true, but not in the way she knew her parents would understand it. She hoped she could get a real job soon and be able to tell them the truth. Surely they would forgive her – and Dot – if she actually had a decent, well-paid position. But that was proving trickier than she would have thought.

The first two replies said that regretfully the positions had already been filled. The third was from a law firm looking for a secretary. It asked her to send in her *curriculum vitae* listing previous experience in the legal sector. She had none. Dot wanted her to make something up: "Darling, you just have to get your foot in the door. You're like me, a quick learner; you'll impress them in no time!"

But Poppy was not prepared to live a lie. What she was doing with her parents was worry enough, but that was just temporary. And surely it was illegal to falsify references… Grace agreed with her that it was.

The fourth reply proved more promising and she was invited to an interview for an assistant manager's position at an Oxford Street stationer's. When she got there and announced she was there for the interview, she was given a quizzical look by one of the counter assistants. He asked if she was in the right place. She said she was. He ushered her into a smoky back office, announced that a Miss Denby had arrived, and quickly withdrew. Through the cloud of smoke, Poppy made out a very austere-looking gentleman with facial hair to match Lord Kitchener's. He didn't bother removing his pipe before asking, "Denby? P. Denby?"

"That's correct, sir. Poppy Denby."

"You should have said."

"Should have said what?"

"That you're a woman, girl. A woman!"

Poppy sucked in her breath and exhaled slowly, giving her time to formulate her response. "The application form did not ask me to specify," she said carefully.

"But it did specify that we are looking for an assistant *manager*, did it not?" The man ran his tongue along his teeth; then, appearing to have found something, he picked at it with his fingernail.

Poppy suppressed a shudder. "It did, sir. And I have some experience helping to manage a charity shop in Morpeth. I have kept books, I have managed stock, I have…"

The man slammed his fist on his ink blotter like a judge's gavel. "You have lied about your gender."

"I have not lied!"

"If we had wanted a woman we would have asked for a manageress. We did not ask for a manageress. Good day, madam."

The man moved his pipe from one side of his mouth to the other and waved her towards the door.

Poppy was incensed. She had prepared herself for pertinent questions that she may have been asked and had even read up on the history of stationery at the British Library. She had not prepared herself for this blatant discrimination.

"But sir!"

"What?" he spat, spraying flakes of tobacco over his ink blotter.

"I am quite capable of doing this job."

"I doubt that. We need someone the staff can look up to; whom they can respect; who can motivate them. We need someone customers can come to for advice, and trust that what they are being told has authority; someone with an agile brain who will not tire easily or be emotionally overcome, who will not be frequently in the family way and have to take extended leaves of absence… in short, madam, we need a man. Good day to you." This time he took the pipe out of his mouth and prodded it towards the door.

Poppy turned on her heel and walked out. She fumed all the way back home to Chelsea, rehearsing what she would have said if she had the chance to do it over. She got herself so worked up that by the time she opened the door of number 137 she was in tears.

After hearing what had happened, Dot was just as incensed. "Grace! Get the motor!"

Poppy expected Grace to try to talk her out of it, but she didn't. Instead she grinned and declared: "Into the breach once more!" and grabbed her hat, scarf and motoring goggles from the hatstand.

On the drive back to Oxford Street, while bumpily applying her make-up in a little vanity mirror strapped to the dashboard, Dot regaled Poppy with a history of their lives as political activists before the war: the demonstrations, the arson attacks on sporting venues, the chaining of themselves to the railings outside number 10 Downing Street. "Those were the days, eh, Grace? We didn't do all of that so that my niece could be humiliated at a job interview."

Grace's eyes narrowed behind her goggles and she shouted over the roar of the engine: "Nor did our friends go on hunger strike, get tortured in prison and get run down by horses. You do know that your aunt's 'accident' was nothing of the sort, don't you, Poppy? A policeman deliberately ran his horse at her. And to this day he's never been charged."

Dot paused, lipstick in hand. "Let's leave that story for another day, shall we, Grace?"

Grace looked across at her friend and nodded in agreement.

When they got to Oxford Street, Grace found a parking spot as close to the stationer's as she could, then she and Poppy offloaded Dot's wheelchair that had been precariously strapped to the back of the motor, balanced on the spare wheel, and helped her into it. The veteran suffragette fluffed her hair, tossed her scarf and pointed her umbrella up the street. "Into the breach, sisters! Into the breach!"

Their advance was slowed by a flight of three steps leading up to the front door of the stationer's. Poppy had forgotten about them. Grace, however, was not surprised. "It's either the tradesman's entrance around the back or the old heave-ho." She grasped one side of Dot's chair and nodded for Poppy to do the same. Dot was no lightweight and it took all of Poppy's strength to hold up her side of the contraption. But they managed with Dot cheering them on. Back on solid ground, she pushed open the door with her umbrella and announced to whoever was on the shop floor: "Take me to the manager!"

The same assistant who had taken Poppy into the back room was still on duty. He nodded at Poppy in recognition, then turned his attention to Dot. "I'm sorry, madam, but the manager has left early."

"A likely story! Show me the way, Poppy!"

Flushing with embarrassment, the assistant stood in front of the wheelchair and blocked the women's advance.

"It's true, madam; he left soon after this – this – young lady left."

"Soon after he insulted her, you mean!"

"I don't know anything about that, madam. But unless you are here to buy stationery, I will have to ask you to leave."

"We are not going anywhere until we have spoken to the manager," said Grace in a voice that would have tamed vipers.

"He's not here."

Grace pushed the chair forward. The man did not move. Dot raised her umbrella threateningly. Poppy feared someone was going to get hurt.

"Let's go, Aunt Dot. Grace. It's not worth it. I wouldn't want to work here anyway. I've still got the interview at the newspaper…"

Dot pursed her lips and jutted her chin. "Don't back down, Poppy."

"I'm not, Aunt Dot. I really don't want to work here."

The assistant smiled smugly. Poppy wasn't ordinarily a spiteful woman, but she could not abide smugness. So she added: "No, I don't want to work here. I have far more ambition than that."

Dot laughed out loud and pointed her umbrella at the man's chest. "Ha! Take that!"

Then she turned her chair around and the three women left in much the same way they had come.

On Fleet Street, Poppy stood at the bottom of another flight of stairs; this one flanked by two brass globes. The plaque on the wall declared "*The Daily Globe*. Established 1900". Poppy took a deep breath, prayed a quick prayer and walked up the steps with as much confidence as she could muster. In the black and white mosaic entrance hall she was greeted by a middle-aged woman behind a polished teak reception desk with a basque relief of Egyptian gods on the wall behind her.

Poppy introduced herself and said she had an appointment with the editor.

The woman ran her finger down a list and nodded. "Indeed

you have, Miss Denby. Take the lift to the fourth floor. Turn right and the door to the newsroom will be in front of you. Go through the newsroom and Mr Rolandson's office will be on the far side. If you get lost just ask anyone for directions."

"Thank you, I will."

Then, as Poppy walked towards the lift, the woman called after her: "Oh, and Miss Denby, good luck." Poppy felt a flush of gratitude and thanked her.

Buoyed, she followed the directions to the fourth floor. In the lift – the first she'd ever been in – she told her twelve-year-old self to stay calm and pretend to be a confident woman who took job interviews in her stride.

She took her own advice and quickly checked her hair in the mirror on the wall. It was a twenty-two-year-old Poppy who stepped onto the landing of the fourth floor and pushed open the doors of the newsroom. She stifled a gasp. It was just as she had imagined it would be. Half a dozen desks were scattered around the room, each within a personal nest of filing cabinets. Typewriters clattered and a telephone pealed. A few hardy pot plants were managing to survive, if not thrive, in the smoke-filled air and there was an underlying stench of sweat. Weary-looking men with loosened ties, rolled-up shirt sleeves and braces looked up from their desks and nodded in greeting. No one seemed over friendly, but neither were they hostile.

Someone answered the telephone and called out: "Bert, it's for you. The Dorchester story." A very large man pushed aside a box of sandwiches, heaved his way out of his chair and shuffled over to the telephone desk. Poppy noticed that under his sagging belly his trousers weren't done up properly. She hoped one of the other men would tell him. They didn't. But one of them did clock that she'd noticed and winked at her. Poppy ignored him as she arrived at a door at the far end of the room marked "Rollo Rolandson, Editor". She took a calming breath and knocked.

"Come in!" A distinctive accent: transatlantic, possibly Canadian, maybe American. Poppy opened the door. At first she didn't see him. The room was so full of piles of newspapers, leaning towers of manila folders, overfull bookshelves, assorted photography paraphernalia and typewriters in various states of repair that she could not have been blamed if she'd thought she'd walked into a storeroom. The transatlantic voice addressed her again from somewhere in the middle of the room. Her eyes focused through the dim light filtering through a filthy window-pane and she saw a shock of red hair above a moon-shaped face.

"Sorry for the mess. Here, take a seat."

The red hair moved from behind what Poppy assumed was a desk and lifted a pile of files off a chair. Attached to the head was a very short, squat body. Poppy, who was five foot five, towered above him. Rollo Rolandson – if that's who it was – couldn't have been more than four-and-a-half feet tall. He dusted off the chair and turned his moon-face up to her with a grin. "Please, Miz Denby, take a seat."

Poppy did as she was bid and waited for the editor to negotiate the obstacle course back to behind his desk. He picked up a sheet of paper which she recognized as her application form and perused it for a moment, making small grunting noises, and Poppy wasn't sure whether they were of approval or disdain.

"You are a little sketchy on your experience here, Miz Denby." He pronounced the Miss with a "z".

Poppy cleared her throat. "I have worked in a mission."

"A Methodist Mission?"

"That's correct." Poppy kept her voice neutral, hoping to deflect the prejudice she was used to whenever anyone heard she attended a non-conformist church.

"So how do you feel about alcohol?"

"I beg your pardon?"

"Alcohol, Miz Denby. I do believe the Methodists are prohibitionists."

Oh dear, thought Poppy, *here it comes*. She folded and then refolded her hands in her lap. "That's not entirely true, sir. Not as a rule of faith. Although a lot of Methodists are teetotallers and support temperance programmes. They have seen the damage alcohol can cause to individuals, families and communities."

He raised his hand. Poppy noted that they were particularly large. "I don't need a lesson in do-goodism, Miz Denby – I want to know whether you personally approve or disapprove of alcohol."

Poppy gave an internal sigh. This was not going as she had expected. Just as she had for the stationer's job she had gone to the British Library and done as much research as she possibly could on the history of the British press. She had read samples of every newspaper that had been published in London in the last two years. She knew, for instance, that there was currently a battle going on in Fleet Street between the evening papers that were financed largely by wealthy benefactors and covered stories of interest to the "gentlemanly" classes and a new class of papers, disparagingly referred to as the gutter press, but which preferred to be called tabloids due to their more compact size. The tabloids covered stories tailored to a broader social spectrum: "jazz journalism", entertainment news and gossip; and on a more serious note, social activism, seeing themselves as watchdogs of the democratic process.

But Rollo Rolandson was not asking about any of that. He was asking about her views on alcohol. Poppy cleared her throat and chose her words carefully. "Well, sir, I don't have a problem with it in principle. I've even been known to have a glass of champagne myself."

"Excellent!" Rollo threw his hands in the air and brought them crashing down on his desk. A precarious pile of files wobbled. Poppy reached out a hand to steady them.

Rollo grinned. "And that, Miz Denby, is why I need an assistant. Your first job will be to organize this office. Can you do that?"

Poppy looked around at the clutter that threatened to engulf them both. It reminded her of the donation room at the mission. It was not quite the cutting-edge job in journalism that she had hoped for, but it was a start.

She nodded decisively. "Yes, Mr Rolandson. I can do that."

"Excellent!" he said again. But this time he stopped before he slapped down his hands. Instead he reached one over the desk. "Welcome to *The Globe*, Miz Denby."

Poppy shook it vigorously. "Thank you, sir. I'm delighted to be part of the team."

CHAPTER 5

There was a knock on Rollo Rolandson's door. He let go of Poppy's hand and called: "Come in!"

The door opened. "Sorry to disturb you, Rollo, but I thought you might like to see – Miss Denby!"

"Mr Rokeby!" Without the bowler hat, Poppy noticed his brown hair and soft, grey eyes. They twinkled in delight.

"You two know each other?"

Daniel Rokeby stepped into the office. He was holding a pile of photographic prints and smiling widely. "I met Miss Denby when she first arrived in London. A month ago, was it?"

"Three weeks," Poppy corrected.

"Well, I'll be. Miz Denby has just joined us at *The Globe*, Dan," Rollo remarked, shaking his head in disbelief.

"You said you'd always wanted to be a journalist," Daniel said, smiling.

"You want to be a journalist?" Rollo raised his shaggy eyebrows.

"I – well – I –" Poppy blushed.

"You're in the right place then. But don't go getting ideas above your station; I need an assistant, not a reporter. I've got plenty of them out there." He cocked his thumb towards the newsroom. "What I don't have is someone to help me sort this lot out."

"Ah, the editor's assistant job," said Daniel wryly.

"It is. And Miz Denby here is all too pleased to take it, aren't you, Miz Denby?"

"I am, sir. Very much, sir," Poppy replied, relieved that she still seemed to have a job despite her "deception".

"Less of the sir! It's Rollo. We're all *mates* around here, aren't we, Danny Boy?"

Daniel and Poppy smiled at Rollo's attempt at a cockney accent.

"Most of the time," said Daniel and raised a conspiratorial eyebrow towards Poppy.

"What you got there, then, Dan?"

"Just the pics for tomorrow."

"Show me at the briefing. After you've given Miz Denby the grand tour."

Daniel gave Rollo a mock salute, then gestured towards the door. "Shall we, Miss Denby?"

"Thank you, Mr Rokeby; I would like that very much."

She tried to ignore Rollo's knowing laughter as they left the office and the equally suggestive looks from the reporters in the newsroom as she accompanied the handsome photographer towards the lift.

Half an hour later, Daniel and Poppy had finished their grand tour. First, they had taken the lift down to the basement where the printing presses droned away day and night. On the ground floor was the foyer where Poppy had first entered the building. As well as the lift, a staircase wound its way up to the fourth floor, where a balcony surrounded the atrium. Egyptian-style bronze and black lacquer statuettes stood sentinel in alcoves overlooking the black and white mosaic floor. It was an entrance hall designed to impress as completely modern, set apart from the other old-style Georgian, Victorian and Edwardian newspapers that occupied Fleet Street.

She was introduced to the kind receptionist, Mavis Bradshaw, who congratulated her on her appointment but asked her if she realized she had been hired as a glorified maid.

"I do, Mrs Bradshaw," Poppy replied, then lowered her voice. "But I don't intend to stay one," she added with a smile. Daniel and Mavis both laughed at this and Daniel added that he had no doubt that a young lady as resourceful as Miss Denby would soon convince Rollo of her worth.

Poppy blushed at this and said, "Please, call me Poppy."

Now on first name terms, Poppy and Daniel toured the rest of the building. Behind the reception area on the ground floor was the typesetters' hall. Half a dozen men stood bent over trays of metal letters, piecing together the copy for the next day's edition from sheaves of typescript. The next floor up, which they mutually agreed to access via the stairs, housed the advertising department and the accounts department.

"This is what keeps the whole thing running," said Daniel. "If our advertisers want us to run a story, it's hard to say no. Someone has to pay the bills."

On the walk up to the second floor, which housed the photography and art department, Daniel warned her to stay clear of the balustrade. It was a little loose and awaiting repair. Then he asked her if she had finished the mystery novel she had been reading on the train. "What was it called? *The Mysterious Affair at Styles?*"

"That's the one," replied Poppy, surprised that he remembered such a small detail. Well, he had remembered her name. And she his… she flushed. "Yes, I have."

"And?" He smiled and looked directly at her. Poppy was not used to such a direct gaze from a man – particularly one with such lovely grey eyes. She felt something flutter in her stomach.

"Er, it was good. I enjoyed it. I enjoy most mysteries," she answered, hoping Daniel would not be able to read her thoughts.

"Oh, why's that?" His gaze was averted as he guided her towards a set of doors off the landing.

Poppy exhaled, hoping he would interpret her erratic breathing as due to the ascent of the stairs. "I suppose it's because I enjoy puzzles. I love to figure out who did it. I'd like to think journalism's a little bit like that too. Following leads, finding out the who, what, where and why…"

He laughed. "Sometimes. Sometimes though it's just writing – or photographing – what you're told to."

Poppy looked a little disappointed and he was quick to add, "Oh, but I'm sure you'll enjoy it. And as soon as you've had a chance to show Rollo what you can do –"

"You mean beyond my filing and cleaning skills."

He grinned. "Yes, beyond that. Once you've written something." He stopped and turned to her, his face alight with a new idea. "Books would be a good start."

"Books?" she asked.

"Yes, books. You should consider writing some book reviews. Our arts editor struggles to produce enough copy for each edition. I'm sure he'd be delighted to receive some submissions."

Poppy was touched that he was taking so much interest in furthering her career. "Are you sure Mr Rolandson won't think I'm trying to rise above my station?"

Daniel laughed. "That's just his sense of humour. He's American; it takes a while to get used to him, but he's a decent fellow."

"What's he doing over here?"

"Came over as a war correspondent and won this paper in a poker game."

Poppy gasped. "He won it in a poker game?"

"He's very good."

"Or very lucky."

Daniel's grey eyes twinkled. "Oh, luck has nothing to do with anything Rollo does. It was strategic. He knew the previous owner wanted to sell, but he didn't like the price being asked. So he offered to play for it. He won."

Poppy laughed, all interest in the grand tour gone. This conversation was far more interesting than how many filing cabinets were in each department. "My, my. I suspected he was eccentric, but…"

"Because he's a dwarf?"

"No, because he gave me this job in light of my views on alcohol."

Daniel threw back his head and laughed, eliciting amused looks from a pair of men exiting the art department. When they were gone, chuckling to themselves and casting knowing glances at the young couple, Daniel lowered his voice and asked, "So, Miss Denby, what exactly are your views on alcohol?"

Poppy straightened her spine and said with affected primness, "Everything in moderation, Mr Rokeby."

"Ha! He'd be relieved to hear that. He threatened to give up his American citizenship when they brought in prohibition over there earlier this year."

Daniel took his watch out of his pocket and checked the time. He put it back in and then turned his full attention back to Poppy. If he had somewhere else to go he did not seem intent on getting there. "So, what got him onto the subject of alcohol in your job interview?"

"He heard I was a Methodist and jumped to conclusions about my views on the devil's brew."

Daniel grinned, then leaned towards her. She did not feel the need to pull away. "I'm an Anglican myself," he said. "At least I was. I don't go to church any more. Not since the war."

Poppy didn't need to ask why. Thousands of men had lost their faith in the trenches, her brother one of them. She had hoped he would get it back after the war, but he didn't last that long. Daniel noticed her silence. He took a step back. "I'm sorry if I offended you. About God, I mean. I did the same at the station, and —"

"No offence taken, Mr Rokeby," Poppy interrupted, hoping he would close the gap between them again. "We each have our own roads to travel." She smiled and cocked her head towards the double door. "Now perhaps you can show me what you do here in the photography department."

But Daniel looked at his pocket watch again and declared they had run out of time and needed to get back for the briefing. Poppy noticed the scarring on his hands as he put the timepiece back in his pocket. "Another time then, Mr Rokeby."

"Indeed. Another time, Miss Denby."

Rollo Rolandson was standing in front of a blackboard with a piece of chalk and a baton. He nodded to Daniel and Poppy as they came in, and briefly introduced her to the team as his new editorial assistant. This was greeted with a knowing chuckle from the assembled men. Pulling out a chair, Daniel whispered to her to ignore them. She smiled at him thankfully and took the seat at the back of the room.

"Let's get started then," said Rollo. "Miz Denby. Get yourself a notebook and pencil. An editor's assistant should take notes of all meetings and type them up afterwards. Do you type, Miz Denby?"

Poppy, who had been preparing for the job not just by researching at the British Library but by practising on Grace's typewriter at home, was truthfully able to say that she did. She declined to point out that that should have been one of the questions he asked at the interview, and instead took a notebook and pencil from one of the reporters with a thankful smile.

"Righto. How are we doing for tomorrow's lead, Bert?"

The large man Poppy had noticed when she first walked in was sprawled in a chair with crumbs down his shirt front. He wiped the back of his hand over his mouth before answering. "It's either the x-ray machine contract or the sex disqualification bill."

"Which one's stronger?" Rollo asked.

"Probably the bill. Got more on it at the moment," Bert answered, taking a loud slurp from his coffee cup.

"And what's your angle?"

Poppy thought she detected a roll of the eyes as Rollo spoke.

Bert put his cup down. "For tomorrow's story, simply that we will soon be having female lawyers and accountants."

"Lord help us all!" someone muttered.

"And you have comment from the Old Bailey?" Rollo asked.

"Uh-huh."

"And that Reynolds woman?"

"I do. But I haven't been able to get a comment from Dorchester yet. Should be this afternoon – just had a telephone call about it. I'll follow up after this."

"Excellent. All right then, we'll go for the sex discrimination story above the fold. What have we got for below?" Rollo stepped away from the blackboard, which was now covered in his near-indecipherable scrawls.

Another voice piped up: "Wimbledon. That Frenchy won again. The one with the short skirt. And Daniel's got a luv-er-ly pic."

On cue Daniel walked to the front of the room and presented a picture of Suzanne Lenglen to Rollo, who in turn showed it to the room. It was met by wolf whistles. No one bothered apologizing to Poppy.

"Can we tie this in to the aeroplane story, Joe?" Rollo addressed his question to a young, dark-haired man Poppy had met earlier on their tour. "Advertising have been on to us to give Instone Airline more column inches."

"I suppose I could mention that she flew in from Paris with them," Joe replied. "They did open the Paris to Hounslow route a few months ago. And I've heard they're also about to transport a racehorse over for the Grand Prix Paris later in the year, and Lenglen's bound to make a bet or two on it, so I can do a follow-up."

"A flying horse? That'll do it. Excellent. Now, arts and entertainment. Where's Lionel?"

"Off sick."

Rollo's thick red eyebrows met in the middle of his forehead. "Sleeping off a night at Oscar's more like it. Did he post a story yesterday?"

Throats were cleared and everyone suddenly appeared interested in their notes.

"I'll take that as a no then. Have we got anything to fill it?" Rollo asked his disinterested audience.

Again he was met by silence.

He swore. Poppy was startled but managed to hide her surprise. Daniel looked apologetically at her. She mouthed, "Don't worry."

"Then what the hell are we going to do?" Rollo started to pace; he was getting redder and redder.

"He's going to blow…" someone muttered.

"I – I – can get you a story on *Midsummer Night's Dream* at The Old Vic."

The whole room spun around to look at Poppy. "I – I – know one of the actresses. I can get an interview."

Rollo stopped pacing. "Can you get it today?"

"I can try."

"Good. Then get on it. Joe, if she can't get it have you got something about Miz Lenglen appearing at some jazz club or restaurant or something?"

"I could whip something up."

"Excellent. But let's give Miz Denby a chance first, shall we?" He poked the baton in her direction. "It's over to you now, Poppy. Let's see what you've got."

CHAPTER 6

Mr Thompson was very grateful to his friend, Mr Jones, for passing on the tip that Willow Park Asylum in Battersea was in need of a new window cleaner. Just south of the river from his usual patch in Chelsea, he and Bess could make it there and back in an afternoon. But today, he had finished his cleaning in double time and left the asylum early because he had something to deliver to an address in Fleet Street.

It had taken him a while to agree to the delivery. He had been told when he first got the job that he should not engage with any of the residents. That was easy enough. He found the men and women wandering around in their nightgowns disturbing. In the men's wing there were young ex-soldiers, shell-shocked and staring, that reminded him of what his son had been through. He didn't want to engage with that at all. Better he stay on his side of the glass, and they on theirs.

But then one day, in the women's wing, he had seen a woman who didn't seem like the others. She would sit quietly by herself and read. She had some flowers on her windowsill that she tended and she would stare out of the window, past him and his ladder, looking longingly at the horizon. From her second-floor window she could not see much beyond the walls of the grounds, as the towers of Battersea Gasworks blocked her view. But she looked, nonetheless.

She was in her mid to late thirties, with pallid skin and long auburn hair worn in a plait down her back. She had large, grey eyes that on another face, living another life, might have been described as intelligent; on hers they simply looked haunted. Mr Thompson thought her face familiar, and it took him a good few visits before he realized where he had seen her before: 137 King's Road, Chelsea; prior to the war she had been a regular visitor. After this realization, the woman started to become a real person in Mr Thompson's mind, not just a white-robed spectre. And before he knew it he was trying to catch her eye. Then one day he did. And she noticed. Nothing happened that first day other than she stopped looking through him and looked at him. But it was enough.

In the following months Mr Thompson and the woman continued to notice each other and gradually became comfortable with it. Last month she had even looked up and smiled when she heard the scrape of his ladder and the clatter of his bucket. He had smiled in return. Smiling did not come easy to Mr Thompson, but nor, he supposed, did it come easy to her.

But today he was surprised when she waved at him to catch his attention and held up a piece of paper to the window, asking: "CAN YOU HELP ME?" He did not know how he could help her, but he nodded anyway. Then she got up, went to her door to check no one was coming, and scratched around in a corner. She emerged with an envelope. As it was a warm day, the window to her room was slightly open. Bars blocked her from escaping, and nails had been hammered into the sash window frame so it could never be opened more than a crack, but there was enough space for her to slip the envelope through. He wiped his hands dry on his overalls and took it. Mr Thompson had had no more than a few years of schooling, but it was enough to read the address: "MR ISAACS, THE GLOBE NEWSPAPER, FLEET STREET."

Near the window she again spoke the words she had written: "Will you help me?"

"I will," he mumbled back.

***

Poppy got the bus to King's Road, ran in to tell Dot and Grace her wonderful news, then jumped on the next bus she could get to Waterloo, where her aunt told her Delilah would be in rehearsal at The Old Vic. Poppy had never been in a real theatre before. The only theatrical performances she had ever attended were Sunday school plays where, inevitably, because of her blonde curls, she was cast as an angel. Poppy hated acting and could barely hold a tune, but as a child who loved making up stories, she did fancy herself as a playwright. She used to secretly write plays to be performed by her two dolls – necessitating the pair of them playing multiple roles – and when that failed, she would make temporary paper stand-ins.

One year she had suggested writing a modern version of the nativity to be performed in the Methodist chapel, but her suggestion was pooh-poohed by her brother, and she feared her parents would agree with him. So the script for *The Three Wise Men of Morpeth* was shelved.

Despite having a famous actress in the family – or perhaps because of it – the world of the arts was treated with suspicion by the Northumberland Denbys. Reverend Denby and his wife did not come from the branch of the church that believed creative activities to be inherently immoral or evil, but they did share the view that unless the arts were employed to teach the Bible or exhort people to faithful Christian service, then there was not much use for them.

So when Dotty Denby flounced off to London to make her debut on the West End stage they were more puzzled than scandalized. They simply did not understand it. Art for art's sake, or pure entertainment, or as an expression of a creative impulse, did not have any place in the world of Reverend and Mrs Denby, so Poppy had wisely kept her compulsions to herself.

Poppy felt a thrill of excitement as she stepped over the threshold and into the foyer of The Old Vic theatre, just down the road from Waterloo station. Her aunt had delighted in telling her the place was run by a Christian woman – Lilian Baylis – who didn't share Reverend and Mrs Denby's view of the arts. Although she did share their views on temperance.

The Old Vic had started as a mission to the working-class men of Waterloo, to give them a wholesome alternative to drinking every night in the pub. Due to Lilian's background in theatre she started staging plays and gained a reputation for being a serious alternative to the elitist froth on offer in the West End. She soon expanded into opera and ballet, and in the same year that Poppy walked through the door to interview the young up-and-coming actress Delilah Marconi, a full-time Shakespearean director had been appointed – Robert Atkins.

In fact, unknown to Poppy, the flustered-looking man she bumped into in the foyer and from whom she asked directions to Delilah, was the great director himself.

"She'll be in the chorus dressing room. That way." He pointed and then strode off, calling: "Has anyone seen Bottom?"

Poppy scuttled in the direction of the chorus dressing room, manoeuvring her way past trunks of props and racks of costumes. She had to stifle a yelp when she almost collided with a man wearing a donkey's head. He hiccuped an apology at her, wafting whisky-laden breath in her direction, then staggered off down the hall.

"BOTTOM!" she heard someone call again.

"Comin'!" slurred the donkey, steadying himself on the wall.

Poppy shook her head and knocked on the door that said "Women's chorus". Someone called "come in", so she entered.

Inside was a long bench covered in boxes of make-up and hairpieces under a long line of mirrors framed with gaslights.

Racks of clothes lined the other wall and there were a number of women in various states of undress.

Then someone called out to her: "Poppy!"

Poppy saw a waif-like creature draped in diaphanous strips of black and grey over a skintight leotard. It was Delilah. Her heavily made-up face with cobwebs drawn on each cheek smiled a warm greeting. In one hand she held a tube of lipstick; in the other a cigarette with red lipstick stains. She transferred both accessories to one hand and reached out the other to draw Poppy to her.

"What are you doing here?"

"Sorry to bother you, Delilah, but would you mind if I interviewed you for the newspaper? I want to do an article on an up-and-coming actress."

"Publicity's never a bother, luvvie," purred another fairy. "And if you want up and coming, I'm going way faster than Delilah!"

Delilah pulled up a seat for Poppy and motioned for her to sit. "Get in line, Edith!" she quipped, and the other actresses laughed.

"The paper? You got the job?"

"I did," squealed Poppy. Delilah squealed too and gave her a hug.

"And you're doing an article already?"

"I am. The arts editor is sick and –"

"Who's the arts editor?" asked Edith.

"Lionel somebody-or-other."

"Lionel Saunders from *The Globe*?" asked Delilah, impressed.

"That'll be the one."

"Drunken old letch." Edith screwed up her face.

"Careful, Edie, you're cracking your make-up," said Delilah and deliberately turned her back on her fellow actress and willed

Poppy to look only at her. She took Poppy's hands and squeezed them tightly. "Well done, you! Look, I don't have time now – we're starting rehearsal in a few minutes – but I'll arrange with Robert for you to watch and we can talk afterwards."

"Robert?"

"Atkins. The director. You haven't done your research, have you?"

"Well – I – it was all rather sudden. I didn't expect to get an assignment the first day and – well – I just sort of thought of you and –"

"It's all right," interrupted Delilah. "I'll get you up to speed. You have at least read the play, haven't you?"

"Well –"

Edith sniggered. Delilah sighed. "Here, read mine."

An hour later, Poppy was sitting in the auditorium completely entranced by what she was seeing on stage. The director had given his permission for her to watch when he heard she was the niece of Dotty Denby.

"Dotty Denby? The most entrancing Titania I have ever had the pleasure to work with. I was her Oberon in 1905 at Drury Lane. Now her daughter's an arts editor!"

"Niece. And I'm not an arts editor. I'm a –"

"Bottom! Where is that ass?"

Atkins rushed off, leaving Poppy to watch the rehearsal. She followed in the script and noted each time Cobweb spoke: there weren't too many occasions. But it didn't matter. The story of the lovers lost in the forest and the rivalry between the king and queen of the fairies was an absolute delight. Poppy knew her parents would think it frivolous; she thought it wondrous.

But then in Act III, scene 1, something unexpected happened. It was Delilah's big moment, when Titania entrusted

Cobweb and the other fairies with the care of the poor man she had just turned into a donkey – the one they called Bottom. Atkins had obviously managed to track down the elusive actor. Being half drunk didn't seem to affect his performance too much; but then, as he was being led off the stage by his fairy companions, Atkins called out, "Make it more playful. Give one of them a piggy back. You, Cobweb, jump on!"

Delilah did as she was bid; but Bottom, who could just about manage to keep himself on his feet, was not prepared for the extra weight – slight as it was – and he and Delilah tumbled off the stage and into the orchestra pit. Delilah screamed, Bottom swore, and everyone else gasped in shock.

Poppy rushed to see if her friend was hurt. She got to the front just as Atkins and some of the other actors were pulling her out.

"I'm fine," she said. "He broke my fall. But he's been sick all over me."

"Eeeeeewwwwww!" came the chorus from the rest of the fairies.

"Lord, give me strength!" said Atkins, then took control, marshalling his troops like a general on the battlefield. "Get him out of there before Lily gets here. And pay him off; he's half tanked most of the time anyway. Who's the understudy? Good. Get into his costume. You, help her wash off that sick. And you" – he pointed to Poppy – "come with me. We need to have a little talk about exactly what's going into your article."

CHAPTER 7

It was nearly four o'clock when Poppy got off the bus at the bottom of Fleet Street and had to wait for a horse-drawn window-cleaner's wagon to pass before she crossed to the sunny side of the street. The sun matched her mood. She had spent a fantastic afternoon with Mr Atkins – although she felt at times he had been directing her instead of her interviewing him – but for her very first article, she didn't mind. She had been going over her notes first on the train and then on the bus and she was wavering between angles: should she go with "Young up-and-coming actress in Shakespearean comedy" or "Top West End director brings serious theatre south of the river". The former was what she had intended and what she knew Delilah was hoping for, but she instinctively knew Rollo would want the "big name". By the time she was a block away from *The Globe* she had decided she would try to blend the two: "Top director takes a chance on new talent". Apparently Delilah wasn't the only new face on the programme, so she felt she could justifiably make it work. Now she just had to write it up.

She was still smiling when she entered the *Globe* foyer and waved to Mrs Bradshaw at the reception desk. Mavis Bradshaw smiled in return. "You look pleased as punch, Poppy. Good first day?"

"Oh, the best! I've just been to Waterloo and –"

A dreadful scream echoed through the atrium, punctuated by a sickening thud. Stunned, Poppy turned to see the body of a man, his limbs contorted like those of a broken doll, in the middle of the black and white mosaic floor. Mavis Bradshaw's screams took over where the man's had stopped and Poppy watched in horror as a red pool spread across the tiles.

"To Bert!"

"To Bert!" Glasses chinked around the table at Ye Olde Cock Tavern, the favourite watering hole of the *Globe* staff.

"Bert Isaacs. The best political correspondent I've ever worked with. Either side of the pond." Rollo downed his whisky, thumped down his glass and wiped his hand decisively over his mouth. "It's a crying shame."

"Will someone tell his family?" Poppy asked Mavis Bradshaw, who sat beside her – the only other woman among the pack of newspapermen who had come to drink to the memory of their late colleague.

"I don't think he had any," said Mavis sadly.

"He didn't," confirmed Rollo. "Married to the job." He poured himself another drink and offered to top up Poppy's. Poppy, who had only taken a sip of the whisky to be polite, covered the glass with her hand. Rollo grunted, but didn't seem to take offence. "Don't worry, Miz Denby. We'll do him right. We're family at *The Globe*." He raised his glass again. "To family!"

"To family!" came the slightly slurred chorus.

Daniel came through the door carrying his camera. Rollo poured him a drink and pushed it across the table to meet him. Daniel swigged it back in one gulp and sat in the vacant seat next to Poppy.

"They finished with you?" asked Rollo.

"For now. They asked me to take some photographs for them. Their fella's on holiday."

"All right for some," muttered one of the hacks.

"What of?" asked Rollo.

"The body from different angles – obviously – the staircase, the broken balustrade –"

"Why the hell didn't I get that fixed?" muttered Rollo, shaking his red head.

Daniel patted him on the shoulder. "You did your best, Rollo. It's not your fault the repairman couldn't come earlier."

Rollo glared at him under his shaggy brows. "He was coming tomorrow. One more day and Bert would still be alive."

"The police think it was an accident," interjected Daniel, happy to distract Rollo from his self-recrimination. "But there'll be a formal inquest."

"They told me that too," agreed Rollo.

That's what they'd told everyone. Mavis's screams had summoned men from every room in the building. Daniel was first on the scene, leaping down the stairs two at a time. He pushed past Poppy, who was fixed to the spot, unable to tear her eyes away from the broken body of the man she had only just met a few hours before. Not wanting to look at his head with the crushed skull and contorted face, she stared at his white shirt with the old food stains and then at his trousers, which no one had bothered to tell him were not properly done up.

Daniel confirmed quickly that Bert was dead and asked Mavis to call the police. As she did, journalists, printers, ad-men and bookkeepers filled the foyer. Poppy allowed herself to be pushed to the back of the crowd. This was not the first time she had seen a dead body – she had helped her mother at a military convalescent home during the war, and she had seen her fair share of dead, dying and grotesquely mutilated men; but it was the first time someone had literally dropped dead in front of her.

When Rollo arrived in the lift – his legs too short to sprint down the stairs the way Daniel had – he took over, leaving the photographer to find Poppy and ask if she was all right. He asked her what she had seen. She told him. Then later she told the police as they interviewed everyone in the building one at a time. As each person was released they went to the pub and waited for the rest of their colleagues.

Mavis had been interviewed just before Poppy. She had the most to contribute. It seemed that she was the last person to see the political correspondent alive. A few minutes before Poppy had arrived, a man came to deliver an envelope addressed to Bert. No, Mavis did not know the man. No, she did not see whether he arrived on foot or by vehicle. No, there was no return address on the envelope. She had called Bert on the interior telephone and he had come down in the lift to collect it. He read the note in front of her, raised his eyebrows in what Mavis described as surprise, then confided that he was thinking of going on a diet. She had teased him that he should be taking the stairs then, not the lift. At this she started crying. "It's my fault! If he'd gone back up in the lift this would never have happened."

The note was found under his body. It was written on very fine paper and had unfortunately soaked up so much blood that the ink was now illegible. The police said they might find out what it said when the blood dried, but they were not hopeful.

The clock above the bar said nine o'clock. It was time Poppy got home, or Aunt Dot and Grace would be worried about her. She had almost forgotten about the theatre story. Should she still write it up, she wondered? Rollo looked more than half drunk and she wasn't sure if she would get a coherent answer out of him. She was wrong.

"You got something for us then, Poppy?"

"Yes. But I still need to write it up."

"Too late for tomorrow. Won't get set in time. But write it up in the morning; I'll have a look at it and if it's any good, we can set it for the next day. I'll have a go piecing together Bert's notes, but we'll still need more copy…" He continued, musing away to himself and anyone who would listen about how he was going to juggle the next couple of editions without Bert's contributions. Poppy marvelled at the editor's ability to separate his emotions from the job at hand. Bert, she assumed, was a friend of Rollo's, yet sentiment would not get in the way of the story. It was a hard world Poppy was entering, this world of journalism. She wondered how she would cope if someone close to her became tomorrow's news. Would it simply be business as usual? Rollo continued to plan the week's papers out loud. Poppy assumed he was finished with her, so she stood up to leave.

"If you don't mind, Mr Rolandson, I need to get home."

Daniel stood up and helped her into her coat. "I'll walk you to the bus stop."

As they were leaving, Rollo called after them, "What's your angle?"

"My angle?"

"The theatre story, Miz Denby."

"Well, I spoke to Mr Atkins –"

"Robert Atkins?"

"Yes. Turns out he acted with my aunt. The most enchanting Titania he's ever seen, he said."

Rollo's drunk eyes slowly came into focus. He looked at Poppy intently. "Denby. Dotty Denby? Don't tell me you're related to one of the most infamous suffragettes of the last decade?" He accentuated his last word with a sweep of his over-large hands, knocking over bottles and glasses.

"Er – yes. Dorothy Denby is my aunt."

"There is a God!" cried Rollo. "Miz Denby, be in my office at eight o'clock on the dot. Not a minute later. And Danny Boy, you be there too."

Daniel and Poppy walked quietly down Fleet Street, past the walkway to St Bride's Church and half a dozen or so printers, publishers and newspaper offices interspersed between more pubs and taverns, some of which had been there from before Samuel Pepys first started writing his diary in 1660. They passed the pub where Charles Dickens had written much of *The Pickwick Papers* when he worked on Fleet Street as a journalist. Then they arrived at the bus stop. Light and laughter spilled from the taverns onto the street, but Poppy and Daniel were in a sombre mood.

"Are you all right, Poppy? After your shock?"

"I am Mr – Daniel – thank you for asking. Not the best thing to happen on a first day though." She forced a smile.

"Indeed."

"Do you think it was an accident?" Poppy asked.

"Of course. What else could it be?"

"Oh, I don't know. Call me silly if you will, but I just have this feeling… Don't you think it was strange that he fell to his death moments after receiving a mysterious letter?"

Daniel laughed, despite the sombre mood. "I think you have been reading too much of that lady mystery writer, Miss Denby."

Poppy flushed. Perhaps he was right. Of course he was right. But she couldn't shake the feeling that something was amiss. "Let's just say, for argument's sake, that it wasn't an accident."

"Poppy…"

"Oh, come on. Humour me."

Daniel craned his neck down the street, then looked at his pocket watch. "All right. Just until the bus comes. So, if it wasn't an accident he must have been pushed."

"Exactly."

"Well that, my learned friend, is where your case ends. There was no one on the stairs or on the landing with Bert. If there was, Mavis would have seen them. And I would have seen them when I heard her scream. They would have been running up or down the stairs either to get away or to pretend they were part of the crowd flocking to see what had happened. I was the first there. It was on the second floor. Just outside the art and photography department. I didn't see anyone."

Poppy absorbed this information and reassessed the situation. "What about the lift?"

"What about it?"

"Did you look in it?"

"Of course not. When I heard the screams I ran out of the department onto the landing, saw the broken balustrade and assumed the worst. I ran down the stairs immediately."

"So you didn't check the lift."

"No, I didn't check the lift."

"And we know that the lift went up to the fourth floor."

"How do we know that?"

"Because Rollo came down in it."

Daniel looked at her quizzically, a slight smile on his face. "Oh, very good, Miss Denby."

Poppy flushed, then immediately felt guilty for feeling so happy discussing the tragic death of an innocent man. But Daniel seemed to be going with the flow.

"So feasibly, someone could have got off the lift on the third floor before it got up to Rollo."

"Perhaps we shouldn't be talking about this." Poppy shook her head. "You were right in the first place. It's disrespectful playing this sort of game."

Daniel took her by the shoulders and turned her to him, looking intently into her eyes. "Not if it helps to find Bert's killer."

"If there was one."

"Yes, if there was one. But whether there was or there wasn't, Bert would want us to get to the bottom of the story."

"I suppose he would."

Daniel checked his watch again. "Do me a favour though: don't mention anything to Rollo just yet. He might think you're overstepping the mark. I'll ask him if he saw anyone coming out of the lift. And I'll ask on the third floor too. That's where we keep the morgue." He laughed at Poppy's raised eyebrows. "Where we keep our archive of old editions and research files."

"When will you ask him?"

"Tomorrow. After our meeting."

Poppy suddenly remembered the summons to Rollo's office in the morning, and despite the tragic circumstances of the day couldn't help a surge of hope rising in her. "What do you think it's about?"

"I'm not entirely sure, but I think it's to do with the story Bert was working on before he died. It had some kind of suffragette, women's rights angle, and Rollo got excited when he heard who your aunt was. So he may want to use your connections in that area to flesh out the story."

"Golly, and I thought I was just going to tidy his office."

"The day Rollo's office gets tidied will be the day he dies."

Headlights flashed as a bus turned the corner at the bottom of the street.

"An unfortunate turn of phrase, Mr Rokeby."

"A slip of the tongue, Miss Denby. Goodnight. Travel safely."

CHAPTER 8

Elizabeth awoke with the strangest feeling, one so alien she almost didn't recognize it. But as she turned over and looked towards the barred window, the first rays of sun pushing through, she felt it wash over her – the possibility that she could soon be free; the hope that she had a future.

She wondered how long it would take the journalist to notify the police and for them to come and free her. Surely not long. But perhaps he might want to see her himself first. Or send someone else to do it. The last time he'd come had not been so successful, after all. It had been about a month ago, just before the last visit by the window cleaner, and she had heard a commotion in the hall outside her locked door. She had crawled along the floor so she wouldn't be seen through the glass panel and pressed her ear to the keyhole. She heard a man's voice claiming to have been given permission to see her. The nurse on duty said she needed to speak to her superior before she could let him in. Elizabeth knew that meant she would have to telephone *him*. The man appeared to assume the same and told the nurse that *he* in fact had been the one who had given permission in the first place, and offered to make the telephone call himself. Elizabeth could not hear what the nurse said in response, but she assumed it must have been positive because she heard them walking towards her door.

She retreated to her bed, lest they realize she'd been listening, and waited to hear the key turn in the lock. But just as she saw the outline of a large man in the glass pane she heard another man shout.

"What are you doing here? Step away from that door."

"He's here to see Elizabeth Dorchester, doctor. He says he's a solicitor. He has permission."

"Solicitor, my eye! He's a reporter. Aren't you? We met at the Marie Curie fundraiser at Great Ormond Street. Abrahams, isn't it?"

"Isaacs," said the journalist, sounding completely unrepentant. "From *The Globe*. What have you got to hide here, doctor? Why is this woman locked up? Has someone paid you to do it?"

"Elizabeth Dorchester is a very sick woman and that is as much as I can tell you. Patient confidentiality, Mr Isaacs – surely even a yellow journalist like yourself has heard of that."

Isaacs' reply was stifled by what Elizabeth assumed was the arrival of some muscle to escort him away. She lay on the bed and listened until she heard the last door slam. And then she cried. She was desperate to make contact with another human being – a sympathetic human being; someone who might see her as she really was, not the fiction created by her medical file.

When she stopped crying she started to think. Why was this Isaacs coming to see her? How had he heard about her? She wondered if it had something to do with *him*. He'd always been newsworthy, never out of the pages of *The Times* for long, and would give social engagements guaranteed to attract press photographers' attention preference over other less glamorous occasions. He had also paraded her in front of the press when she was a young and beautiful debutante; but all that changed when she managed to get herself onto the front page of *The Times* all by herself – chained to the railings of number 10 Downing Street. He had been appalled and attempted to have her locked up, claiming she must be mentally deranged. He hired three different psychiatrists to testify to her instability in front of a judge. But the judge did not accept it and dismissed the case. That time.

Elizabeth no longer knew what he was up to out there in the world, but she doubted he was any less prominent than he was before the war; before he'd finally succeeded in having her sectioned under the 1913 Mental Deficiency Act after that most terrible of affairs.

Elizabeth shook her head. She did not want to think about that now. She did not want images of feeding tubes and tortured women filling her waking hours as they filled her dreams. She did not want to see the broken body of her friend on a railway line. She tried to sink back into that elusive feeling she had glimpsed when she awoke, but it was fading fast. Mr Isaacs from *The Globe* had better do something quickly, because if he didn't there was only one course of action left to her. She closed her eyes and started to wander down the well-worn paths of fantasy in which she worked out the intricacies of her Plan B – her suicide plan. *Please hurry, Mr Isaacs; please hurry.*

When Poppy arrived in Rollo Rolandson's office at 8 a.m. sharp, she found him staring moodily into a cup of thick black coffee, wearing the same shirt, bow-tie and braces as the previous night. Poppy doubted he'd had a wink of sleep.

"Miz Denby," he growled, and motioned for her to sit. "Dan will join us in a minute. He's just sorting out his equipment."

Poppy looked around at the piles of files in danger of crushing the diminutive editor at any moment. "Do you want me to get started on the clean-up?"

Bleary-eyed, Rollo looked up from his coffee, his unshaven top lip glistening with droplets of the brew. "Later. Got something for you to do first. You and Dan. Your aunt *is* Dotty Denby, right?"

"That's right."

"And has she ever mentioned a Melvyn Dorchester to you?"

Poppy thought for a moment. Dorchester. Melvyn Dorchester. No, she couldn't say she had. But then suddenly Poppy remembered her aunt slamming down *The Globe* newspaper a week or so ago and clattering the tea tray. Grace had looked up from the accounts she was doing on the other side of the room. She had asked what was wrong.

"The Dorkmeister!" Dot declared. "Lord snake-in-the-grass Dorchester. Who would have thought that Curie woman would fall for it?"

"Perhaps you should speak to Marjorie Reynolds about it," Grace mumbled before returning to a column of figures.

"Perhaps I shall," Dot had fumed. When Poppy asked her about it she said she would tell her later. She didn't want to give herself indigestion so late in the afternoon. But she had never got around to telling her. Poppy told Rollo what had happened.

"Good. Just what we need. You can get the details from her later, Poppy. And see if she's prepared to be quoted. For now, all you need to know is in here." He pushed a file across the desk. "The highlights are: Lord Melvyn Dorchester, Tory peer and business tycoon, was a very vocal opponent of the women's suffrage movement before the war. There were even suggestions that he put pressure on the Home Office to get the police to use strong-arm tactics on some of the women."

Poppy immediately thought of her aunt's accident. "Strong-arm tactics?"

"Ask your aunt. And read the file. But nothing's been proven."

Poppy absorbed the information.

"Are you taking notes?"

Poppy whipped out a notebook and pencil from her satchel. "Yes, sir." She started to scribble.

"That's just background. There's more to it and we will get to the bottom of it, but for now the story Bert was working on is that Dorchester has just been awarded a contract to supply London hospitals with X-ray equipment. He's in some kind of partnership with the Radium Institute in Paris."

"Marie Curie."

"Right on, Miz Denby. The thing is, Curie is a known feminist and it seems strange – no, let me rephrase that – downright *bizarre* that she would approve it."

"Have you spoken to her?"

"We have. And she said Dorchester has come around to seeing the justice of the women's cause. She points to his recent backing of the Sex Disqualification (Removal) Act."

"Which my aunt probably thinks he's faking."

"Well, he can't fake his vote, but his motives seem highly dubious. The contract, apparently, is worth millions."

"Hmmm," said Poppy. "So you want me to interview my aunt about this."

"I do. But first I want you to go and see Dorchester himself."

Poppy had not expected that. She took a few moments to gather her thoughts while Rollo took another slurp of his coffee.

"Er – when do you want me to go?"

"This morning. Dan will go with you. He's already been briefed. I've put a list of questions in the front of the file. Nothing too in-depth – it's well-trodden ground. Keep it sweet. Just say you're there to clarify a few points from Bert's notes before we go to print. I've also included a copy of the story you can lead him to believe we're going to print –"

Lead him to believe? Poppy didn't like the sound of that. She was never comfortable with deceit. Rollo must have read her thoughts.

"You'll have to leave your Christian qualms behind, Miz Denby, if you want to make it as a journalist." His voice softened a little as he saw her looking perturbed: "You believe in truth, Poppy. And justice. So do we. This is just a means to an end. And it's not an outright lie. It *is* what we're going to print – just not all of it."

Poppy absorbed that for a moment and then nodded her agreement. "All right, I'll do my best."

"Good girl."

"But why are you sending me? Surely there are more experienced people that could do it." She cocked her head towards the newsroom just as the door opened and Daniel entered.

"There are," agreed Rollo. "But none of them will get up Dorchester's nose like you will."

"And why's that?" asked Poppy.

"Because you're a woman," said Daniel, swinging his camera case by its strap.

"*And* you're Dotty Denby's niece," added Rollo. "Wait until the very end of the interview, then let that little gem slip and see how he reacts. If anything will knock his composure, that will. He hates women. I know he does. And you're just the gal to bring it out of him."

Poppy raised her eyebrows in alarm. Daniel put a comforting hand on her shoulder. "Don't worry. That's why I'll be there. He won't do anything in front of me."

"I hope not," said Poppy quietly.

"Will you do it?" asked Rollo.

Poppy looked around at the "housekeeping" that awaited her if she declined. Then she thought of poor Bert, lying on a cold slab, unable to finish the story he'd started. And finally she thought of her aunt and her friends, and the untold sacrifices they had made to give young women like her a chance to follow their dreams.

She looked straight into Rollo's bloodshot eyes and nodded decisively. "I will."

CHAPTER 9

Poppy had never been in the sidecar of a motorcycle before; it was very exciting. Daniel helped her put on the leather helmet and button it under her chin. He paused for a moment to twirl his finger in one of her curls and push it under the leather. Poppy's eyes widened at the familiarity; he apologized with the look of a chastised puppy, making Poppy laugh.

Daniel had parked the motorcycle in the alleyway behind the *Daily Globe* building, through the double doors of the basement where delivery vans backed up to receive each day's edition. Poppy knew that today's edition would have an obituary on page 3, written by Rollo last night and typeset himself just before midnight after he had called "stop press" on the printers. Poor Bert Isaacs. She'd barely known the man, but she felt a sudden fondness for him, and, as she gripped the file of research on Dorchester, a sense of responsibility that she was taking on his mantle, at least temporarily, and helping to finish the story he had started.

The question of whether or not his death was an accident was still to be pursued. Daniel did not have a chance to talk to Rollo about it before they left; he promised he would do so when they returned after the interview.

Daniel lent Poppy his scarf – a hand-knitted one in purple, orange and blue stripes. She wondered who had knit it. His mother? His wife? No, not his wife. She hadn't seen a wedding ring on his finger. She inhaled the smell of him and smiled to herself, remembering the touch of his finger as he fastened her helmet and the weight of his hand on her shoulder in Rollo's office. Good heavens! What was she thinking? She had a job to do and could not be distracted mooning over a man she had only just met. But then he helped her into the sidecar and covered her legs with a rug, tucking it tightly down the sides of her legs. Oh, that was too much. She pushed his hands away.

"Thank you, Mr Rokeby. I can manage."

He looked at her askance, shrugged and then straddled the motorcycle. He lifted his leg like a dog and kicked down on the starter. The engine roared into life.

"Ready?" he shouted.

"Ready!" she called back and then grasped the edge of the sidecar as they slalomed their way between barrows and bins down the alley and into Fleet Street.

Dorchester lived out west in Windsor. It took Poppy and Daniel just over an hour to get there from central London. Once out of the gridlock of the city and on the open road, Daniel pulled back the throttle and pushed the motorcycle towards its full potential. Poppy had never felt anything so exhilarating in her life. She laughed and smiled at Daniel – which he took as a cue to go faster. She laughed again and threw back her head, wishing she could take off her helmet and allow her hair to fly in the wind. All tension between the two of them was gone and they were united in their love of speed and the open road.

She was disappointed when he finally slowed down on the outskirts of Windsor and joined the traffic skirting the edge of Ascot. Dorchester – apparently the owner of a string of champion racehorses – lived on an estate only a few miles from the racetrack. Outside the imposing wrought-iron gates marked with the family crest of a crow and a rose, Poppy and Daniel had a last-minute discussion about the approach they were going to take. Rollo had telephoned ahead and given Dorchester the bad news of Bert's death and asked him if he minded if *The Globe* sent someone over to clarify a few points before going to print. They also wanted a photograph. Dorchester was notoriously vain and could never say no to a picture that might get him on the front page of a daily – even if it was a tabloid. Rollo had of course failed to mention that the person he was sending over was a woman.

The cycle advanced slowly up the gravel drive to the imposing façade of a sixteenth-century manor house, set amid perfectly manicured gardens. A butler was waiting for them on the steps at the front door and he took Daniel's camera and tripod from him as the photographer helped Poppy out of the sidecar and unstrapped her helmet. Then he swapped the helmets for the camera and they followed the butler up the granite steps and through the front door.

They were quickly ushered into a large library, which was bigger than Poppy's parents' entire two-storey house in Morpeth. But before Poppy could take in the grandeur of the book-lined room they were met by a pencil-thin man striding towards them, wearing a steel-grey morning suit and navy blue cravat. He was in his early sixties but had the gait of a much younger man. His dark-blond hair had only the slightest suggestion of grey, and his sharply trimmed sideburns none of it.

"Mr Rokeby and Miss Denby from *The Globe*, sir," intoned the butler before backing out of the room.

"Ah, Rokeby! You did a splendid job on those King's Cross memorial photographs. Everyone's been commenting on them."

"Thank you, sir," said Daniel and took the gentleman's hand.

"And may I introduce Miss Poppy Denby. Miss Denby, Lord Melvyn Dorchester."

Dorchester did not extend his hand, but gave a stiff little bow, punctuated by a twitch of his mustachioed upper lip. "Miss

Denby." Then he turned his attention back to Daniel. "Dreadful business about Isaacs. Dreadful."

"We're all very shocked, sir."

"I see Rolandson's wasted no time in promoting you."

"Promoting?" asked Daniel.

"To chief reporter. Isaacs' old job" – he looked at Poppy briefly – "and a new assistant, I see. Was she Bert's before yours?"

Poppy bristled at being spoken of as if she were property. "Actually, I am Mr Rolandson's assistant. He has asked me to –"

"Ah. Thank you for clarifying that, madam." Dorchester put his arm around Daniel, turning his back on Poppy.

"Shall we get on with this then, Rokeby? I'm due at the stables in half an hour."

He ushered Daniel towards one of two winged armchairs on either side of a marble fireplace and indicated that Poppy should take a smaller chair nearby. Above the mantelpiece was a life-size painting of two children. The clothing suggested turn of the century or soon before. The boy, about ten, looked like a child version of Dorchester: the same blond hair, the same aquiline nose and cool grey eyes. The girl was a few years older, with thick auburn hair falling loosely over her shoulders; she was fleshier than her brother and although she had the same colour eyes, they were larger and set further apart. They were clearly related, but perhaps cousins rather than siblings; or maybe one took after the father and the other the mother.

"My children. Alfie and Lizzie, when they were younger," said Dorchester. "Now, let's get on."

Poppy suddenly realized that she had been standing staring at the painting and neither man felt he could sit until she had done so first. She made her way towards her allocated seat, but Daniel redirected her to the armchair and then pulled up the other chair for himself.

"Miss Denby," he smiled.

"Thank you, Mr Rokeby," she smiled back.

"May we *please* get on now?" said Dorchester crisply, flicking out his jacket tails and then turning his attention to Daniel.

Daniel nodded at Poppy. She reached into her satchel and took out her notebook, where she had transcribed the questions Rollo had written out for her. She left the file out of sight in the bag.

"Lord Dorchester ..." she started.

With a sharp intake of breath he pursed his lips and looked down his nose at her, clearly frustrated by what he considered another interruption. "Madam, do you mind? Rokeby, can you ask your – assistant to –"

"She is not my assistant," said Daniel lightly. "In fact, if anything I am hers. I have not been 'promoted' as you assume, Lord Dorchester; I am a photographer, not a reporter, and am happy to remain so. Miss Denby here is *The Globe*'s newest journalist. And she –"

"Rolandson's sent a – a –" – Poppy was sure he had been about to say "woman", but he pulled himself back just in time – "*novice* to interview me?"

"Well, I –" started Poppy.

Daniel interrupted her. "Sorry, Poppy. If I may..." She nodded. "You are not Miss Denby's first assignment by any means. She has most recently interviewed Robert Atkins and is highly connected in certain – how should I put it? – *political* circles. In fact she comes highly recommended."

"Well, I –" tried Poppy again.

"Does she indeed?" droned Dorchester, once again not even looking at her.

Poppy remembered suddenly the Lord Kitchener look-alike at the stationer's and what she had wanted to say to him if she had the chance to do it again. Well, this was her chance. And while she appreciated Daniel defending her – as she had her aunt – what she really wanted, no, what she really *needed*, was to do it herself.

"Thank you, Mr Rokeby. Lord Dorchester. May we please get started?" She said it with the forcefulness of a school headmistress, and before the two surprised men could comment any further she poked her pencil at the first question on her list and asked, "Could you confirm, sir, that you have won the contract to put new X-ray machines into London hospitals and that the first hospital to receive one will be the Royal London?"

Dorchester looked for a moment as though he were going to question her authority once more, but then with a terse look at his pocket watch appeared to decide against it. "Yes, I can confirm that."

"And can you confirm that…"

For the next twenty minutes Poppy went through Rollo's list of questions – as well as a few of her own – that essentially clarified the article Bert was writing before he died.

"Well, that just about covers it. Thank you, Lord Dorchester."

With another quick look at his pocket watch, Dorchester stood briskly and smoothed down his jacket. "Right, where do you want me for the photograph, Rokeby?"

"However," said Poppy, looking at her notes, "I have one more question."

Dorchester bristled. "Well, I have no more time, madam."

"It shan't take a moment. And in case you've forgotten, the name is Denby, Poppy Denby. Is the name familiar to you?"

"No. Should it be?"

"We have a mutual acquaintance. Dorothy Denby is my aunt."

Dorchester's thin nostrils flared ever so slightly.

"And it is she who has inspired me to ask this: have you now changed your mind about women in the professions? Women such as Madame Marie Curie, one of the world's leading scientists?"

"I do not know what you mean, madam," said Dorchester, glaring at Daniel with a look that suggested he should get his "filly" under control.

Poppy was flicking through her notebook and then stopped at a particular page. "Is it not true that in the House of Lords in 1910 you declared that, and I quote, 'women do not have the mental capacity to fulfil the roles that have been rightly reserved for men for millennia' and that you would – and I again quote – 'withdraw from the House if ever women were given the right to vote'?"

"Well, I –"

"Did you or did you not say that?"

"I did. And it is on record. But you misquote me. I hope you are not going to make a habit of this so early in your – *journalistic* – career. What I said, in context, *Miss Denby*, was that I support the advancement of women in as far as they are mentally able – as Madame Curie certainly is, and certain other women are too."

"Certain other women? Such as Marjorie Reynolds?"

"Indeed. Marjorie Reynolds is an exception to the rule."

"So, Lord Dorchester, would it be correct in saying that you still consider the vast majority of women intellectually inferior to men and incapable of professional advancement?"

"No, madam, it would not." He pulled himself up to his full height and towered over her. "And be assured I shall be putting in a formal complaint to your editor."

Dorchester and Poppy glared at one another, their feet almost toe to toe. She would have stood, but he did not give her sufficient room to do so.

"Ahem." It was Daniel. "Should we take the photograph at the stables then?"

An hour later Poppy and Daniel were sitting in a tea room in Windsor and he was pouring her a cup of Earl Grey from a floral teapot.

"Oh, Poppy, you were splendid, just splendid," he chuckled as he put down the pot and offered her a slice of lemon.

"But he said he would put in a complaint to the editor," said Poppy glumly and sucked on the lemon before she remembered where she was and put it down politely on her saucer.

"I know. Isn't it marvellous? Rollo will be delighted. You have all the instincts of a first-class newshound, Miz Denby," he drawled in a mock New York accent.

Poppy giggled. "I thought for a minute this hound was going to be taken outside and shot!"

"Pompous ass."

Some elderly ladies, whose fashion icon was clearly the late Queen Victoria, tutted at him. Poppy stifled another giggle.

"Pardon me, ladies," Daniel apologized.

"You've obviously met him before."

"Dorchester?"

Poppy nodded.

"He pops up all over the place. Can't get enough publicity, that one. And of course I know his son."

"Alfie?"

"Yes. He's a year or two older than me. We served in the same regiment in Flanders. Used to see him – and his father – a lot when I attended regimental dinners. Don't bother with them any more now." He rubbed his forefinger over some of the scar tissue on his right hand. Poppy wanted to ask what had caused it, but sensed this wasn't the time.

"He's insufferable. If you think Melvyn's bad, you should meet his son."

"Oh?" said Poppy, leaning in and turning her shoulder to block the view of the two Victorian ladies.

"Won the Victoria Cross."

"That's impressive."

"It is, but he never shuts up about it. Neither does his dad. Surprised he didn't bring it up today."

"He was obviously distracted."

Daniel raised an eyebrow in what Poppy's mother would have described as a rakish manner. "I don't blame him."

"Mr Rokeby!" Her tone was chastising, but the twinkle in her eyes betrayed her. The disapproving ladies tutted again and Poppy heard mutterings of "Well I never" and "The youth of today", before they gathered their hats and parasols and left the shop.

Both Poppy and Daniel sighed their relief and refilled their teacups.

"So what did he win it for?"

"Seems he fought off a nest of Huns trying to save his men."

"Were you there?"

"No," said Daniel, still rubbing his hands. "I'd been sent home a few months before. But I would have been." He stopped rubbing and looked out of the window at the passers-by, many of them dressed for the races in top hats and tails.

Poppy sat in silence, waiting for him to continue or to change the subject. She'd met enough patients at the military convalescent home to know that they would speak when they wanted to speak.

"They were good lads. The lot of them. Thirteen of them died that day. Alfie was the only one who survived. They thought he was dead at first and loaded him onto a wagon with the rest of them. But then someone heard him and –" He paused, and started rubbing again. "More tea, Miss Denby?"

"Thank you, Daniel, but I think I've had enough," she said quietly, wanting to take his hands in hers. "We should probably get back. I've got to write up these notes and finish the theatre story."

Daniel laughed, the ghosts of the past once again at bay. "Only two days on the job, eh?"

Poppy laughed too. "I know! Can you believe it?"

Daniel stood and held out his hand for Poppy. She took it. They stood for a moment, their hands linked over the table. Embarrassed, Poppy grappled for something to divert their attention.

"Er – you said you knew Alfie. Did you ever meet the daughter? What did he say her name was? Lizzie?"

Daniel shook his head. "No. Apparently she's ill. Some kind of long-term mental condition."

"Oh?"

Daniel helped Poppy into her coat. "She's been in hospital since before the war. I heard Alfie mention it once. Not sure what it's about. You should ask your aunt."

"My aunt?" asked Poppy, surprised.

"She was a suffragette. Tied herself to the railings of 10 Downing Street and then firebombed Lord's cricket ground. Was sent to Holloway, I think. Dorchester was mortified. His wife had been a feminist too. She'd left him."

"Why am I not surprised?"

"Indeed. I think she died on the *Titanic* or something."

"Oh, how tragic."

"Yes, it is. But they say Dorchester never batted an eyelid."

"Delightful man."

Daniel grinned. "Let's get back to the office, Miss Denby. There's work to be done and deadlines to keep."

"Stop press!" cried Poppy and they both laughed.

CHAPTER 10

Poppy spent the rest of the day writing up her notes from the Dorchester interview and then finishing off the *Midsummer Night's Dream* story. She showed both to Rollo, who seemed to have caught his second wind after lunch – and a spell in Ye Olde Cock – and was looking much brighter. He declared the theatre piece to be a good first effort and after a few minor edits sent it to be typeset.

"This will be your first byline, Miz Denby. Well done."

Poppy flushed in delight.

However, he declared that the Dorchester piece needed a bit more work and he would take over.

"You did well though, Poppy. Dan told me you've got a natural flair for it. And of course Dorchester rang…"

Poppy felt her pulse quicken. "What did he say?"

"The usual. We'll be hearing from his solicitor and so on."

"Oh dear," Poppy said, taking a deep breath.

"Don't worry. I'll handle it. We've got solicitors too. You did exactly what I asked of you." He looked around him at the piles of files and then turned and winked at her. "The best editorial assistant I've ever had. Now get home and interview your aunt. Can you telephone in her comment before six o'clock? You do have a telephone, don't you?"

"We do. And I'll try, sir."

Aunt Dot's first comment was too rude to be printed but was finally amended to:

*Leading WSPU member Dorothy Denby sheds doubt
on Lord Dorchester's motivation at supporting the Sex
Disqualification (Removal) Act, suggesting he may have
ulterior motives. "A leopard does not change its spots," Miss
Denby said.*

Rollo seemed happy enough with it. As Poppy put down the
phone she heard raised voices coming from the parlour. It was
Aunt Dot and Grace.

"Why are you trying to antagonize him, Dorothy?"

"Because he's never been held to account. I thought you
would have wanted me to do it. For Emily. For Gloria. For Ellen."

"I do. But I don't think mud-slinging in the press is going
to achieve it. It just makes you look like a – a hysterical woman.
Just what he wants."

"Hysterical?" asked Dot, her voice rising. "You think I'm
hysterical?"

"I don't. But he will. We need to show we can be just as
professional as men."

"Ha! You sound just like them. Women are too emotional.
Women are too unpredictable. Well, let me tell you something,
Grace –"

"I – I'm sorry if I've caused any bother." Poppy stood in
the doorway and looked from one friend to the other. Dot was
sitting in a patch of evening sun beside the bay window. Grace
was standing near her in the shadows. She turned to Poppy, her
thin shoulders rising and falling in resignation.

"No, I'm sorry. You haven't caused any bother, Poppy. I'm
very proud of you." She reached out her hand to her wheelchair-
bound friend. Dot took it and squeezed.

"We both are," continued Grace. "You're doing what we
could only have dreamed of doing when we were your age."

Dot looked at Poppy intently, her blue eyes awash with concern. "Are you sure you're all right after what happened yesterday? It must have been quite a shock to witness such a thing on your first day." She patted the window seat beside her. "Take a seat, darling."

Poppy sat down heavily. "Yes, it certainly was a shock." She shook her head. "I didn't even know Mr Isaacs, but seeing him that way was... awful."

Dot took Poppy's hand and squeezed it warmly. Poppy smiled gratefully. "But I'm fine, really, Aunt Dot." She released her grip from Dot's hand and flexed her fingers. "It's made me more determined to see his story through." She looked at Grace then Dot, wondering if she dared stoke the fire further. But she didn't have a choice, not if she wanted to do the story – and Bert – justice. She took a deep breath and asked as nonchalantly as possible: "So... what can you tell me about Melvyn Dorchester?"

Dot looked up at Grace. "Can I tell her? Is it all right?"

Grace nodded and took a seat.

Poppy, positioned between the two women, suppressed the urge to take out her notebook.

"I think we need to see the photograph and the medal, please, Grace," said Dot.

Grace got up, went to the sideboard and returned with the artefacts. Dot put on a pair of pince-nez.

"This was taken in 1909. There's the WSPU banner and our motto –"

"'Deeds not words'. It's on Emily's grave," observed Poppy.

"That's right. But she was alive and well here. And there's Emmeline and her daughter Christabel. I think Sylvia took the photograph."

"She did," confirmed Grace.

"And there's Frank and, of course, Grace."

"And you," Poppy added.

"Yes, and me, pet." Aunt Dot smiled wistfully as she looked at the younger, slimmer, more mobile version of herself wearing the white suffragist uniform.

"I don't remember who that other man is. Do you, Grace? The one at the back?"

"A friend of Sophie's, I think. He wasn't one of us; he just slipped in for the photograph. He was a journalist. Jewish."

Poppy's curiosity was piqued. She took the photograph and stared at the man partly obscured by the banner. Could it possibly be a younger, slimmer version of Bert Isaacs? All she could remember of him was his dead eyes and his overhanging belly. She made a mental note to ask if she could take the photograph with her to show Daniel and Rollo. But for now she gave it back to Aunt Dot, who held it like a child on her lap.

"Now, the rest of them we do know. We were called the Chelsea Six. We should have been the Chelsea Seven, but people forgot to count poor Frank."

There was a sharp intake of breath from Grace, and Poppy made another mental note to finally get around to finding out what happened to "poor Frank". As far as she knew he was still alive. She wasn't sure whether he and Grace were divorced or just separated.

"Well, moving on," said Aunt Dot with forced brightness. "The Chelsea Six. It was Maud Dorchester who brought us together. There she is there. She was Irish with the most beautiful auburn hair. A great fan of the theatre. She and I met back in 1905 – at a reception after *Midsummer Night's Dream*, in fact! Did I ever tell you –"

"Dorothy, you digress."

"Indeed I do. But I must link up with Robert again. Perhaps we can go to Delilah's opening night…"

"I have tickets," Poppy added.

"You do? Splendid!"

"Dorothy!"

"Sorry. Yes, Maud O'Sullivan, or Lady Maud Dorchester as she became, was a good friend of Emmeline Pankhurst. And she also knew Frank."

"He was Dorchester's accountant," contributed Grace. "Well, we both were, but he was the one 'on the books', so to speak."

"If Dorchester had found out that a woman was managing his finances he would have gone through the roof," Dot exclaimed with a chuckle.

"Well, he did. But that was later. Carry on with the story, Dorothy. I'm sure Poppy has got better things to do than listen to two old ladies like us."

"Oh, I've nothing better to do," said Poppy in all seriousness. "Do carry on, Aunt Dot."

"Well, Maud was already sympathetic to the feminist cause – she'd read Mary Wollstonecraft and had even wanted to become a doctor. But her father, an Irish peer, had put his foot down and married her off to Melvyn Dorchester. She did the usual: got married, had children, supported her husband in his political career; but when the children were in their teens and the boy was off at Eton, she had more time on her hands and started going out. She met Emmeline and became a card-carrying member of the WSPU. There's a lot more to it of who met whom when, but to cut to the chase, Maud recruited Grace and Frank and her daughter Elizabeth too."

Dot pointed to a beautiful, full-figured young woman in her early twenties, whom Poppy recognized as an older version of the teenage girl in the painting. She put her finger on the photographic image and pointed to Elizabeth.

"What happened to her, Aunt Dot? I heard she became ill."

"She did. I'll get to that in a minute. So, where were we? Ah yes, Maud recruited first Grace and Frank and then Elizabeth. Soon afterwards I joined. And then I recruited Gloria Marconi." Dot pointed to an Italian-looking woman with long black hair under a felt hat. "She was an actress who married the nephew of the famous Guglielmo Marconi, the head of the Wireless Telegraph and Signal Company. He's just about to launch a public radio service too! Apparently he needs voices. Delilah told me all about it! I think I might audition… What do you think, Poppy?"

"Dorothy!" Grace reprimanded. "Oh, you're incorrigible. Let *me* finish the tale."

Dot squinted through her pince-nez at her friend and sniffed. "Oh, all right. If you must."

Grace pushed back a strand of hair that had strayed onto her forehead and slicked it down as smoothly as the rest. "So now we have Maud, Elizabeth, Frank and me, Dot and Gloria. The final member of the cell – because that's what we were; a political cell of the Women's Social and Political Union based here in Chelsea and operating from this house – was Sophie Blackburn." She pointed to a plump, sensible looking young woman in her early twenties with hair pulled back into a bun. "Sophie was a friend of Elizabeth's. She, like Maud, had wanted to be a doctor but ended up working as a nurse. She was with us for just a couple of years before she left for Belgium. She joined Marie Curie and her daughter, and helped them with their mobile X-ray wagons travelling around the battlefields. We haven't heard from her since 1914 but believe she's still with Madame Curie in Paris."

Poppy's ears pricked up again at the mention of Marie Curie and X-ray machines. She made another mental note.

"So there you have it. The Chelsea Six, excluding Frank, were Maud, Elizabeth, Grace, Dorothy, Gloria and Sophie. If you read press clippings of the time you'll discover we were quite famous. We initiated a number of campaigns, including the chaining of some of the sisters to the railings outside 10 Downing Street. Elizabeth was at the forefront of that. Her father went ballistic."

"And took it out on her mother," said Dot darkly.

"Yes, he could be – how should I put it? – a *traditional* husband; not scared of disciplining his wayward wife."

"He was a brute," added Dot. "We had to take Maud in after the worst of the beatings. Sophie nursed her back to health. We would have taken Elizabeth too, but Dorchester locked her up."

"Oh?" Poppy's ears pricked again.

"He wouldn't let her out of the house. She managed to escape a few times though. She got out on the day of the Epsom Derby. When poor Emily was killed. She was involved in the demonstrations soon afterwards – she bombed a pavilion at Lord's – and got sent to Holloway. The poor girl was force-fed. Drove her mad. She lost her mind and we've never seen her since."

"Where is she now?"

"A mental hospital in Battersea."

Poppy made another mental note. "And Maud?"

"She died the year before: 1912. We all agreed that it wasn't safe for her to stay in London. She decided to go to America to help the sisters in New York. She tried to get Elizabeth to go with her, but wasn't able to. She died on the *Titanic*."

Dot's eyes welled up and Grace passed her a handkerchief. "And then –"

"And then Gloria was killed too," Grace finished for her. "She was in Holloway with Elizabeth. They were released at the same time under the Cat and Mouse Act. But like Elizabeth, she seemed to have lost her mind."

"She threw herself under a train," Dot whispered.

"Dear God. That's poor Delilah's mother," said Poppy and felt tears welling up. She composed herself and asked, "But what has all this to do with Dorchester?"

"Apart from his beating his wife and locking up his daughter?" asked Grace.

"Yes, apart from that. There's more, isn't there?"

Grace nodded. "There is. Your aunt's so-called accident. It was 1910 – 18th November to be exact. And Asquith, the prime minister at the time, had dragged his heels on some very important legislation that he had promised to bring before the House – the Conciliation Bill. It would have given the vote to certain propertied women. Not the universal suffrage we wanted, but it was a start. But Asquith pussyfooted around so much they never got to it before parliament shut down for the season – and it would have been too late for the next General Election. Emmeline was furious. Asquith had given her a personal assurance that the bill would be presented; so she went into Westminster to confront him."

"In the meantime," continued Dot, "about three hundred of us sisters –"

"And some brothers –"

"Yes, some men too, congregated outside. The police set up a cordon to keep us out. We pushed. They pushed back. Then all hell broke loose."

"It was brutal," continued Grace. "They called it Bloody Friday. There were pictures in the press of women being beaten. They were manhandled – intimately too. Some people were seriously injured. One of the sisters –"

"Ellen Pitfield, God rest her soul," Dorothy added solemnly.

"– died later of her injuries. She was injured at the same time as your aunt. At least a dozen witnesses saw a policeman deliberately ride his horse into a crowd. Ellen was crushed by people trying to get away. And your aunt – your aunt –"

Dot took her friend's hand. "I was crushed under the hooves, pet." She held up a medal and showed Poppy. Her hands were shaking. "I was awarded this for conspicuous bravery by the WSPU."

Grace was openly weeping now. "You were more than brave, Dorothy. And that bastard has never been tried."

"The policeman?" Poppy asked, incredulous.

"PC Richard Easling. Yes, him – and Dorchester. Maud told us that he had boasted to her that he had bribed some police officers to target her and her friends on Black Friday. But we never had any proof. There was nothing written down. He was too clever for that."

Poppy thought about the man she had met that morning and did not have to stretch her imagination too far to see him orchestrating an act of brutality against anyone who opposed him. She was just about to tell Dot and Grace what Rollo had told her – that he intended to get to the bottom of the allegations about Dorchester instigating strong-arm tactics against the suffragettes – when the doorbell rang.

Grace went to answer and a moment later Delilah Marconi skipped into the room looking as fashionable and exotic as ever. She was carrying a dress bag.

"Oh, there you are, Poppy! Just the girl I wanted to see."

CHAPTER 11

"Oh, Poppy! You look absolutely divine."

Poppy stood in front of the full-length mirror in her bedroom and stared at her reflection in disbelief. She was wearing a sleeveless shift dress in sheer red satin with a Vandyke hem that brushed the top of her knees and revealed lines of tantalizing flesh between the fingers of fabric. The shift was overlaid with navy blue lace and cobalt blue beads appliquéd in abstract swirls. On her feet she wore red satin shoes with Cuban heels, and a matching evening bag with beads and tassels was slung over one shoulder. The bag was only just big enough to contain a small make-up compact, a tube of bright red lipstick and a comb, as well as a small purse. Poppy doubted she'd need to use the comb, as her mass of curls had been trimmed into a bob – with a pair of scissors that Delilah produced like a genie out of a bottle – and tamed by a red satin hairband with a paste ruby and feather brooch.

"Are you sure the theatre won't mind you borrowing it, Delilah?"

"Not at all! I would have given you one of mine, but you are a couple of sizes bigger than me."

Poppy raised a recently plucked eyebrow.

"Not that you're big. Good heavens, I'd never say that. It's just that –"

Poppy laughed at the petite beauty beside her. "I know you wouldn't. I am bigger than you. In all directions. How do you keep so slim?"

"Ciggies, darling!" said Delilah and produced a foot-long cigarette holder. "Want one?" she offered Poppy.

"I'd rather not, thanks."

Delilah didn't take offence but posed with the cigarette holder held between two fingers and her legs crossed at the ankle as she took in her handiwork. "Divine!" she declared again.

If anyone was divine it was Delilah, thought Poppy. The actress wore a black velvet shift dress with silver threads running from neckline to hem, finished off by a fringe of tassels in alternating black and silver. She wore silver satin shoes and an elaborate diamante headdress. Her black hair had been recently cut and the square bob framed her heart-shaped face beautifully. Her make-up was as exotic as it had been the first time Poppy met her and her dark brown eyes smouldered like polished ebony.

Poppy rubbed her lips together, unaccustomed to wearing make-up, but not wanting to offend her new friend. "I don't know, Delilah. Don't you think it's a bit much? I'm not used to wearing all of this."

"It looks like a lot now, darling, but when you're in the club the lights will be dimmer and you will look like a ghost unless you put on a bit of slap. Trust me."

Poppy smiled nervously. She had already lost the argument about going out on a "school night" when the Lord knew she needed an early night. She had tried to tell Delilah that she was exhausted from her new job, but the girl had pouted and declared that she had absolutely no one else to go with, as she was currently between suitors and it was too late to rouse any of her girlfriends.

"And I must go, darling. I must! I've heard Mr De Mille might be there. And even Mr Chaplin!"

Poppy knew that she referred to famous film directors and assumed that she wanted to try to catch their eye. Poppy didn't have the heart to disappoint her.

"All right then, I'll come. But I must be back before midnight."

With a clap of her hands Delilah proceeded to jazz up Cinderella, and within an hour they were both ready to go to the ball.

Aunt Dot and Grace both declined to accompany them. They were subdued after their emotional recollections and said they would both go to bed early. Grace checked that Poppy had her key and then locked the door behind them as they left.

Out on the street Delilah looked longingly across the road at the Electric Cinema Theatre and declared that one day she would grace the screens like Mary Pickford and Clara Bow. Poppy had no doubt that she would.

Oscar's was thrumming; the music burst out of the club in spurts as the double brass-plated doors opened and closed. As usual, the queue to get into the hottest spot in town went halfway around the block. Delilah made her way to the front with Poppy in tow and caught the eye of the doorman, who winked at the two girls and ushered them in. Inside, the roar of the partygoers duelled with the raucous ragtime of the band. Dinner was over and the dancing had begun. But instead of taking to the floor, Delilah made her way to the bar.

"Can I get you anything?" she shouted at Poppy.

"Champagne?"

"You have expensive taste!" Delilah laughed and ordered two glasses of pink bubbly from the barman, who also winked at her. Poppy wondered if he and the doorman were two of the suitors Delilah had spoken of. But Delilah, it seemed, had her sights set a lot higher.

"There he is!" She clutched Poppy's arm and directed the blonde girl's gaze.

In the middle of the floor, surrounded by bright young things, stood Charles Chaplin: film director, producer and actor. Poppy had seen him recently on the silver screen when she had accompanied her aunt to the Electric Cinema. Apparently he was in London to promote his new film *The Kid* – the first time he'd been back in England for ten years. Poppy had been following his story in *The Globe* and knew that he received a lot of criticism as a "draft dodger". However, the fawning socialites seemed to have forgiven him. As had Delilah.

"Oh! Isn't he a dream? He looks nothing like the Tramp. That silly moustache must just have been a costume. Hold on, I'm going to get his autograph." And before Poppy knew it, Delilah had left her at the bar and sashayed her way through the crowd to whisper something in Chaplin's ear. Chaplin looked down at Delilah and gave her one of his most dashing smiles, then kissed her on the cheek and signed the napkin she proffered.

"She knows how to make an impression, doesn't she?"

Poppy turned at the sound of the upper-class male voice to see a man in his early thirties sporting a tuxedo, white bow-tie and black and white snakeskin jazz shoes. He had slicked-down blond hair and light grey eyes and held a cigarette in one hand and a glass of whisky in the other – which he raised to Poppy.

"If you didn't already have a drink, I would offer to buy you one."

"Thank you," Poppy said, flushing. She wasn't really sure if it would be considered "fast" to accept a drink from a strange gentleman in a club, so was grateful she didn't have to make the decision.

"I haven't seen you here before." He leaned in closer. Poppy could smell the whisky on his breath. She wondered if he was squiffy.

"I've been once before." She clutched the stem of her glass tightly.

"I'm sure I would have noticed if you had."

Poppy shifted slightly, but did not want to make a scene. The man did not take the hint and moved in closer still. He put an arm around her shoulders and whispered in her ear, "You look swanky."

She ducked from under his arm, spilling some of her drink down the front of his shirt.

"Oh, you little slapper!"

"I beg your pardon, sir! That was an accident. But your arm around my shoulder was not. You, sir, are a cad."

"Take that!" said Delilah, joining her friend and pulling her away from the bar. "Stay away from him, Poppy. He's no gentleman."

But the "gentleman" in question was too busy dousing his shirt front in soda water and dabbing at it with a bar towel to respond with more than an "Oh, shut up, Delilah."

"Who's that?" asked Poppy as the dark-haired girl found them a table near the bandstand.

"A former suitor. He showed his true colours before I let him put his shackle on me."

Poppy looked alarmed and Delilah laughed and pointed to her ring finger on her left hand.

"A shackle is an engagement ring. Don't they call them that in Northumberland?"

"I've never heard it before." The girls sat down. "So he asked you to marry him?"

"He did, but he was drunk. Even if I hadn't said no, his father wouldn't have let him go through with it."

"Why's that?"

Delilah shrugged and pursed her lips. "Long story. I'll tell you about it sometime, but tonight I don't want to think about Alfie Dorchester." Then she giggled. "Who needs an Alfie when you can have a Charlie!" She produced the autographed napkin excitedly.

But Poppy hardly focused on the scrawled signature. Had Delilah really said Alfie Dorchester? Poppy looked across the club at the young aristocrat at the bar – who by now had recovered from the spillage and was making a move on another unaccompanied young lady – and saw immediately the similarity between him and the man she had met that morning. *My, my,* thought Poppy. *The plot thickens.*

It was just before midnight when Poppy managed to convince Delilah it was time to go home. They waved to Oscar, who made Poppy promise to give his regards to her aunt, and stepped out of the overheated foyer into the cool Chelsea night. A bank of camera flashes nearly blinded them.

"It's not them!" someone shouted and was greeted with a barrage of expletives.

"Who did they think we were?" asked Poppy as the girls scurried aside.

"Dunno. Could be anyone. I saw Suzanne Lenglen inside. And of course Chaplin."

Delilah took Poppy's arm and the two girls started heading up King's Road, which was double-parked outside the jazz club for at least a quarter of a mile. Taxis and chauffeured private vehicles were picking people up and, incredibly to Poppy's mind, dropping people off. It seemed as if Oscar's only started warming up after midnight. They were well away from the scrum of photographers when Poppy stifled a yawn.

"Past your bedtime?" said a familiar voice from the curb.

Poppy squinted through the dim gaslight. Her heart sank. Alfie Dorchester was sitting in a silver Bentley racing car that was more suited to the tracks of St Moritz than the streets of London.

"Do you want a lift?"

"We're fine," said Delilah tersely.

"I wasn't talking to you," drawled Alfie. "I've already *had* you. I want to try your little friend."

Delilah gave a sharp intake of breath, then exhaled slowly.

"Just ignore him," whispered Poppy, and the two girls kept on walking.

But Alfie wasn't one to give up easily. He vaulted out of his car and stood in front of them, blocking their way.

"Excuse me," said Poppy and shifted to the left. Alfie moved too.

"Come on, cherry, I bet you taste sweet. Just one little kiss for Alfie." He reached out his hand to touch Poppy's face. Before she could react, Delilah had slapped his hand down.

"Keep your filthy paws off her."

Alfie rounded on Delilah and caught her wrist in his hand. "Ohhh, still the little vixen, I see."

"Let – go – of – me!" hissed Delilah through gritted teeth.

"Let go of her!" ordered Poppy. Alfie just laughed.

Like father like son, thought Poppy. She grabbed his arm and tried to force him to let go of Delilah. Alfie pushed her away with his other hand. She stumbled but held her ground, then pivoted round on her Cuban heel and brought the other down on his foot. He yelped, let go of Delilah and raised his hand to strike Poppy.

Suddenly a camera flashed, stopping Alfie mid arc. "What the hell?" He pulled out of the blow and stepped away from the girls.

"I think we might just have our front page pic, eh Lionel?"

Poppy's heart raced. Daniel! He stepped into the gaslight and rounded on Alfie. A small, mousey man in an oversized evening suit scampered after him. "Oh, I'm sure that won't be necessary, Rokeby," the man squeaked. "I'm sure the viscount was only jesting."

"Lieutenant Rokeby to the rescue," observed Alfie. "Stand down, soldier."

Daniel turned on him and Poppy could see it was taking every bit of his self-control not to swing the heavy camera case at him.

"The war's over, Dorchester. Go home."

"Rokeby!" squeaked Lionel again. "I'm sure the viscount has a perfectly reasonable explanation…"

"I'm sure he does. He specializes in *reasonable explanations.* Don't you, Dorchester?"

The two men – one blond, one dark-haired, of equal height and build – stared at each other like champion boxers sizing each other up for a fight, while Lionel scurried around, wringing his hands, like a match referee.

Poppy had had enough drama for one night and simply wanted to get home. "It's all right, Daniel. We're fine. Aren't we, Delilah?"

"Yes, we're fine. But thank you for your help, sir. Who knows what could have happened if you hadn't intervened."

Alfie shot Delilah a venomous look but then allowed a serpentine smile to turn up the edges of his thin mouth. "My apologies, ladies. A misunderstanding. There's no need for this to go any further, is there, Lionel?"

"Absolutely not. This is not the sort of thing we put in the entertainment section of *The Globe*, is it, Rokeby?"

Daniel took a step back but raised his camera box. "The camera doesn't lie, Dorchester. Stay away from these girls."

Alfie nodded mockingly. "Aye, aye, lieutenant." Then flicked a salute at Delilah and Poppy and vaulted back into his Bentley.

Relieved, the girls thanked Daniel and, less effusively, Lionel for their help.

"I'll walk you home," said Daniel and swung the camera case over his shoulder.

Suddenly there was a roar from outside Oscar's. "Charlie!" someone screamed. Lionel started running and called to Daniel over his shoulder. "Come on!"

Daniel looked back at the girls, uncertain what to do.

"Go," said Poppy decisively. "We'll be fine."

"You sure?" he asked.

"Yes!" Poppy pushed him playfully.

He grinned and raised his hat. "Good night then, ladies," he said and then ran to catch up with Lionel.

Poppy and Delilah watched him go.

"My, my, Poppy. Who is your knight in shining armour?" Delilah took Poppy's arm and they continued up the street as nearby church bells struck twelve.

"Oh, just someone I work with," said Poppy nonchalantly.

CHAPTER 12

The next day at work Poppy could barely keep her eyes open. It didn't help that she spent most of the morning in the fusty atmosphere of Rollo's office where she finally started to tackle the mountain range of files. Rollo left her to it as he was organizing Bert's funeral and fielding some follow-up questions from the police. He instructed her to leave anything that was either on or within two feet of his desk. Everything else was to be sorted first by date, then alphabetically by slug. A slug, Poppy learned, was a short codename for a story that appeared on each piece of copy and on the back of related photographs. So, for instance, her *Midsummer Night's Dream* article was slugged "Midsum'" and the publicity photographs and the poster she'd been given by the theatre were called Midsum pic. 1, 2, 3, etc. Another code she learned was coined by Rollo and specific to *The Globe*: JF.

"It stands for Jazz Files," said Rollo. "It's what we call any story that has a whiff of high society scandal but can't yet be proven. We've got a whole filing cabinet of them downstairs, going back twenty years. We hang on to them because you never know when a skeleton in the closet might prove useful to a story we're working on now."

"Downstairs" was the morgue archive on the third floor. After a few hours of sorting, Poppy piled her files onto a wheeled trolley and took the lift down to the third floor. The lift bell clanged and she pulled back the concertinaed iron grille gate. She held it open with one hip and pulled the trolley backwards onto the landing.

"Need a hand there?" It was Daniel.

Her heart skipped a beat. But she kept her voice casual as she said, "If you can keep the gate open, that'll be a help, thanks."

Daniel did as he was asked, then closed the gate. The lift bell clanged again and the arrow above the door moved from 3 to 2 to 1 to "G" then to "B" – basement. Suddenly Poppy was reminded of Bert's accident and the query she had regarding the lift. Daniel must have thought the same.

"I've asked Rollo, by the way, and he said he didn't see anyone getting in or out of the lift on the fourth floor. I was on the second, so that just leaves this one. I was just heading in to see Ivan."

"Who's Ivan?"

"Hasn't Rollo introduced you yet?"

Poppy shook her head.

"Hmmm," said Daniel. "He should know better than to send you in without forewarning. Ivan can be, how should I say, *temperemental?*"

Temperemental, eh? If Poppy hadn't been so tired she would have been intrigued by this mysterious Ivan. But this morning she didn't really care. She just wanted to offload the files, then have a cup of coffee before the editorial briefing scheduled for midday.

"All right; I'll do it then," declared Daniel and like the day she first met him at the station, he took the trolley from her without asking and pushed it through the double doors, expecting her to follow. *Why should I?* she thought grumpily. *He has a habit of pushing me around, doesn't he? And just because he's charming and good looking he thinks he can get away with it. Well, let me tell you something, Mr Daniel Rokeby, I can look after myself. I can…* But she didn't have the energy to make a feminist statement, and meekly followed.

"What do you think you are doing?" someone bellowed in a thick, Russian accent.

Poppy stopped in her tracks. "I – I –"

"Not you. Heeem!" A large bear of a man with shaggy grey hair and an unkempt beard stood arms akimbo in the middle of the morgue.

"Calm down, Ivan. I'm just dropping off some files."

"Dropping off? Dropping off? How many times have I told that Yankee? There is no dropping off! Appointments must be made. Applications submeeted! I have a seeestem! *Ya ne vyezzháyu!* I 'ave 'ad eeenuff!"

Then he grabbed a mackintosh and fedora hat from a hat stand and stormed out, leaving Poppy quaking in his wake.

"Is that him?"

Daniel grinned. "That's him. Ivan Molanov. A White Russian émigré. Don't worry – he's just blowing off a little steam. He'll probably be going to hunt down Rollo."

"Golly! Should we warn him?"

"Rollo? Nah, he can handle himself."

"He'll probably sack him if he talks to him like that!"

Daniel laughed. "Rollo sack Ivan? Hell'll freeze over before that happens. No, they're old sparring partners. Ivan needs this job or he'll be in trouble with the Home Office. They're under pressure from the Bolsheviks to send back any 'traitors to the Revolution'. An unemployed Rusky on the streets of London would be easier to round up than the employee of a London newspaper."

As he was talking, Daniel positioned the trolley next to Ivan's regimentally organized desk.

"Do I put the files away?" asked Poppy.

"No. Ivan will do it later. After he's hauled Rollo over the coals. He'll be calmer then, and he might just show you around. There's some fascinating stuff down here."

"Like the Jazz Files?"

Daniel raised an inquisitive eyebrow. "Yes, like the Jazz Files. But I wouldn't go sniffing around by yourself. Ivan keeps a tight ship."

"So I see," observed Poppy. Then she had a thought: "So would he know if anyone was visiting the morgue on the day Bert died?"

"He would. We can ask him when he comes back."

"Ask me what?"

Poppy and Daniel turned around to see Ivan hanging his hat back on the stand. He looked a lot calmer than he had a few minutes ago. He shrugged, as if by explanation. "Mavis said Rollo was out. I see him later." Then he smiled, showing a top row of gold teeth, and thrust out a bear-sized paw towards Poppy. "I am Ivan Molanov. Archivist."

Poppy marvelled at how hot and cold the archivist could blow in such a short space of time, but thrust out her hand too. "Hello. I'm Poppy Denby, editorial assistant."

Ivan flicked over her hand and brought it to his lips. "I am very happy to make your acquaintance, Mees Denby."

"Er, Daniel – Mr Rokeby – said I should just leave the files here and you will sort them. Is that correct?"

"It is. Have you sorted them by slug and date?"

"I have."

"Good, good. Then that is all I need. Thank you, Mees Denby."

"Oh no, thank *you*, Mr Molanov. And I'm sorry Mr Rolandson didn't tell you about me – or the files."

"Ah, that not your fault." He smiled again, and despite the gold teeth and fearsome facial hair, there was a warmth about him. Poppy was beginning to like Ivan Molanov.

"Right then," said Daniel. "Let's get a cup of coffee before the ed meeting."

"Erm, yes, but – while we're here, shouldn't we ask Mr Molanov about Mr Issacs?"

"Bert? What you want to ask about Bert?"

"The day he died," said Poppy. "Did you see him?"

"As I told police, no, not since morning. He was looking at a Jazz File."

"Oh? Which one?"

"The one of Elizabeth Dorchester."

Poppy's ears pricked up. "Do you have it? Can I see it?"

Molanov's shaggy brows collided. "Why you want see it?"

"Because I have – er – taken over from Mr Isaacs on a story he was writing."

Daniel cleared his throat. "Well, Poppy, I wouldn't say you've taken over…"

"Well, perhaps not taken over, but I helped Rollo finish Bert's last article and –"

"It matters not. The file is gone," Ivan interrupted.

"The Elizabeth Dorchester Jazz File is gone?" asked Poppy incredulously. "When?"

"I don't know. Maybe Bert took it without asking. Maybe it is in his papers. But it is gone."

Poppy ignored Daniel's body language, which was strongly suggesting they bring the conversation to a close and go and have coffee. "All right. Thank you, Mr Molanov. But if you don't mind, one more thing."

"Just one more. I am very beesy, Mees Denby."

"Of course. On the day Mr Isaacs – Bert – died, did anyone get off the lift at the third floor? I mean in the moments before or after he fell."

Ivan looked surprised. "Have you been talking to police, Mees Denby?"

"I have not."

"Well, that is strange. They ask same thing."

"And what did you say?"

"I said I did not see anyone. But I hear them. I hear bell on lift. But no one came in here. I did not see them."

Poppy absorbed this information.

Daniel was now looking interested. "I saw you in the foyer, Ivan, just after Bert's fall. Did you run down when you heard the screams?"

"I did, like everyone else."

"Everyone perhaps except the man in the lift."

"What man in lift?"

"The one you heard but didn't see," said Poppy. "Did you run down the stairs or go in the lift?"

"The stairs."

Poppy looked excitedly from one man to the other. "So technically, the mysterious man in the lift could have hidden there until Ivan left, and then slipped in here in all the chaos."

"He could have," agreed Daniel. "But to what end?"

"The Elizabeth Dorchester Jazz File," Ivan said.

Poppy grinned. "Ah, Mr Molanov, you've hit the nail right on the head."

A detour to the powder room showed dark rings under her eyes. Poppy regretted not bringing Delilah's compact with her to work, finally acknowledging that foundation powder might have a good use after all.

She ran her fingers through her newly cropped curls. The haircut alone would be enough to alarm her parents, but champagne, jazz, and a dead journalist would send them into a cadenza. She stifled a giggle. Well, what else did they expect, sending her to live with Aunt Dot? The former actress was renowned for her party lifestyle. But it wasn't just her social life she was hiding from them. Poppy sighed. She knew she would have to tell them about her new job sometime, but she had enough to think about for now. She would send them a telegram at lunchtime saying all was well and that she would write a proper letter in a couple of weeks. That would hold back the tide for a while. And hopefully, when she got her first pay cheque and was able to send some money home to help the mission, they would see the wisdom in her taking a more highly paid job. And it was a respectable job.

She splashed water on her face, pinched her cheeks to bring up some colour and left the powder room.

Poppy returned to the canteen, where Daniel was chaperoning a pair of coffee cups. His face lit up. Her heart warmed.

"If I may say so, Miss Denby, you are looking lovely, despite your late night."

Poppy sighed. "I'm not used to them. But I didn't have the heart to say no to Delilah. I'll have to be a little firmer next time." She sat down, picked up her coffee, and took a restorative sip.

He grinned. "Your friend… is she one of the Marconis?"

"She is. A friend of my aunt's. She's the actress I went to interview for the *Midsummer* piece."

"Ah, that explains it. I met her great-uncle Marconi last year. I was with Bert. He was doing a story on the proposed British Broadcasting Company. It's opening next year – or perhaps the next – at Marconi House."

"So I hear. Radio into every home in the country."

"That's the plan. Anyway, he offered me a job."

"Did he? What did you say?"

"I thanked him for his kindness but said I was very happy at *The Globe*."

"And are you? Very happy here?" Poppy lowered her cup and looked into his handsome face.

Daniel looked into his coffee as if searching for an answer to her question there. "Mostly. The hours are tricky and it's difficult to manage things at home, but Rollo's a great boss and, like Ivan, I owe him."

Poppy had picked up on "manage things at home" and immediately wondered what he meant. But she felt it would be overstepping the mark to ask him. So instead she asked Daniel what he meant by owing Rollo.

Daniel rubbed his scarred hands and took a deep breath. "We met in a field hospital in Flanders – 1915. Ivan and I were in the same tent. I'd had a run-in with a phosphorous grenade. He'd been found shot and lying in a ditch on our side of the Maginot line. It was thought for a while he was a spy. Rollo convinced the Brits he wasn't and they let him go."

"Was Rollo a patient too?"

Daniel laughed. "Not if you discount treatment for a hangover, no. He was covering the war for *The New York Times*. His cameraman had been shot – not fatally – and was at the hospital too. He was eventually discharged and went back Stateside. Rollo, Ivan and I hit it off. Rollo gave me his contact details and told me to let him know if I ever needed a job. I'd spent some time with the American photographer before he left and he showed me some of the tricks of the trade. I couldn't do much with – with these at the time," he splayed his hands, "but I remembered what he showed me and when I got back to England I took up photography. I stayed in touch with Rollo and when he won *The Globe* in that poker game, he offered me a job. That was 1916. I've been here ever since."

"And Ivan?"

"Late '17. After the October Revolution. It became clear he could never go home."

"What about his family?"

Daniel started rubbing his hands again. "All dead. Supporters of the Tsar."

Poppy was suddenly overwhelmed by the sadness of it all: Ivan and his family, Bert and his lack of family, Maud and Elizabeth Dorchester, Delilah's mother, the dead soldiers from Daniel's unit, her brother… *Oh God,* she prayed silently, *where were you? Where are you?* Typically, there was no answer. She had not heard him speak to her for a very long time. She sighed and had another sip of coffee.

Five minutes later, she and Daniel were sitting with the rest of the editorial staff in the newsroom. Lionel Saunders, the arts and entertainment editor, was staring daggers at her. She ignored him. Rollo – pointer in hand – went through what she was beginning to realize was the daily agenda of checking in with each section to see what was going into the next day's edition. When it came to arts and entertainment she was surprised that he singled her out and congratulated her on her first byline for the *Midsummer Night's Dream* piece. There was a smattering of ironic applause, then Lionel piped up: "Actually, Rollo, I've been meaning to speak to you about that. I would have appreciated it – really appreciated it – if you could have passed that with me first."

"And I," drawled the American, "would have appreciated – really appreciated – if you'd come into work that day. If it hadn't been for Poppy your ass would have been on the line – pardon the French, Miz Denby – so you should be thanking her."

"Thanking her!" squeaked Lionel. "She nearly lost us the Chaplin pic last night, didn't she, Rokeby?"

"Well – not really, Lionel. We got the pic and –"

"No thanks to her and her distractions. You should have seen what she was wearing."

Sniggers and wolf whistles erupted in the newsroom. Poppy flushed as brightly as her namesake.

Rollo grinned, enjoying the raucous humour, but brought the meeting to order. "All right, fellas, that's enough. Dan, you did get the picture of Charlie, didn't you?"

"I did."

"No thanks to *Miz Denby*," muttered Lionel sarcastically.

"And no thanks to Alfie Dorchester," declared Poppy. She was not going to take all the blame for this; she was absolutely not.

"Oh?" said Rollo, suddenly serious. "What about Alfie?"

"He was making – well, he was making *inappropriate* advances on me and was quite put out when I turned him down."

"Good for you," said Rollo thoughtfully.

"And if it hadn't been for –" started Daniel, but Rollo interrupted him.

"Can I see you in my office after this, Poppy? I think I might have another assignment for you."

CHAPTER 13

After the meeting Poppy went to Rollo's office as instructed. However, she had to wait outside because during the editorial meeting Mavis Bradshaw had shown up a police detective who wanted to see Rollo and would not take no for an answer. Poppy got this information from Mavis, who seemed quite put out by what she had described as the detective's "rude manner".

"He wasn't like the police officers who were here after poor Bert died, Poppy. They were very sympathetic, knowing what a shock we'd all had. This one should learn some manners," she humphed, before making herself a cup of tea and taking it back down to reception.

Poppy took a seat outside Rollo's office and waited to be summoned. She could hear raised voices – one English, one American – but could not hear exactly what was said. "Obstruction of justice" and "freedom of the press" were two phrases that popped out, but she couldn't make much sense of the in-between. She was just beginning to let her eyelids droop when the door to Rollo's office was slammed open and an angry man in a cheap blue suit and black chesterfield coat stormed out. He rammed a black bowler hat onto his head and glared at Poppy.

"Do I know you?"

"N-no – sir."

He growled and blasted his way out of the newsroom.

Poppy turned to see Rollo leaning wearily on the doorframe. He ran his hand over his thick red hair and sighed. "God help us, Miz Denby. God help us." Then he gestured for her to come in. He stood in the middle of his office, raised his arms as though he were about to fly and turned slowly round. "Space. Good job, Poppy."

"Still a way to go, sir."

"Rollo."

"Still a way to go, Rollo. I took a trolley-load down to the morgue. There's at least five or six loads more."

"Yes, Ivan nabbed me on the way up. Gave me a good rollicking about the files, but he seems to be quite taken with you."

"Oh?" Poppy flushed.

"Don't worry. You'll be quite safe with Ivan. He's not the romantic sort."

Poppy remembered the chivalrous kiss to her hand which from another man might have been construed as lecherous or rakish. "But a gentleman, nonetheless."

"Ivan's been described as many things, but I'm not sure 'gentleman' is one of them." He gestured for Poppy to sit.

"Do you know who that man was?" Rollo asked.

"The man that stormed out? No, I've never seen him before."

"That is Chief Detective Inspector Richard Easling of the Metropolitan Police. He's investigating Bert's death. He's convinced it was suicide and wants access to Bert's files to prove it."

Richard Easling… Hadn't Poppy heard that name before?

"Do you think it was suicide?" Poppy asked.

"I don't. And neither do you from what Ivan's been telling me."

"I-I-I. . ." Poppy stuttered.

Rollo raised his hand. "It's all right, Poppy. I know you were going to tell me eventually."

"It was just a theory, really, but now that Ivan has said he heard someone in the lift…"

"It's a good theory. It could still of course have just been an accident, but I'm not prepared to rule out foul play just yet."

"But now the police think suicide."

"No," said Rollo, templing his fingers and flicking them back and forth under his chin. "DCI Richard Easling thinks it's suicide. PC Plod and his pals are happy to call it an accident."

"Why is Easling so keen to call it suicide then? And what does he expect to find in Bert's files?"

"That, Poppy, is exactly the question. I've been going through them and can't find anything more than I've given you already. But there must be something we're missing. And as for the suicide – the *alleged* suicide – well, I can't say for sure, but I think Easling is trying to discredit Bert. If Bert can be shown to have killed himself, then that suggests an unstable frame of mind. And if he was unstable, that would discredit any theories he might have had or articles he might have written."

"But why would a police detective do that?" asked Poppy, completely flummoxed by this whole line of thinking.

"Because it's Richard Easling. Have you heard the name before, Poppy?"

"It sounds familiar, but I'm not sure…"

"Well, he seemed to think he had seen you before. Or someone quite like you…" Rollo sat back in his chair and looked at her over his templed fingers.

"My aunt?"

"Well done, Miz Denby. You're a little slow today, aren't you? Must be your late night fighting off advances from Alfie Dorchester." He grimaced. "Richard Easling was the police officer who rode the horse that crippled your aunt. He was a plain mounted police constable back then. Now, let's see how awake you are. What is Richard Easling's connection with the Dorchesters?"

Poppy screwed up her eyebrows and tried to think. "He was supposedly in Lord Dorchester's pay?"

"Give the prize to the little lady! Co-rrect! But nothing was ever proved, nor was it likely to have been if Bert hadn't dug up the old Jazz File on it while he was looking for background material for the Dorchester/Marie Curie story."

Poppy was suddenly awake. "You have evidence that Dorchester paid to have my aunt attacked?"

Rollo dropped his hands and pursed his lips. "I don't. And neither did Bert. But I think he was on to something. Here…" He pulled open a drawer and took out a thin manila folder. He opened it to reveal a single sheet of bloodstained writing paper. "I got this from one of Easling's colleagues last night. That's why Easling was here. He wanted it back. He said his colleague had made a mistake by giving it to me. That it was still evidence. But I wouldn't give it to him. He's gone off to get a court order."

"Will he succeed?"

"He might. But our legal lads will keep him at bay long enough for us to follow this up."

"What is it?" Poppy leaned in to have a closer look in the dusty light, making a mental note to clean Rollo's windows when she had a chance…

"It's the letter that was delivered to Bert on the day he died. I've just had Mavis in and she's identified it."

"What does it say?"

Rollo pushed the letter towards her. There was very little to see. "Well, as you can see, the ink has been obscured by all the blood. Apart from the odd word here and there" – he pointed to a couple of scrawls – "which make no sense in isolation, the only thing we can see for sure is this." He pointed with a letter opener to something that might have been "Batte" and "illow" in the place where an address might have been.

"What is it?"

"I'm not entirely sure. But there's also this –" He pointed to part of a word in the place where a signature might have been: "lizabe".

"Is that Elizabeth, do you think?"

Rollo nodded. "Indeed I do. Elizabeth Dorchester is in a mental hospital in –"

"Battersea," finished Poppy, and she told Rollo what her aunt had told her.

Rollo nodded with interest, but didn't say whether any of this was new to him. Instead he said, "Don't you think it strange that Bert received a note from someone who might have been Elizabeth Dorchester on the day he died?"

"I do," agreed Poppy. "And add to that the missing Jazz File that Ivan told us about –"

"And the sudden appearance of Richard Easling on the case –"

"And the sudden interest of Alfie Dorchester –"

"Well no, Poppy, that's probably just a coincidence. Alfie's simply a cad."

"But his father isn't."

"No, he isn't," said Rollo thoughtfully, his fingers forming a pyramid. "He's far worse than that."

It was a glorious late afternoon in early July and Battersea Park was full of picnicking families, footballing youths and young couples walking arm in arm. From the top of the bus Poppy watched as a nursemaid picked up a screaming toddler who had fallen face first into his ice-cream and an old man nodded off to sleep on a nearby bench while his ageing Labrador kept watch beside him. The bus skirted the park and passed the gasworks towers. Rollo had told her the bus-stop she needed was the one just after the towers and – according to the map they had looked at in his office – the Willow Park asylum was a fifteen-minute walk south from the stop.

It had been her idea to visit the asylum. Initially Rollo had been reluctant – concerned about the potentially violent twist the investigation was beginning to take – and suggested she wait for Daniel to go with her the following day. He was currently on an assignment covering the opening of the Imperial War Museum by the king at Crystal Palace. However, Poppy had an idea of how she could get in under cover, and thought the presence of a known press photographer might work against her. She had read in *The Globe* that the Red Cross was asking for books to take to hospitals. So she decided to give Willow Park a ring and ask if they would be willing to accept a donation from "a Methodist Mission". Poppy felt slightly uneasy that she allowed the person she spoke to to believe she was from the Methodist Mission in Chelsea – which she as yet had not got around to visiting – but she put her scruples aside, deciding that in the greater scheme of things God would forgive her this indiscretion in pursuit of truth and justice. Needless to say, Rollo agreed.

So Poppy dropped home to pick up the box of books she had been planning on donating to the Red Cross before catching the next bus to Battersea. Neither Grace nor Dot was in, so Poppy did not have to explain herself – which was a relief. She still didn't know why Grace and Dot had never visited Elizabeth. Perhaps they had tried and been turned away. As Poppy approached the tall, wrought-iron gates of the asylum, she prayed that the same fate would not befall her.

The gates were locked. She spotted a bell and rang it. A few minutes later a uniformed security guard arrived and asked her her business. She said her name was Poppy Plummer (her mother's maiden name) and that she had a delivery from the Methodist Mission. The man looked her up and down and noted the box of books, which was getting heavier and heavier.

"They could have sent someone to help you with that, miss," he observed, then opened the gates. Inside he took the box from her and told her to follow him. Poppy looked up at the hundred-year-old red-brick building, designed in the Gothic style, and noted that if she ever changed careers and went into architecture this would be the last thing she would consider building as a place for sick people to get well. Although there were no gargoyles on the turrets, Poppy imagined that they were there anyway, snarling down at her and the guard as they walked up the gravel path. To left and right the gardens sloped down to the high perimeter wall and there was a smell of jasmine in the air as Poppy entered the asylum.

CHAPTER 14

It had been three days since Elizabeth had given the note to the window cleaner – and still no Mr Isaacs. But she wasn't ready to give up yet. Plan A was still very much a possibility. She had asked God to help her, and she wanted to give him – and Mr Isaacs – a chance. At least that's what she thought when hope flowed in her; but, like the moon and the tide, it soon threatened to wane. She'd asked God to help her many times before – during those long years of abuse she and her mother suffered at the hands of her father; in those dreadful days when her mother's ship sank and she waited to hear if Maud was one of the survivors; during those tragic days when she sat at Emily Wilding's bedside, praying she would come out of the coma; and during those torturous months in Holloway.

She thought he'd come through for her when the warden, without explanation, tossed her and Gloria out, declaring they'd been released – for now – and the strange hope had risen again. Then as she and Gloria, both weakened, feverish and emaciated, planned their next move, she'd felt some kind of divine direction; at least that's what she'd thought at the time. But had it been divine? Or diabolical? What God would lead her and Gloria to make a plan that would end in the death of one and the incarceration in an asylum of the other?

And yet here it was again: that creeping hope. She picked up her old leather-bound Bible that had once belonged to her mother – the only possession they'd let her keep both in

Holloway and Willow Park – and laid her hand on the embossed cross on the cover. She closed her eyes and mouthed a prayer, daring to believe – just one more time.

Poppy was surprised at how easily she had got into the asylum. The guard had escorted her to reception and then deposited the box on the counter, suggesting the receptionist find a trolley for the lady. While riding over on the bus, Poppy had envisaged a number of scenarios of what might happen if her cover was exposed, including arguing, running, hiding, and, in a fleeting hyperbole of fantasy, fighting. She had laughed at herself and instead rehearsed one or two alternative cover stories in case the staff at the asylum decided to check out her claim about a donation from the Methodist Mission. It turned out she needed none of them. The middle-aged man behind the counter appeared charmed by the pretty young Christian girl who was giving up her time to help those less fortunate than herself. Poppy had a twinge of guilt, but suppressed it, and, taking inspiration from Delilah, flashed him her most endearing smile.

The receptionist called a porter – a surly youth who soon brightened when he saw Poppy – to escort "the lady". The receptionist then adopted a paternal air when he suggested that the men's wing might contain sights inappropriate for an unmarried miss, and had directed the porter to take her to the women's wing only. As this was Poppy's goal anyway, she just smiled again.

The porter told Poppy that some of the women were in secure units and she would not be allowed to see them for her own safety. She was desperate to ask if Elizabeth was in one of those units, but knew that to do so would have blown her cover. So instead she prayed a quick prayer – trusting God wouldn't hold her recent deception against her – and hoped for the best.

An hour later and her devil-may-care attitude was well and truly subdued. It must have been the saddest place she had ever been – and that included the military convalescent hospital. Some of the women she had seen were desperately lonely, grateful beyond words that someone bothered to spend a little time with them, suggesting this book or the other; others were vacant and unresponsive and no matter how many times she flashed her pretty smile she couldn't engage with them. Again, others were surly or passively aggressive, giving furtive looks at the porter when he warned them to behave. Poppy wondered what might have happened if he hadn't been there. She reminded herself that these were not the worst of them and she shuddered at what she might have seen in the secure unit.

Eventually she was led to a room just off a nurses' station. The porter took a key from his belt and unlocked the door. He stuck his head in and said, "Liz, do you want a new book?" A voice replied in the affirmative and Poppy was ushered in. There, sitting near the window, looking out, was a woman in her mid-thirties with a long auburn plait down her back. She turned to see who was visiting her and Poppy had to stop herself from gasping when she saw the large grey eyes of Elizabeth Dorchester looking back at her – just as they had from the painting and the photograph.

Elizabeth raised her eyebrows curiously and said, "Hello. Who are you?"

"I'm Poppy Den – Plummer. I'm Poppy Plummer. I was wondering if you wanted a new book?"

"I do. What do you have for me?"

Poppy wheeled the trolley over to her. She looked back at the porter standing at the door. She wanted to speak to Elizabeth privately. Her mind whisked through a few options until she settled on: "Excuse me. Would it be possible to get a cup of tea? I'm parched. Would you mind awfully making a cuppa while I speak to… to… Liz, is it?"

Elizabeth nodded.

The youth looked uncertain. "Er – well, miss. I – well, I probably shouldn't leave you alone with the patient."

"Oh, I'm sure it will be all right," said Poppy in her most soothing voice and blinking her blue eyes in a way she hoped was particularly charming. "I'm sure Liz and I can keep ourselves busy for a few minutes."

The youth still looked uncertain.

"*Please…*"

He melted. She rewarded him with her most dazzling smile.

"All right," he said. "But I'll have to lock you in. Liz is harmless, but she tends to wander, don't you, Liz?" he said loudly, as if talking to a deaf person or an imbecile.

"Liz" glared at him, but offered no words of contradiction.

Poppy waited until the door was locked. Then she noticed a nurse pop her head up to look through the glass pane. It was clear that although they might be out of earshot, they were still being watched.

Poppy exhaled nervously, then busied herself with the trolley. She ran a hand along the shelf and picked up *Jane Eyre*. She thought of Mrs Rochester in the attic, and stifled an impulse to giggle.

She offered the book to Elizabeth, who took it wordlessly while staring intently into Poppy's eyes.

"Do I know you?" she whispered.

"You don't," whispered Poppy in return. "But I think you know my aunt. Dot Denby?"

Elizabeth's eyes widened in recognition. "Dot!" She looked over Poppy's shoulder to the door, where the nurse's face was still framed in the window pane. "Is she here?"

"She isn't," said Poppy. She too looked over her shoulder at the door. She knew she didn't have long. "Are you Elizabeth Dorchester?"

Elizabeth nodded.

"And did you write a letter to Bert Isaacs at *The Daily Globe* three days ago?"

Elizabeth nodded again.

"I thought so. I work for *The Globe* too."

"Is Mr Isaacs…"

"I'm afraid Mr Isaacs is – he's, well – he's – had an accident."

"Oh," said Elizabeth, sounding deflated.

"But he's sent me instead. The only problem is. . . well, the letter you sent got wet and we couldn't read what it said. Only who it was from. Can you tell me what it said, Elizabeth?" She looked over her shoulder again and whispered, "We don't have much time."

Elizabeth nodded her understanding. "It said – I said – that I had been falsely imprisoned here by my father –"

"Melvyn Dorchester."

"Yes. And I want to get out. No one here believes me. I think Mr Isaacs will. I think I met him once, many years ago."

"With the WSPU?"

"Yes. I heard that he came to visit me, but he couldn't get in. I think – well, I hope – he suspects something isn't right. And it's not. I need to get out."

Poppy nodded. "I'm not sure how we can help…"

Elizabeth's eyes turned from soft grey to flint. "You must. I can't live like this any longer." Then her eyes flitted to the Bible on the windowsill beside her. "I can make it worth your while. I can give your newspaper a – what do you call it? – a scoop."

"Yes, a scoop, but we don't need –"

"I have information that proves Melvyn Dorchester has been involved in criminal activity."

Poppy's newshound ears pricked at this, but she was cautious. "Ah. Well, no offence, Miss Dorchester, but your information will automatically be – well – be *tainted* by your present circumstances."

Elizabeth smiled mirthlessly. "You mean no one will believe the woman in the loony bin."

Poppy blushed. "Well, yes, I'm sorry, but that's how it is."

There were voices outside the door and a key was turning in the lock. Poppy and Elizabeth looked at each other and an unspoken "Hurry!'" passed between them.

"Are you a Christian woman, Miss Denby?"

"I am," said Poppy.

"Then will you pray with me?"

"Well, I" – the door opened – "yes, of course."

"Good." Elizabeth reached out and took her Bible. She held it on her lap and took Poppy's hands and held them over the good book. She looked up at the porter standing with a cup of tea. "We're just praying. Take a seat," she said with the imperious authority of one born to wealth and privilege.

The porter looked as if he was about to argue, but then complied as one accustomed to taking orders. He gave Poppy the cup of tea, then sat down in a chair near the door and started picking studiously at his pimples.

Poppy put down the cup of tea on the floor beside her.

"Our Father," said Elizabeth, "I thank you that you have brought your daughter, Poppy, here today to encourage me. Thank you for her generous spirit and the gifts she brings…"

Poppy nodded her assent to the prayer. Then she felt something slip under her hand. She peeked open an eye to see a folded sheet of paper. She quickly glanced at the porter to see if he had noticed. He hadn't. She took the paper and slipped it into the pocket of her dress. Elizabeth squeezed her hands and continued praying.

"Father, I pray too for my sister here, that she may receive from you knowledge to lead her in the path you have chosen as she carefully studies the sacred text laid before her. I pray too that justice and truth will prevail, in the name of the Father, the Son and the Holy Ghost. Amen."

"Amen," said Poppy, and opened her eyes.

Suddenly Elizabeth's foot shot out and kicked over the cup of tea, smashing the cheap china against the wall. "Oh my! Look what I've done! Clumsy me."

The porter jumped up and looked at the women suspiciously.

"Better clean that up before someone cuts themselves – or someone else," said Elizabeth. "We wouldn't want anyone to get the blame for putting our guest in danger now, would we…" she said, holding the porter's gaze.

"I'll do it," said Poppy, understanding the game. "Have you got a dustpan and brush?" she asked the porter, who looked confusedly from one woman to the other.

Poppy gave him her "calming" smile, the one she had used in the convalescent home with soldiers who were in pain. "Get a dustpan, will you? I'll sort it out. And don't worry. No one has to know…" She tapped the side of her nose with her finger.

"All right," said the lad. "Just a tick." And he unlocked the door.

The women knew they only had half a minute or so. Elizabeth grabbed Poppy's hand. "Take that to *The Globe*. Tell them there's more where that came from. I've hidden it – outside, in a box, in a safe place – but you will have to get me out of here before I tell you where the rest is. Do you understand?" She squeezed Poppy's hand until it hurt.

"I understand," said Poppy and then turned to take the dustpan from the porter, who had just returned.

Five minutes later and Elizabeth and the room were just as Poppy had found them, with the addition of a copy of *Jane Eyre,* which lay beside the Bible on a sunlit windowsill. Poppy said "goodbye and God bless" as she had to all the patients that day, and with the help of the young porter wheeled her book trolley out of the room and continued with her delivery round.

As she left, she didn't see another visitor arrive to see Elizabeth. Alfie Dorchester, who had been flirting with a red-haired nurse while his sister was choosing a book from a do-gooder, raised his eyebrows in recognition as he saw the pretty blonde girl emerge from Elizabeth's room. He thought of calling out to her, but stopped. Best he speak to Lizzie first, lest the little slapper make a scene. But he'd be having words with Poppy Denby; oh, she could bank on that.

Half an hour later and Poppy thanked the guard with a sunny smile as he locked the gate of the asylum behind her. She had left the trolley of books in a common room and promised to come back in a few months with more. She'd meant it. Elizabeth or no Elizabeth, she had been deeply touched by what she'd seen today and wanted to reach out in some small way to help the people she'd met. But for now, she had a job to do. She walked twenty yards or so down the road and waited until she could no longer feel the admiring gaze of the guard on her back. Then she slipped her hand into her dress pocket and retrieved the tightly folded paper.

The moment Poppy unfolded it, she knew what it was. The columns of figures, names and dates were an extract from a ledger – much like the one she had kept at the mission in

Morpeth. The jagged edge down one side suggested it had been torn out in a hurry. An asterisk and squiggly line in the middle of the page caught her attention. It underlined an entry for 3rd October 1910. To one R.Easling, the sum of fifty pounds.

Poppy stopped dead in her tracks, almost causing a man with a barrow of vegetables to career into her. She waved an apology and then focused again on the page. A chill ran down her spine. Was this evidence of a bribe to Police Constable Richard Easling? She scoured the page, front and back, to see if Dorchester's name was on it anywhere – it wasn't. But she was almost certain it had come from one of Dorchester's ledgers and that Elizabeth had somehow managed to acquire it before she was taken into hospital. Perhaps she had smuggled it in in her Bible. Had she been waiting all these years to show it to someone? And she said there was a box somewhere with more of the same. Could she finally have proof that Dorchester had paid Richard Easling to run down her aunt and the other suffragettes? She needed to get the page to Rollo as quickly as possible.

She looked up and saw the clock tower in Battersea Park marking ten minutes to four. If she hurried, she could catch the four o'clock bus back to Fleet Street. She refolded the ledger page and slipped it into her satchel, then looked quickly to left and right before she crossed the road. There was a silver motorcar coming towards her from the direction of Willow Park, but she would easily make it to the other side in time. But suddenly, the motor sped up and swerved onto the wrong side of the road. Poppy sprinted to get out of the way, but it was too late: the vehicle rammed her from behind and hurtled her into the air. The last thing Poppy remembered was the crack of her skull as her head hit the cobbles.

CHAPTER 15

Poppy was swimming in the sea at Whitley Bay. Her brother was with her. The waves lifted them up and down, their legs kicking frantically under the water to keep them afloat. Their mother called to them from the shore: "Be careful! Don't go too far out!" and their father waved to them, a pease-pudding and ham sandwich in hand. It was getting dark, and a light swept over them in a wide arc: it was coming from St Mary's Lighthouse.

Suddenly her brother cried out and disappeared under the waves. Poppy waited for him to pop back up or to grab her ankle and pull her down, pretending he was a shark. She waited. And she waited. The light from St Mary's came faster and faster. She looked to shore, but could no longer see her parents. She thought she could still hear her mother's voice, distantly calling: "Come back, Poppy; come back!" But she couldn't leave without her brother. So she dived under the water to find him.

As her eyes adjusted to the murk, she saw him below her, face down, his arms and legs splayed like a turtle in his red and white striped bathers. His blond hair was spread out like a halo. She dived down further and grabbed his collar and pulled him up. His body rotated until he faced her, his eyes and mouth wide and lifeless. The light above her was getting brighter. She dragged her brother towards it, but as she burst through the surface she lost her grip and he drifted away from her, back below the waves. She flipped herself over to dive again, but then someone grabbed her shoulders and pulled her upwards. She fought, she screamed and then she felt a sharp prick in her arm. The waves calmed, the light dimmed and she saw her brother smiling up at her. She turned on her back and floated away.

Poppy was awake before her eyes opened. She could hear voices rising and falling on the waves of an argument. "He shouldn't be here." … "I have every right." … "Family only." … "Police business." … "Call the doctor." … "Is she awake?" … "Oh, thank God! She's awake!"

Poppy reluctantly opened her eyes. The first person she saw was Grace, leaning over her, her brown eyes fraught with worry. "She's awake, Dorothy. She's awake!"

"Oh, thank you, God! Poppy! Darling!"

Grace stepped back so Aunt Dot could lean in from her chair at the side of the bed. She reached out and touched Poppy's face. "How are you feeling, darling?"

How was she feeling? Her head throbbed like a giant thumb that had been whacked by a hammer. Her mouth was dry and her throat was struggling to hold back billows of nausea. Below her neck her right shoulder ached and below that she had a sharp twinge in her ribs if she moved even slightly to either side. And below that… below that she wasn't sure what she could feel…

"W-water."

"Water! Of course. Grace, pass the water."

A glass appeared and Aunt Dot held it to her niece's lips while cupping her chin with her other hand. Poppy drank a little and spilled a little, but it was enough.

"Thank you," she mouthed.

"Excuse me, can I have some room?" A man in a white coat, accompanied by a woman in a winged nurse's hat, appeared at her bedside. He asked her some questions, to which she seemed to give satisfactory answers, then he produced a torch and shone it in her eyes like the beam from St Mary's Lighthouse. She flinched, which he declared "good, good". He looked at her shoulder and poked at her ribs, announcing, "Nothing's broken, just badly bruised"; then he moved down her body until he reached her toes.

Again, Poppy noted there was very little feeling. She looked to Aunt Dot when she said this and the older lady gave her a reassuring look, but there was worry in her blue eyes.

"Is everything all right, doctor?"

"Yes, everything's fine."

"But she says she can't feel much…"

"Everything is normal, Miss Denby. There appears to be full nerve and motor function. The subdued feeling is a result of the painkillers and muscle relaxing medication we gave to your niece. It will eventually wear off."

Then to Poppy: "You have had an X-ray, Miss Denby, and nothing appears to be broken or internally displaced. But you have severe bruising and a mild concussion, and will need to stay in the hospital for a few days."

Poppy nodded.

"Do you remember what happened?" the doctor asked.

"She was hit –" started Aunt Dot, but the doctor silenced her with a raised hand.

"Do *you* remember what happened?"

Poppy closed her eyes to try to sort the clutter of images and memories: Whitley Bay … her brother … the lighthouse … the smell of jasmine … wrought-iron gates … gargoyles … a woman in a white gown … then the clock tower … it was ten to four … she wondered what time it was now …

"Miss Denby? Miss Denby? I think she's had enough for now. We'll let her rest. I'll tell the inspector to come back later."

"Tell the inspector to send someone else. I will not have that man near my niece. I will not!"

"Shhhh, Dorothy. Poppy is going to sleep …"

The next time Poppy opened her eyes it was nearly dark. Daniel and Rollo were talking quietly together near the window, Daniel leaning on the windowsill with both elbows so that he didn't tower above the editor. She attempted a cough. They both turned.

"Poppy?" Rollo walked over to the bed and peered intently into her face. "You know how to make a statement, Miz Denby, you really do." He chuckled, but there was a note of worry in his voice.

Daniel leaned in towards her. "How are you feeling?"

"Like I've been run over by a bus," she whispered.

"Funny you should say that… do you remember what happened? Your aunt said you didn't answer when the doctor asked before."

"Aunt Dot?"

"She and Mrs Wilson have gone to the café for a cup of tea. They asked us to keep an eye on you until they get back," Rollo said.

"So do you, Poppy? Do you remember?" asked Daniel, scouring her face as if he could find the information there.

"I – I think I was run down. By a motor. A silver motorcar. Outside the asylum. It swerved – on purpose – and hit me."

"Oh, I don't think it was on purpose, Miss Denby."

Poppy, Rollo and Daniel looked up and saw the silhouette of a man in a bowler hat standing in the doorway.

"Is that –"

"Detective Chief Inspector Richard Easling. We met briefly outside Mr Rolandson's office yesterday. I don't know if you remember."

"I remember," whispered Poppy. And she also remembered the ledger page. She looked around, trying to spot her satchel.

Easling continued. "A witness says you weren't looking where you were going and you stepped out right in front of it. The poor driver didn't have a chance to avoid you."

"What witness?" asked Daniel, his voice filled with scorn. "Alfie Dorchester? Don't you think he's a little biased, Inspector?"

"No. Another witness. A vegetable vendor who has corroborated *Viscount* Dorchester's version of events. I don't know if you know yet, Miss Denby, but you owe your life to the viscount. After you stepped in front of his motor –"

"I didn't step in front of his motor. He deliberately –"

"After you stepped in front of his motorcar," Easling repeated more forcefully, "he immediately administered first aid. As an army captain, who has won the Victoria Cross, he has experience of such things."

Rollo gave a derisive snort.

Easling glared at him. "And then he picked you up and brought you here in his Bentley. If it hadn't been for his quick thinking –"

"Quick thinking? He deliberately ran me down!" Poppy's voice was getting stronger.

"Hear that?" said Daniel. "He deliberately tried to run her down. I demand that you arrest him."

Easling sucked in his cheeks and then puffed them out like a blacksmith's bellows. "You demand? You have no authority to demand anything. Rolandson, keep your man in order."

Daniel launched himself at Easling and grabbed him by the lapels.

"Unhand me, sir, or you will be arrested!"

"Cool it, Danny; cool it." Rollo wheeled his way between the two men, put a hand on each of their bellies, and pushed them apart. Daniel continued to hold on to Easling's lapels until a whimpered "Please, Daniel" from Poppy convinced him to let go.

"Can you all please go?" asked Poppy, sounding as if she was about to start crying. The men looked at each other, daring the other to go first. "Not you, Rollo. I need to speak to you. But Daniel, can you come back later please? And Inspector, can this wait until the morning? I've had a dreadful shock."

Easling grunted, but then nodded his assent. "All right. But Rolandson, talk to this young buck or he'll be taking photographs inside a prison cell."

Daniel looked as if he was about to retort, but didn't. Easling gave a sniff of victory then turned and left. He stopped in the doorway: "I'll take your statement in the morning, Miss Denby."

"I suggest, Inspector, you make sure Miz Denby's aunt isn't here when you do. I don't mind stopping Danny boy here from decking you, but I wouldn't dream of denying a lady the opportunity." He grinned and winked at Poppy.

Easling's eyes narrowed and he pointed a quivering finger at Rollo, saying, "You're on borrowed time, Rolandson." Then he left.

Daniel flopped down in a chair and swore. "Sorry, Poppy."

"It's all right, Daniel. Thank you for defending me. But I really need to speak to Rollo alone."

Daniel looked offended.

"Go on, Dan," said Rollo, tossing his shaggy red head towards the door.

"All right. I'll see if your aunt and Mrs Wilson need anything."

"That's a fella."

Poppy waited until Daniel had left the room before saying to the editor, "Do you know where my satchel is, Rollo?"

Rollo looked quizzically at Poppy. "Hang on, I'll look for it." He had a scout around the room, opened a cupboard or two and returned with Poppy's satchel.

"Look inside," she said. "There should be a folded piece of paper. It's a page that's been torn out of a ledger."

Rollo had a dig around inside the bag but shook his head. "Nothing."

"Are you sure?"

Rollo emptied the contents of the satchel onto the bed and sorted through them so that Poppy could see. "Nothing. What is it? What are you looking for?"

"Elizabeth Dorchester gave it to me. It's a page from a ledger." She then went on to tell Rollo what had happened when she went to visit Elizabeth and the deal she had made with the woman to try to get her out. "So do you think you can still do it? Even without the ledger page?"

"I'll take your word for it, Poppy, yes. And I'll speak to our legal team about overturning the sectioning order. But I don't imagine it will be easy. You say there's a box of evidence somewhere."

"Yes, but she won't tell us where until we get her out."

"Understandable. The problem is, Alfie is now likely to know about it. If he's got the ledger page he'll be showing his father. It's just a matter of time until Elizabeth is silenced."

"Silenced?" asked Poppy, not wanting to consider what lengths the male Dorchesters would go to to keep Elizabeth quiet. They'd kept her locked away for seven years, but now that was no longer enough.

"We've got to get her out, Rollo."

"I know. I'll do my best. But don't worry about it now, Poppy. You need to get better." He took her hand and patted it with paternal warmth. "I should never have let you go there on your own. What was I thinking? You could have been…"

Poppy squeezed his hand. "Stop, Rollo. It was my choice, and I'm glad I went – even if it does mean I'm stuck here for a few days."

He grinned, and Poppy couldn't help thinking he looked like the Cheshire cat from *Alice in Wonderland*. And come to think of it, she felt a bit like Alice after she'd fallen down the rabbit hole.

"Promise me you'll get better, Poppy."

She smiled gently. "I'll do my best, Rollo."

"Good. Because my office isn't going to clean itself!"

They both laughed until Poppy winced from the effort.

Rollo frowned in sympathy. "Do me a favour. Don't tell anyone else about the ledger page."

"No one?"

"No one. I think we might have a mole at *The Globe*. There's the missing Jazz File – and of course Bert's 'accident' – but beyond that, someone seems to be one step ahead of us. How did Dorchester know you were going to be there?"

"Maybe it was just a coincidence."

"Maybe. But just to be on the safe side, keep this between us."

"And Daniel."

"No, not Daniel. I don't like saying this, but no one is above suspicion. Not yet. And even if he is, he's a bit too – how should we say? – emotionally involved with you to not do something stupid. We need clear heads on this, Poppy. Agreed?"

"Agreed," said Poppy and yawned.

Later, after Rollo had left and Poppy drifted off to sleep, her thoughts were not about Alfie or Elizabeth Dorchester, nor even of Bert Isaacs or Richard Easling, but of Daniel Rokeby. Emotionally involved? Really? Now that was a nice thought.

CHAPTER 16

"Oh, you look better!"

Aunt Dot wheeled into Poppy's hospital room, followed by Grace. It was late morning and Poppy had already had one visitor: DCI Richard Easling. True to his word he had been there first thing, and after a brief consultation with the doctor, he had taken her statement. Poppy outlined exactly what had happened outside the asylum and her belief that Alfie had deliberately swerved to the wrong side of the road to hit her. Easling dutifully wrote down what she said, but Poppy doubted the statement would ever see the inside of a courtroom. Then he asked her why she had been to see Elizabeth Dorchester. Rollo had prepared her for this and she followed his script to the letter: she had been following up a lead on a story, the details of which fell under press privilege.

Easling pursed his lips under his pencil-thin moustache, not hiding his frustration. "I can get a court order, Miss Denby…"

"You do that, Inspector. And if there is nothing else, I would like to eat my breakfast in peace. Nurse, can you show the inspector out please?"

The nurse, already perturbed that Easling had muscled his way in outside of normal visiting hours, was only too happy to oblige.

By the time Aunt Dot and Grace came to visit her she had eaten her breakfast, been examined by the doctor – who declared her to be pleasingly on the mend – and had received a bed bath. A bouquet of flowers had also been delivered. The card said: *"My dearest Miss Denby. Please be more careful. You are too pretty to be lost to the world. Wishing you a speedy recovery. Alfie Dorchester."*

"Please be more careful? Oh, the cheek of it! Shall I get rid of them for you?"

"Yes please, Aunt Dot. Perhaps you can give them – without the card – to another patient who needs cheering up."

"Good idea, darling. You are always so very thoughtful. Even at times like this."

"How are you feeling?" asked Grace, pulling up a chair to the bedside.

"I've been better," said Poppy, gingerly fingering a throbbing lump on her head. "But the doctor said there's no permanent damage and I can leave in a few days."

"Oh, that's such a relief," declared Dot. "And the feeling in your legs? Has it come back?"

"It has. Just like the doctor said."

"You had one of those new-fangled X-rays, didn't you? I wonder if I'd had one they would have been able to save my legs…"

Grace laid a hand on Dot's knee. "I don't think so, Dorothy. An X-ray can only take a picture of what's already there, not reverse any damage. Isn't that right, Poppy?"

"That's right," agreed Poppy, "but it might have helped doctors see where the damage was so they could treat it more effectively."

Aunt Dot sighed and shook out her curls: "What's done is done. No one can undo the past, can they, girls?"

Grace agreed that they couldn't, but Poppy wondered whether it would be possible to at least reverse some of the damage. If not physically, then emotionally. She thought again of Elizabeth Dorchester and the secrets she carried, and wondered what the two women in front of her knew. She had promised

Rollo not to tell anyone about the ledger page, but surely Grace and Aunt Dot would have put two and two together and realized where she had just come from when Alfie knocked her down.

"Do you know where I was yesterday when I had the accident?"

Dot and Grace looked at each other and a wordless message passed between them. "Well, darling, we didn't want to bring it up until we knew you were on the mend, but the truth is, we're not very happy, are we, Grace?"

"No, we're not. If you were going to visit Elizabeth you could at least have told us. She was our friend, you know."

"Then why have you never visited her?"

"Oh darling, we tried. Didn't we, Grace? We really tried, when we heard she'd had a breakdown – and who wouldn't after seeing what happened to poor Gloria? Apparently she was there when Gloria jumped in front of the train – did you know that?"

"I surmised as much."

"She got such a shock she ran off. They didn't find her until the next morning. Nearly frozen to death, she was. They took her to the hospital, but even when her body was better, her mind wasn't."

"How do you know? Did you see her?"

"No, they wouldn't let us in, would they, Grace? We tried. Here and at Willow Park, but they said we were on a 'forbidden visitors' list. There was nothing we could do."

"Then how do you know what state of mind she was in?"

"Well, Gloria told us – she came to see us, you know, before she died, to ask for a ticket for Elizabeth to go to America. When they got out of Holloway Elizabeth was too scared to go home. She thought her father would try to have her locked up again –"

"And he has –"

"Yes, but this is different. I've no doubt he's the one who's driven her mad, but mad she is. Poor woman."

"Well, I wonder about that —"

"She was," interjected Grace. "You asked how we knew, Poppy — well, apart from what Gloria told us, it was confirmed by Sophie. She was a nurse and she worked in this very hospital."

"So Sophie saw her?"

"No," conceded Grace, "she was also on 'the list'. But some of Sophie's colleagues told her Elizabeth was hysterical and needed more specialized treatment."

"In Willow Park?" asked Poppy.

"It's one of the best mental hospitals around," offered Dot with a plaintive look that begged Poppy not to judge her too harshly for not visiting her friend.

Poppy lay back on her pillows and absorbed this. "All right," she said after a while. "So she was hysterical after she'd seen her friend killed by a train. But that doesn't mean —"

"Who wouldn't be, darling? Oh poor, poor Gloria! If only we'd stopped her going back. Or if one of us had gone with her."

"Then why didn't you?"

Dot and Grace looked at each other again. A steely, almost accusatory tone inflected Dot's voice. "Well, I wasn't there when Gloria arrived, was I, Grace?"

Grace elongated her neck, sniffed and looked down her nose at her friend. "I thought we'd laid this to rest, Dorothy…"

"Laid what to rest?" asked Poppy.

"Well… Grace —"

Grace raised her hand to silence Dot. "I'll tell her. On the day Gloria came home, your aunt was at the hairdresser's. Only Frank, Sophie and I were home. We didn't know Gloria had been released from Holloway — she still had another month on her sentence — so it came as a shock when she arrived on the doorstep. She'd been on hunger strike, like most of the sisters, and looked like a half-starved waif."

"Haunted, you said, Grace. You said she looked haunted."

"Yes, she did. That's the very word to describe her. When we heard later she had… she had… well, she had done what she had done, none of us were that surprised. But I'll never forgive myself for letting her go on her own. Your aunt knows that, Poppy. And even though she says she's forgiven me, I'll never forgive myself."

"So why didn't you go with her?"

"She begged me not to. She said Elizabeth was disturbed – 'paranoid' was the word she used – and she thought that if I went with her Elizabeth would get spooked. She saw her father's agents behind every bush."

"And not without reason," observed Poppy.

"So true," agreed Dot, and tears welled up in her eyes.

But Poppy was not ready to let up. "So, to summarize, Elizabeth and Gloria were released suddenly from Holloway. Elizabeth feared her father would try to have her locked up again, so she asked Gloria to book passage for her to America."

"That's right," agreed Grace. "Frank, Sophie and I agreed that this was probably the safest course of action, so after she'd had something to eat, I took Gloria to the shipping agent. We got the ticket and then I dropped her off at Paddington station. She said that once she'd delivered the ticket to Elizabeth in Slough, she would come back. But she never did."

"Poor Delilah! I'd got back by then and heard what had happened. I sent a message to Delilah's father. They came round to wait with us. But Gloria never came. Oh, you should have seen the look on the little mite's face when the policeman arrived. She thought it was her mother. But it wasn't. It was the most dreadful news."

Aunt Dot was now openly crying. A nurse popped her head around the door and asked if everything was all right. When she was assured it was, she tapped her fob watch and said that visiting time was nearly over. Aunt Dot and Grace both got ready to go. But Poppy wasn't finished yet.

"Did Gloria mention a box, Grace?"

"A box? No, I don't believe she did. Dorothy, did Frank or Sophie say anything about a box?"

Dot dabbed at her eyes with a frilly handkerchief. "I don't recall. I don't think so. Why do you ask, Poppy?"

"Nothing. I was just wondering. And I'm not feeling too well again, Aunt Dot. Do you mind if I get some sleep?"

"Of course not, darling. We'll come back to see you tomorrow."

"Thank you. And don't forget the flowers."

Dot grimaced at the ostentatious display as Grace picked it up and deposited it on her lap. Then, as they wheeled out, Dot raised her hand to stop Grace. She looked over her shoulder and said, "You can tell us more tomorrow, darling, but how was she? How was Elizabeth?"

"Quite sane," said Poppy. But before she could expand further, the nurse came and announced that visiting time was now, most definitely, over.

At the mid-afternoon visiting time, a large bunch of yellow roses appeared in her doorway, held by a grinning Daniel. "Glad to see you on the mend, Poppy."

"Oh, how lovely! Are they for me?"

"No, they're for Rollo, but he didn't like the colour."

Poppy laughed and then winced.

Daniel rushed to her side. "Are you all right? Do you need the doctor?"

"No, I'm fine; just bruised ribs. You will need to be exceedingly dull today, or I shan't survive it."

"Don't joke about it, Poppy. I've been beside myself with worry."

"You have?" She sounded pleased. And he looked pleased that she was pleased.

He grinned like an overgrown schoolboy and announced, "Righto. Let me get a vase for these."

He popped out and returned a few moments later with the flowers in a cheap white china vase. He put them on the table that Alfie's expensive bouquet had previously occupied. Poppy thought they looked much better.

"They really cheer the room up. Thank you, Daniel."

He pulled up a chair. "So when are you getting out?"

"Not really sure. The doctor said a few days yet."

"Just as well. There's influenza going around the office – half the staff called in sick today."

"Oh dear," said Poppy, sounding worried. Ever since the Spanish influenza two years previously, the mere mention of the word conjured up images of plague-like proportions.

Daniel matched her tone. "Hopefully it will just be the common or garden variety this year."

"I'll be praying."

Daniel didn't respond to that. Instead he absent-mindedly started pleating the bedspread with his scarred hands. After a while he asked, "So, what were you doing in Battersea?"

"Visiting Elizabeth Dorchester."

"You didn't tell me you were going."

"I didn't have time. Rollo and I came up with the idea suddenly – and you were at the Crystal Palace."

"You could have waited…"

"I could have, but I thought it would be best to go on my own."

"Oh." He sounded hurt.

"Rollo thought it best too."

"Did he now?"

"Perhaps I should have waited, but I thought it would be easier for me to get in on my own. I pretended I was there on behalf of the Methodist Mission. It would have been harder to come up with a cover for both of us. Besides, you're quite well known –"

"Not at Willow Park. I've never been there before." He continued pleating the bedspread.

"No, but you *have* been covering some hospital stories lately, haven't you?" She willed him to look at her, but his gaze remained lowered.

"Is that what Rollo said?"

"It is. Look, Daniel, don't be offended."

He stopped pleating and looked up at her, his brown eyes filled with hurt. "I'm not."

"You are."

He gave a wry grin and smoothed out the bedspread. "Oh, all right, I am, a little. But not for professional reasons." He looked at her intently.

"Oh? Why then?" She tried to keep her voice nonchalant, but failed.

"Well, Poppy, I've… well, I've… not made it much of a secret that I find you very charming."

Poppy flushed with delight.

"And I was hoping that you perhaps might be beginning to feel the same way about me."

"Well, you are charming, Daniel. I'll give you that."

"Charming enough for you to go out to dinner with me?"

Poppy looked mockingly around the hospital room. "What – Now?"

"You're not making this any easier for me, are you, Miss Denby?"

"Most definitely not, Mr Rokeby. But it will be easy for me to say yes when I'm free to do so."

"When you're out of hospital – and, of course, fully recovered –"

"I would be delighted to go to dinner with you, Daniel."

Daniel's face lit up. "Then that's a date." He took her hand. "Now you'd better hurry up and get well."

"Now that I've got something to motivate me, I shall."

Poppy and Daniel looked at each other, cheesy smiles on both of their faces.

"Ahem. Sorry to interrupt you two love-birds…"

Poppy and Daniel looked up to see Delilah in the doorway, her voice tight with forced joviality. There were the remains of mascara streaks down her cheeks.

"I've just been to see your aunt and Grace. They told me you've been to see Elizabeth Dorchester."

"I have," said Poppy. "Are you all right, Delilah?"

Delilah looked from Poppy to Daniel. "Do you mind if I speak to Poppy alone?"

Daniel stood up and offered Delilah his chair. "Of course not. Have a seat." Then he leaned over and kissed Poppy's cheek. "I'll see you later."

And despite being worried about her friend, Poppy's heart welled with happiness. "Don't get the flu!"

"I'll try not to," he said, then nodded at Delilah and left.

"Things have been progressing, I see," said Delilah, taking off her coat and hanging it on the back of the chair.

"The lengths I'll go to to get some attention, eh?"

"Don't joke, Poppy. I heard you nearly died."

"Well, that's a bit of a stretch. But yes, it could have been worse."

"Dot said it was Alfie. That he did it on purpose. Did he?"

"I think so."

"But why?"

"Because I visited Elizabeth. I think he and his father have got something to hide – and Elizabeth knows about it."

"So do I," Delilah whispered. She took Poppy's hands in hers; they were shaking. Then her shoulders began to quiver and she started to cry.

Poppy squeezed her friend's hands. "Oh Delilah, what is it?"

"H-has… have they – have they told you about my mother?"

"They have. I'm so sorry, Delilah. I'm so sorry."

"Elizabeth was the last person to see her alive."

"I believe so, yes."

"And you've just seen her. How was she?"

Poppy thought about this for a moment. She'd made a promise to Rollo – and she wouldn't mention the ledger page – but surely she could tell Delilah something. "She was much better. Sad, but sane."

"Then why is she still locked up?"

"I don't know. She believes her father's behind it."

"Do you?" Delilah's eyes were swimming in tears.

"Probably. We only spoke briefly. But my boss at *The Globe* is looking into it."

Delilah wiped the back of her hand over her eyes, spreading black streaks over her olive skin. "Do you think I could see her? I've got so much I want to ask her. I was told she was mad, that you couldn't get any sense out of her, but you say she isn't."

"No, she isn't. But I'm not sure how you could get in to see her. Apparently there's a 'forbidden visitors' list made up of the people Elizabeth used to know from her WSPU days. You're probably on it. But even if you're not, they'll be upping security on her after what happened yesterday."

"Oh." Delilah looked crestfallen.

Poppy reached out her good arm – the one that wasn't hit by the motor – and put it around Delilah's slim shoulders. "Don't worry, we'll make a plan. I'll speak to Rollo and we'll see if he can arrange something. But it might take a while…"

Delilah's eyes lit up with renewed hope. "I've waited seven years. I can wait a few days more."

CHAPTER 17

The next day there were no visitors. The administrators had made a decision to shut the hospital to outsiders as a precaution against the influenza. Although no one was officially saying this was a return of the Spanish variety, the memory of a quarter of a million people in Britain alone – a quarter of a million people who had been celebrating the end of the war with friends and family and soldiers who had miraculously survived the trenches – was not easily laid to rest.

Poppy spent the day quietly reading a new book that Aunt Dot had brought in for her. It made her cry and she wondered if Dot had actually read it before giving it to her. In every line of Wilfred Owen's poems, published two years after his death in 1918, she saw her brother Christopher. He was the youth in the "Anthem for Doomed Youth"; he was the unnamed soldier losing his faith in "Exposure". She thought of Daniel, and wondered if this too had been his experience:

Since we believe not otherwise can kind fires burn;
Now ever suns smile true on child, or field, or fruit.
For God's invincible spring our love is made afraid;
Therefore, not loath, we lie out here; therefore were born,
For love of God seems dying.

To-night, His frost will fasten on this mud and us,
Shrivelling many hands and puckering foreheads crisp.
The burying-party, picks and shovels in their shaking grasp,

Pause over half-known faces. All their eyes are ice,
But nothing happens.

Poppy laid aside the book and stared at the blank wall opposite and listened to the sounds of the hospital around her. Nothing happened.

The next morning she received a visit from the doctor, who declared her fit to go home. She was instructed to call someone to pick her up, because she was not yet ready for the rigours of public transport. At the nurses' station she used the telephone to call Grace and Aunt Dot. There was no answer. Then she tried *The Globe*. Mavis Bradshaw informed her that both Rollo and Daniel had called in sick. "I'm sure it's just a common cold, Poppy; nothing to worry about. Would you like me to arrange a taxi for you?"

"No thanks, Mavis. I'll do it myself." Poppy hung the earpiece in the cradle and held the telephone like a goose with a wrung neck. She was just about to ask the nurse for a number for a taxi when she thought about Delilah. She rang the operator and asked for the number for The Old Vic theatre. The receptionist there informed her that the cast were currently having a tea break, but managed to call Delilah. Delilah said she wouldn't be needed for a few hours, as the director wanted to polish some scenes with the lovers. She would come and pick her up.

Half an hour later Delilah carried Poppy's overnight bag to the hospital carpark.

"I've borrowed a friend's motorcar," she announced. "He's playing Demetrius – quite a dish." She flashed a smile at Poppy, who was glad to see that her friend's spirits were buoyant again.

"How long have you been driving?" asked Poppy as she gingerly climbed into the passenger seat, trying to ignore the painful twinge in her ribs every time she moved.

"I've just started!" declared Delilah blithely. "It's really not hard though. I got stuck on Waterloo Bridge, but some friendly gentlemen helped me get it started again."

Poppy wondered if it was too late to call a taxi.

"It's really quite simple." She took hold of the crank lever, turned it a few times and then leapt into the driving seat, pulled out a few stops, swore briefly when the exhaust let out an almighty belch, then laughed uproariously when the contraption shuddered forward. "See? Simple!"

Poppy, who was used to Grace's subdued driving style, saw her short life flash before her eyes at least three times during the journey from the hospital to Waterloo. It was only when they were halfway over the bridge that she realized they were going the wrong way.

"Home's the other way, Delilah." She pointed westwards and winced at her aching shoulder.

Delilah shouted over the engine. "I hope you don't mind, but I need your help first. Would you mind coming with me to the theatre? It won't take long."

Poppy reluctantly agreed.

They pulled up outside the theatre a few minutes later and Poppy sent up a quick prayer of thanks that they'd made it in one piece. Delilah cut the engine and turned to her friend. Her dark eyes behind the circular motoring goggles made her look like a bushbaby.

"I've been thinking about what you said about us being on a 'forbidden visitors' list at Willow Park. Well, I've got a plan."

"Delilah, I don't think this is wise…"

Delilah's bushbaby eyes started filling with tears. "Please, Poppy. I need to see her. I'll go on my own if I have to, but it would be so much better if you could come with me. Of course, if you're really not up to it, I'll understand."

Poppy looked at her and sighed.

Delilah nodded. "I'm sorry, Poppy, I should have thought. You've just got out of the hospital and –" She glumly reached for the crank.

Poppy stopped her. "It's not that I don't want to help you, Delilah. I will of course be happy to go with you –"

Delilah's face lit up. "Oh, will you really? Are you sure you feel up to it? I can go on my own if you like –"

"No, I'll be fine. I'm a bit sore, but nothing I can't handle. But that's not the point. It's not about how I feel; it's that we won't be able to get in."

Delilah cast her a mischievous glance and said, "Ah, but that's where you're wrong."

An hour later Poppy and Delilah were standing outside the wrought-iron gates of Willow Park. They were wearing nurses' uniforms and wigs, borrowed from the costume department at The Old Vic. Delilah was now a plump, mousey blonde and Poppy a brunette. As an added precaution Poppy was also wearing spectacles.

Poppy froze when she saw the guard who had let her in a few days ago. She held her breath and let Delilah do all the talking. One of Delilah's many former suitors worked as a junior doctor in the men's wing of Willow Park. Delilah had asked him to arrange passes for her and a fellow actress, as they were doing research for a new role. The young doctor had been reluctant at first, but when Delilah promised him dinner and a chance to woo her back, he had come up with the goods.

Their cover story was that they had been sent by "the agency" to fill in for staff off sick with the flu. The guard, who was sneezing into an already drenched handkerchief and muttering that he could do with someone filling in for him, didn't think twice about letting them in. So, for the second time in three days, Poppy walked up the gravel path towards the Gothic asylum.

Inside, Poppy was relieved to see a different receptionist. They showed their passes, repeated their cover story and were waved in the direction of the women's wing. Poppy had told Delilah that she thought their best bet was to get hold of a linen trolley and change bedding. She doubted their ability to answer medical questions if they claimed to be administering treatment. She got her bearings and led Delilah up to the second floor and the area where Elizabeth was held. She remembered seeing a linen cupboard near the nurses' station. True enough, there it was. Delilah boldly walked past the nurses' station and headed straight for the cupboard. She had told Poppy during the drive over that the key to inhabiting a role was to believe you really were that person and not to feel you had to convince anyone of it. She had explained her theory of method acting: "If you don't question yourself, no one else will."

So the two girls headed straight for the linen closet and each armed themselves with a pile of clean bedding. The nurse at the station did not look up from her magazine. Then Poppy led them to Elizabeth's room. She looked through the glass pane and saw the auburn-haired woman in bed. *Good,* thought Poppy, *she hasn't been moved to the secure unit.* She turned the doorknob, but it was locked.

The nurse looked up. "What are you doing?"

"Matron told us to change the bedding," said Delilah.

"Matron told me no one was to go in there," said the nurse.

"When did she tell you that?" asked Delilah.

"About an hour ago."

"Well, she told us to change the bedding ten minutes ago. Should I go and get her, to confirm it to you?"

A flicker of fear flashed in the nurse's eyes, no doubt considering what Matron would say if it was known her authority was being questioned. But she wasn't going down without a fight.

"Who are you? I haven't seen you before."

"The agency sent us. Flu cover." Then they produced their passes.

The nurse peered at them intently. Poppy was convinced they had been caught out. But then the nurse pulled up suddenly and sneezed. They blessed her. She thanked them, then came and unlocked the door before blowing her nose and returning to her magazine.

Poppy and Delilah approached the bed. Elizabeth appeared to be asleep. Poppy shook her gently by the shoulder.

"Excuse me, miss. We need to change the sheets."

Elizabeth opened her eyes and stared blearily at Poppy.

"Sorry to wake you," said Delilah, her voice quivering.

Poppy and Delilah helped Elizabeth up and moved her to an armchair. The older woman moved sluggishly. As she slumped into the chair Poppy looked into her eyes. They were vacant and staring.

"I think she's been drugged," she whispered to Delilah. "You change the bedding and I'll talk to her."

Delilah started stripping the bed but kept a close ear on what was being said. Poppy flicked a glance through the door to the nurses' station. They weren't being watched.

"Elizabeth," she said softly, "it's Poppy Denby. I came to visit you a few days ago. Remember? I'm Dot Denby's niece."

"Dotty?" Elizabeth's eyes focused for a moment. "You still look so young."

"No," said Poppy, "I'm not Dotty. I'm her niece. And I've brought someone else to see you. This is Delilah Marconi. Gloria's daughter."

Poppy took over making the bed while Delilah kneeled down beside the drugged woman.

"Gloria? Gloria? I thought you were dead!" Her voice was raised.

The nurse looked up. Poppy made a big deal of flapping out the sheets. The nurse returned to her reading.

"Shhhh," said Delilah. "We need to whisper. Can you whisper?"

"I can," said Elizabeth, but there was still a note of excitement in her voice. "Is it a secret?"

"It is," said Delilah. "Elizabeth, do you remember me? I was about fourteen the last time I saw you. Before you went to Holloway."

"Holloway," repeated Elizabeth.

"Yes, Holloway. You were there with my mother. Do you remember?"

"Gloria."

"Yes, Gloria."

"I thought you were dead!"

"No – no – I'm not Gloria. I'm –"

"Just go with it," said Poppy as she stuffed a pillow into a fresh pillowcase. "We don't have much time."

Delilah nodded her understanding. "Yes, I'm Gloria. I need to ask you what happened that night in the train yard."

"But you were there!"

"I know, but – but – I don't remember. I lost my memory. I'm trying to get it back."

"You don't remember?"

"No."

"Do you remember the box? You were going to give it to Dotty and the rest of them. I was going to give it to you."

Delilah looked confused. "What box?"

Poppy interjected, remembering that she hadn't told Delilah about the box or the ledger page. "Yes, Elizabeth, she remembers the box. But you didn't give it to her. Why didn't you give it to her?"

Elizabeth's eyes widened and she looked past Delilah. "The shadow," she whispered.

"What about the shadow?" pressed Poppy, indicating with a flick of her head that Delilah was to take over making the bed while she knelt beside Elizabeth.

The older woman turned and fixed her eyes on Delilah. "It pushed her under the train."

Delilah dropped the sheet she was holding, all pretence of making the bed gone. "Someone pushed her? I mean me – someone pushed me?"

"The shadow."

"The shadow's a person?" asked Poppy.

"Yes."

A voice came from the nurses' station. "Are you two finished yet?"

"Nearly!" called Poppy and then she said more quietly to Delilah, "Hold it together."

Delilah carried on making the bed, her hands shaking as she smoothed down the bedspread.

"Who is the shadow, Elizabeth?"

Elizabeth looked fearfully from one to the other. "It's one of you."

"How can the shadow be Gloria, Elizabeth? It pushed her."

"No, not Gloria. You. Us. The Chelsea Six."

"The shadow is one of the Chelsea Six?"

Elizabeth nodded.

"How do you know?" asked Poppy.

"Quick, she's coming," mumbled Delilah through gritted teeth as the nurse got up from her station.

Poppy repeated her question as she picked up the pile of dirty laundry from the floor.

"Because no one else knew about the box," said Elizabeth. Then suddenly her eyes came into focus and her voice became more lucid. She stared again at Poppy. "It's you. The journalist."

"That's right," said Poppy.

"You promised to get me out of here."

"We will," said Poppy as the nurse strode into the room.

"What do they teach you in the agency?" She cast a critical eye over the bed and then at Elizabeth. "Are you just going to leave her there?"

"No, of course not. Here –" Poppy took Elizabeth by the arm.

"Oh, get out of here!" said the nurse. "I'll do it myself. Come on, Liz. Back to bed."

Delilah and Poppy stood with their arms full of dirty linen.

"Don't just stand there gawping. Out!"

Reluctantly, they left as the nurse helped Elizabeth back into bed. Poppy tried to catch the older woman's eye, but couldn't.

"Come on," she said to Delilah, and they left.

Chapter 18

"**I** thought you said she was sane."

Delilah and Poppy were sitting in the motorcar overlooking Battersea Park, well out of sight of the asylum.

"She is. She was completely lucid the last time I saw her. She's been drugged. Today – at the end – she knew who I was."

"At the end. It's the bit in the middle that worries me. All that about the shadow…" Delilah reached up a shaking hand, removed her blonde wig and tossed it on the back seat. "If it's true, then all these years when I thought my mother had killed herself have been a lie." Delilah turned to Poppy, tears welling in her eyes. "Do you know what it's like to lose someone, Poppy?"

Poppy thought of Christopher. "I do. I lost my brother."

"But he didn't choose to kill himself, did he? He didn't decide that you, his family, weren't worth living for, did he?"

"No," said Poppy quietly, "he didn't. But we don't know if what she's saying is true."

"You said she was sane."

"I did. And she is. I really believe that. But that doesn't mean everything she tells us is the gospel truth. I mean, if it was, that means my aunt or one of her friends is a murderer."

"Your aunt couldn't have done it. She's in a wheelchair."

"No, but Grace isn't."

"Or Frank. Or Sophie. But I can't imagine any of them hurting my mother. They all loved her. Everyone did." She stifled a sob. "If Elizabeth's sane, could she simply be lying?"

Poppy nodded thoughtfully. "She could be. She wants to get out of that asylum and who knows what she will say to make sure that happens? Or she could simply be confused. She's been locked up for seven years. And that night – that night at the train yard – she was definitely confused. Everything I've heard suggests she was half starved and sick. She could have hallucinated the whole thing."

"But what if she didn't?" asked Delilah. "What if what she's saying is true? What if one of the Chelsea Six is a murderer?"

"Then we'll need to prove it."

"How? We only have her word for it. There's no physical evidence."

"Well, actually, there might be…"

Delilah grabbed Poppy's shoulder. Poppy winced, but Delilah didn't notice. "What do you mean? What aren't you telling me, Poppy? And what was all that about a box?"

"It's something that the newspaper's following up. But I promised my editor I wouldn't tell anyone."

An edge came into Delilah's voice. "My mother may or may not have been murdered, Poppy. I think I have a right to know."

"All right. But you must promise not to tell anyone about it. Particularly my aunt. You know she can't keep quiet about anything."

Delilah nodded gravely. "I promise."

Poppy went on to explain about Bert Isaacs and how they found the letter that led to the asylum – and then the ledger page, Richard Easling, Alfie and Melvyn Dorchester and the alleged box.

"What's in the box?" asked Delilah.

"I don't really know, but whatever it is, it might corroborate Elizabeth's version of events."

"If it exists."

"Yes, if it exists. Neither Grace nor Dot remembers anything about it."

The Battersea Park clock struck five o'clock. Delilah looked up. "Crikey! Robert's going to kill me! I promised I'd be back to go over a scene with him."

She jumped out of the motorcar and grabbed hold of the crank lever. "I'll drop you home."

"No, it will take too long. You're on the right side of the river. Just go to the theatre. I'll get home by myself." Poppy got out, opened the boot, and took out her overnight case and satchel.

"Are you sure?" asked Delilah.

"Yes; just go."

Delilah smiled her thanks.

"And Delilah, don't worry. We'll get to the bottom of this. I'll tell Rollo about it. I'm sure he'll know what to do."

Delilah finished cranking the engine, gave her a brief hug, jumped in the driver's seat and pulled down her motoring goggles. "All right, we'll talk about it tomorrow. Toodles!"

"Toodles," said Poppy, and waved her friend goodbye.

An hour later and Poppy was carrying her satchel and little suitcase up Fleet Street. Her whole body was beginning to ache, but she knew she wouldn't be able to rest until she had had another look at Bert's files.

According to the clock outside Barclay's Bank, it was after six o'clock, so she wasn't surprised that the front door to *The Globe* was locked. She went around the back in the hope that the service doors from the alleyway were still open. She wasn't disappointed. Printers worked in shifts at *The Globe*, and the new crew were setting up the presses for the next day's edition. They looked surprised to see Poppy, but didn't question her as she walked through the basement to the stairwell. But before she left them, she turned and asked, "Were any of you on day shift when Bert Isaacs died?"

Two men – one approaching retirement age and another, a young apprentice – indicated they had been. She questioned them as to whether or not they had seen anyone come in or out of the basement shortly before or after his fall. They said they hadn't, but that one of the printing presses had jammed and all hands were needed on deck to fix it. They admitted that someone could have slipped in or out without anyone noticing as they were all distracted by the broken printer at the time.

"Why are you asking, miss?" asked the older man. "Do you think Bert's death wasn't an accident?"

"Well, the coroner hasn't given his report yet, so Mr Rolandson and I are just considering the options."

She used Rollo's name to give herself some authority, in case the men questioned her right to ask – or even to be there. They didn't. She thanked them and went up the stairs. She stopped on the ground floor and went and stood in the middle of the deserted foyer, where she had been when Bert fell to his death. She looked up into the high-ceilinged atrium and noted that the balustrade on the second floor had finally been fixed. Could Bert simply have leaned on it, exhausted after his efforts to climb the stairs, and fallen through? Or was he pushed?

She mentally recapped the layout of the building. In the basement, the printing presses. On the ground floor, reception and the typesetting hall. On the first floor, the finance and advertising departments. The second floor was art and photography. The third floor was the morgue archive, and finally the fourth, editorial. But it was the second floor that interested Poppy. She went up there in the lift.

The art and photography department was the only part of the building she had not yet visited. She stepped out of the lift and went over to the balustrade, noting where it had been repaired. She looked over and down onto the black and white mosaic two floors below. The swirling Egyptian patterns made her feel dizzy. She stepped back. *Poor Bert*, she thought again. There was nothing else on the second floor other than the double doors to the art and photography department. So if Bert had been pushed, the killer had either to have come from in there or from the lift. Ivan Molanov had heard the lift around the time Bert fell, but that could have been the killer – if there was one – making his or her escape, or, in all the confusion, trying to get to the third floor to steal the Elizabeth Dorchester Jazz File. That was the theory so far. However, no one seemed to have considered the possibility that someone could have come out of the art and photography department, pushed Bert over, then jumped into the lift.

Daniel had already told her that no one else was on the second floor landing when he came out, hearing Mavis's scream. That's when she'd suggested the person might have hidden in the lift. But until now she had never considered that the assailant might have gone back into the department. She walked the few steps across the landing and pushed open the double doors.

Inside were half a dozen or so desks, some light tables, easels and a long central table with various mock-ups of illustrations. A door at the back of the room was marked "Dark room". She assumed that was where the photographs were developed. She went in. It was indeed dark, and she felt around for a light switch. As the light came on she saw a number of trays filled with liquid. She didn't know what any of it was, but by the acrid stench in the air, there were obviously some chemicals in use. Across the small room was strung a clothes line with pegs. But instead of clothing, photographs were hung out to dry. A quick perusal told her they were linked to various stories the paper was working on. But then one of them caught her eye: two young women, dressed to the nines, coming out of Oscar's jazz club. It was her and Delilah. It must have been when Daniel and Lionel were trying to get a shot of Charlie Chaplin. *Gosh, that dress was short!* thought Poppy and chuckled to herself.

She really didn't know what she was looking for, so if something was out of place, she wouldn't know. She turned out the light and closed the door. Back in the main office she wondered which desk was Daniel's. It was impossible to tell. Some desks had framed photographs of family members – wives and children, she assumed – some didn't. Some desks were tidy, others messy. She didn't know Daniel well enough to know which one his might have been. She pulled herself up: *Stop thinking about Daniel.* But then a thought occurred to her. Daniel had said he was first out of the department when he heard Mavis scream. She walked towards the doors, as if retracing his steps, and pushed them open. But what if he hadn't come out of the doors and had been on the landing already? What if… Good heavens, what was she thinking? Impossible! And yet… and yet… what did she really know about Daniel?

She let the doors swing shut again and paced up and down on the landing. Rollo had suggested that perhaps he was not to be trusted with the information about the ledger. Why not? What possible connection could he have to the story? Well, for one thing he had a history with Alfie Dorchester. They had been in the same regiment and there was no love lost between them. What was it that Daniel knew about Alfie that made him question his version of events on the day he won the Victoria Cross? And how had he been injured and why had it led to an early discharge? And finally, why was he so evasive about it all?

There was a lot she didn't know about Daniel Rokeby and his relationship with Alfie. Could Bert have uncovered something? All the more reason to take another look at his files.

The editorial office was two floors up. She thought of taking the stairs, but her aching body prompted her back into the lift. She went in and pressed the button for the fourth floor. However, on the way up it stopped at the third floor – someone must have pressed the button. But no one opened the gate to come in. Curious, she pushed the gate open herself and had a look out. There was no one on the landing and the doors to the morgue remained firmly shut. She shrugged and went back into the lift and pushed the button again for the fourth floor.

One floor up she stepped out onto the landing. She suddenly thought that whoever had pushed the button for the lift on the third floor might have changed their mind and decided to take the stairs instead. She quickly looked down the stairwell, but it was empty. Perhaps they were up here already… She looked at the doors to the editorial department, her throat tightening, her palms sweating, and considered backing down and returning tomorrow when more people were in the building. Rollo might be back by then and she could talk it all through with him. But Rollo might still be sick, and she was here now… She pushed open the doors.

Inside, she was relieved to see no one was there. Perhaps the person on the third floor – possibly Ivan – had gone *down* the stairs. Yes, that made perfect sense. Ivan Molanov had been working a little late and was now going home. He might have seen that the lift was going up and didn't want to waste time going up before he went down, so had simply taken the stairs. She was sure that's what must have happened; she would confirm it with him in the morning. She looked around again to check she really was alone and went to Bert's desk. She searched through the piles of papers, sandwich wrappers and empty coffee cups, but could not find any notebooks or files. Rollo must have taken them. Yes, that would make sense. Hadn't he said that Easling wanted to have a look at Bert's files? Of course the editor would have taken them.

She walked across the newsroom and tried the door to Rollo's office. It was locked. However, on the day Rollo was out arranging Bert's funeral and had left her alone to sort out his office, he had given her a key – which she was to return to him when she had finished. That was the same day she had gone to the asylum; the same day she had been knocked down and taken to hospital… She had not had a chance to return the key! She scratched around in her satchel and found it, still attached to the house keys for 137 King's Road.

To the casual observer, Rollo's office was a warzone. However, in the hours she had spent there she had come to realize that despite the apparent chaos there was a loose filing system and she had an idea of where to look for Bert's files. A few minutes later she had located them.

She cleared an oasis on Rollo's desk, turned on the desk lamp and started to read. It didn't take her long to realize that Rollo had been right: there was nothing more there than she already knew and which had been condensed into the summary file he had given her the day she went to interview Melvyn Dorchester. There was also very little on Elizabeth Dorchester, but she did find a note in red pencil: "See EDJF for more" – see Elizabeth Dorchester Jazz File for more? Ah, but that was the file that was missing. Would that have given her any more clues as to who the Chelsea Six mole was? Or in fact if there even was a mole? Why had Bert been trying to gain access to Elizabeth in the days before his death? What did he think she knew that he didn't? And how, if at all, was this connected with his death?

Her head throbbed. She lay down for a moment with her forehead on her arms, stretching out her neck and lower back.

She should probably get home. If Grace and Dot had telephoned the hospital to see if they could visit they would know by now that she had already been discharged and would be worried as to where she was.

She sat back up. But as she did, she realized something was stuck to the inside of her arm: an envelope smeared with what looked like the remains of one of Bert's jam sandwiches. She peeled it off. It was postmarked Paris and addressed to Bert at *The Globe*. She opened it and read:

17th of May, 1920

Dearest Bert,

I'm sure it will come as a surprise that I am contacting you again after all these years. I hope it is not too unwelcome. I realize that things were not well between us the last time I saw you, and for that I am deeply sorry. As you know, in 1913 I became involved in things for which I am deeply ashamed and I thank you for keeping your silence about it all these years. It was more than I deserve.

However, I feel it is time to make it up to you. I cannot give you specific details lest I personally implicate myself and open myself up to criminal charges, but I can tell you that you should look more carefully at the recent deal between the Radium Institute and our old friend Melvyn Dorchester. I'm sure a journalist of your calibre will soon find the evidence you need. I hope this goes some way towards making up for what I did in 1913 – of which, I say again, I am deeply ashamed. I hope you find it in your heart to leave my name out of your story when it is finally published.

Sincerely,
Sophie Blackburn

Poppy was stunned. She reread the letter, then read it again. Was this evidence that Sophie Blackburn was the mole? Was the thing of which she was so deeply ashamed the murder of Gloria Marconi? And had Bert known about it back in 1913? Why had he not reported it? And now that it had resurfaced, would he really have been prepared to keep her name out of it for the sake of a scoop about Melvyn Dorchester and the Radium Institute deal? Perhaps he hadn't been. Perhaps that's why he was trying to see Elizabeth to find out what had really happened back in 1913. Perhaps that's why he was killed…

A shadow appeared in the frosted glass pane of Rollo's door. Poppy looked up. It was too tall for Rollo. Poppy quickly slipped the letter into her satchel, slung it over her shoulder and looked for a place to hide. But there was no point. The light was on and whoever was outside would have already seen her through the glass pane. She stood up and waited. The doorknob turned.

"What are you doing here?" The skinny arts editor stood in the doorway striking a melodramatic pose with an accusatory finger pointed at her.

"I am Mr Rolandson's assistant. I'm picking up some files to take to him at home. He's got the flu." She closed Bert's file and slipped it into her satchel.

Lionel Saunders sneered. "A likely story. I thought you were still in the hospital."

"They discharged me this afternoon."

"And the first thing you did was come here and rifle through Rollo's files. Who are you working for, Miss Denby? The WSPU, or" – his eyes widened – "*The Courier*? That's it! You work for *The Courier*. They're setting a honey trap."

"A honey trap? I have no idea what you are talking about."

"Oh, don't play the innocent with me, missy. That outfit you wore the other night proves otherwise. And now here you are in a foxy little nurse's uniform –"

Drat! Poppy had forgotten she was still in costume.

"Well, you won't get far seducing me. Rollo, on the other hand, is a sucker for anything in a skirt, and Danny's out to find a replacement."

"A replacement? What on earth do you mean?" She held up her hand. "Actually, I don't want to know. I'm tired, Mr Saunders, and I want to get home. I'll drop this over at Rollo's on the way back."

Lionel strode towards her, holding out his hand. "Hand it over."

"What?"

"Bert's file."

"I... well... I – hang on. How do you know it's Bert's file?"

There was a fleeting look of panic on Lionel's face before he regained his composure, but it was enough for Poppy. She straightened her shoulders and put a protective hand on the satchel.

"Excuse me, Mr Saunders, I'm leaving. And I'm taking this with me – as per Rollo's request. You can ring him if you like." She indicated the telephone. "Or perhaps I should. I'll tell him you're here, harassing me." She reached out to take the phone by the neck.

Lionel grabbed it from her. She refused to let go. They grappled for a moment, then she let go, taking him by surprise, and he fell backwards, knocking over one of Rollo's stacks of files. The pile, which nearly reached the ceiling, toppled onto him.

She wondered for a moment if he was hurt, but judging by all of the swearing coming from under the avalanche, he was fine. She took her chance and ran.

CHAPTER 19

Poppy did not stop running until she was well down Fleet Street. She didn't stop when the printers called to her and she didn't stop when she nearly ran into a group of choirboys heading to Temple Church for Friday night choir practice. She only stopped when the pain in her ribs was so acute she could hardly breathe.

She pulled up in the doorway of a pub and took in sharp, painful breaths, looking down the street to see if Lionel was following her. If he was, she planned to go into the pub and ask for help. A damsel in distress in a nurse's uniform was sure to illicit sympathy from the male clientele. But Lionel was nowhere in sight. She had heard him running after her down the four flights at *The Globe*, but by the time she got through the basement she could no longer hear him. And when she got onto the street she was too scared to look back.

As her breathing evened out she realized she felt sick. Physically sick. She leaned her forehead against the stone lintel and closed her eyes until the feeling passed.

"Are you all right, miss?" Two men and a woman were looking at her, concerned.

"I'm feeling a little ill."

"Do you want a glass of water?"

"No, thank you. But can you call me a taxi?"

"Of course."

Poppy sank down on the step. The woman sat beside her while one of the men hailed a taxi.

"Are you sure you're all right to travel, love?" asked the woman.

"Yes, thank you," said Poppy, who could think only of her bed.

Half an hour later, Poppy was shakily paying the taxi driver outside 137 King's Road. Aunt Dot and Grace were waiting for her in the hall, beside themselves with worry. They demanded to know where she'd been, why she hadn't called, if she was all right – and why on earth she was wearing a nurse's uniform! Poppy waved them off and said she was sorry about everything and she would tell them all about it in the morning. But for now she was going to bed. Goodnight.

The next morning Aunt Dot and Grace brought Poppy breakfast in bed. Poppy had already decided that she couldn't tell them much – there was too much up in the air and she wanted to thrash it out with Rollo first – but she had to tell them something. So as she munched on her toast and marmalade she told them a series of half-truths. She had been unexpectedly released from hospital. Her own clothes had somehow got lost in the hospital laundry, so she'd borrowed a nurse's uniform. Delilah had come to pick her up after she'd called home and discovered they weren't there. But then Delilah's motorcar had broken down – she made a quick mental note that she would need to square this with Delilah in case Dot asked her – and then she had made her way back on public transport. There had been a traffic jam in central London (highly plausible, as everyone knew) and it had taken her hours to get home. She had not been able to telephone because she could not find a public booth. Dot seemed to take this at face value, but Grace gave her a curious look. Poppy sipped her tea.

And then Delilah arrived. Poppy cursed her timing. However, thanks to Dot's effusive greeting of "Delilah, darling!

Thank you so much for picking Poppy up yesterday. How's the motor by the way? Call our mechanic – he's marvellous, he'll have it fixed in no time", coupled with a warning look from Poppy, the young actress quickly picked up the script.

"Thank you, Dot, but my friend – the one I borrowed it from – has already got it sorted."

"I didn't know you drove," observed Grace drily.

"Well, I'm just learning. Apparently I flooded the engine. Silly, silly me. I'm just sorry Poppy had to get back using public transport."

Ah yes, thought Poppy. *She doesn't know that I didn't come straight home. Best leave it like that.*

"Well, it did take it out of her," said Dot. "A day in bed, methinks. Are you staying for breakfast, Delilah? Or you could come over later for lunch. I'm sure Poppy would enjoy the company."

"I'd love to, Dot, but Robert went through the roof yesterday when I missed my rehearsal. So I've got to get in extra early today and stay extra late. I'll come and see you as soon as I can, Poppy." She gave the blonde girl a knowing look. "Rest up."

So Poppy did. Until about eleven when Grace came to tell her that she and Dot were going to lunch with Marjorie Reynolds and they wouldn't be back until later that afternoon.

"Is there anything you need?"

"No, thank you, Grace. I'm feeling much better. I think I'll get up and make a few phone calls, if that's all right."

"Of course." Grace kissed her on the forehead.

Poppy was taken aback. Grace was not one for physical affection. The older woman seemed to have surprised herself too. "We were worried about you, Poppy. Please don't do anything silly."

"I won't, Grace," said Poppy. But even as she said it she knew it was a promise she would soon break.

The first phone call Poppy made was to *The Globe*. She knew that Mavis would be on reception until one o'clock, because the older lady had told her Saturday morning was the busiest time for people coming in to buy classified advertising: items for sale, baby announcements, funeral arrangements, lonely hearts… She asked Mavis for two home telephone numbers: Rollo's and Daniel's. She wasn't sure if Daniel had a telephone at home, but was pleased when Mavis told her he had. She felt terrible about accusing him of Bert's death – if only in her mind – and now she was convinced that the mole at *The Globe* was Lionel Saunders, she wanted to apologize to him. Well, of course she couldn't actually apologize, as that would require her admitting she'd suspected him in the first place, but it would settle things on her side if she at least spoke to him. She was worried too about how ill he might be with the flu, and of course there was the dinner invitation …

But before she rang Daniel she decided to catch up with Rollo. After a few rings a croaky voice answered: "Rolandson."

After exchanging a few pleasantries and enquiring about each other's health, Poppy filled Rollo in on the events of the last twenty-four hours.

"Lionel Saunders? Well, wadya know? But it fits. He's always had contacts in high society, which is why I kept him on when I took over, but obviously they go deeper than I thought."

"Do you think he's responsible for Bert's death?"

She was answered by a hacking cough. "Sorry, Poppy." Rollo cleared his throat. "Right. Lionel and Bert. I don't honestly know. I can buy that he's been snooping around for Dorchester – and he's probably the one who took the Jazz File – but murder? I don't know, Poppy. The man's a weasel, but I don't think he'd go that far."

"But he might have."

"Yes, he might have. Or it could have been someone else. Or no one at all."

A shiver went down Poppy's spine as she thought about what might have happened to her last night in Rollo's office. "Even so, is there some way you can suspend him so he doesn't come into work until this is all sorted?"

Rollo wheezed out a sigh. "I don't know. Possibly. But there's no evidence of anything."

"But –"

"Hang on, I didn't say I didn't believe you, but the legal department will want more than that before they approve his suspension. He'll be lawyered-up, suing us for unfair dismissal in no time. And that can get expensive…"

Poppy was irked that Rollo was thinking about money at a time like this. But he was, first and foremost, a businessman.

"But I can understand you not wanting to be around him. Perhaps it's better if you take a few days off."

"I've had a few days off! I'll be ready to get back to work on Monday. I'm ready today."

"Hold on there, missy, I haven't finished. What if I send you away somewhere on assignment?"

Poppy relaxed a bit. "What do you have in mind?"

"Paris is lovely at this time of year."

"Paris? You mean… you mean –"

"Yes. I want you to go and speak to Sophie Blackburn. I'd go, but I'm in the middle of reapplying for my visa and I can't leave the country."

"But I don't have a passport."

"You don't? Hmmm." Rollo was quiet for a while, mulling this over, punctuating the silence with an occasional sniff.

"Take down this address."

Poppy did so.

"There's a guy there called Bobby Smith, who owes me a few favours. He's got connections in the passport office. I'll give him a call now and get him to arrange a temporary travel document for you. You can pick it up this evening."

"This evening?"

"Yes, there's a ferry leaving for Calais tonight. I want you on it."

"But I –"

"Don't worry, I'll arrange the ticket. And some spending money. You can pick those up from Bobby too."

"But my aunt – she'll be worried. What am I going to say to her?"

This silenced Rollo for a while as he sniffed and thought. "Is she in?"

"No. She won't be back until late this afternoon."

"Then leave her a note saying you're off on an assignment. Doing a feature on a getaway in Leamington Spa. I'll give her a call to confirm it. I'll tell her the paper was offered a few days there in return for a review – which is true, but we haven't taken them up on it yet – and that I sent a motor for you. I'll pitch it to her as a convalescence."

"All right. She might buy that. So when can I expect the motor?"

Rollo hacked out a laugh. "Who do you think you're working for? *The Times*? No, Miz Denby, we're not made of money. You can get the train to Dover. Get a ticket from Charing Cross and keep the receipts."

They finished their conversation with a discussion of the angle she would take with Sophie Blackburn, and Poppy promised to telegraph him from Paris when she got there.

"See you in a few days, Poppy. And be careful."

As Poppy put down the telephone she was assailed with worry. Was she really fit enough to travel? What if she missed this Bobby Smith and couldn't get the documents she needed? She'd never been out of the country before – would she know what to do? She only had school French and had never actually spoken to a real, live French person before. Would they be able to understand her? Would she understand them? Poppy suddenly felt very young and very small.

Only a month ago she had been leaving her parents in Morpeth. They had only agreed to let her go because she was going to be staying with her aunt, who was supposed to look after her. Now here she was working as an investigative journalist, on a story that may involve two murders, having survived at least one attempt on her life, and she was leaving the country. And she couldn't tell her parents any of it.

Aunt Dot had told her that she telegraphed them to say she'd had "a little accident" and that they said they would come down to see her. But that would take a few days to arrange and the earliest they could be here was Tuesday. How long would she be out of town? The last thing she needed was for them to arrive in London while she was still in Paris. She would send them a telegram when she got to Charing Cross, telling them they shouldn't bother coming as she was now out of hospital and feeling fine. She would tell them she was going to Leamington Spa for a few days with a friend and that they should book a telephone call with the Morpeth Post Office and she'd speak to them when she got back.

Oh, how she wished she could speak to them now and tell them everything. She yearned for someone to confide in. Delilah was in rehearsal, Grace and Dot were out (and besides, they were possibly implicated anyway), so that only left one person: Daniel. Rollo had told her not to tell him about the ledger page, but now that it was almost one hundred per cent certain that Lionel was the mole, surely that no longer applied? There was lots he already knew; what harm would there be in telling him more? Poppy unhooked the earpiece and dialled Daniel's number.

"Hello? Hello?" It was a child's voice.

"Let me! Let me!" A second child.

"Hello, is this the right number? I'm looking for Daniel Rokeby."

"DADDY!"

"Daddy can't come to the phone right now." A woman's voice. "Who is it? Hello? Can I help you?"

"Er – hello. I'm not sure if this is the correct number. I'm looking for Daniel Rokeby."

"This is the Rokeby residence. May I enquire who's calling?"

"Er – my name's Poppy Denby. It's to do with work. I'm from *The Globe*."

"Well, Miss Denby, Daniel is sick. He's sent in a sick note. I'm sure if you check your files you'll find it. Good day to you." She put down the phone.

Poppy looked at the earpiece, not believing what she had just heard, then she quietly put it down. She leaned against the wall in the hall for support while she steadied her breathing, then slowly slid to the floor. As her bottom hit the tiles she began to cry, great wrenching sobs that hurt her ribs with each breath. But she didn't care. And she cried until there was nothing left in her.

CHAPTER 20

Poppy mounted the gangplank of the *Fleur-de-lis* with the upper-class passengers while some motorcars were being winched onto the ferry by a crane. Unlike most of the travellers, who were accompanied by valets and maids, Poppy carried her own suitcase. She had had to borrow one of Aunt Dot's, as she had left hers in Rollo's office when she fled from Lionel – yet another thread that if pulled would rapidly unravel her story. How long she could keep this up, she had no idea, but the desire to pursue the truth took the edge off her guilt.

She was surrounded by cut-glass accents in English and French, and ladies who looked as though they were on a Parisienne runway, not a Dover gangplank. Poppy was conscious of her dull travelling clothes – the same ones she had arrived in from Morpeth – and wished Delilah had been on hand to give her a makeover. She was not dressed for the company she would be travelling with and had not been prepared for it. Knowing Rollo's predilection for doing things on the cheap, she was surprised when Bobby Smith handed her a first-class ticket – all he could get at short notice, he told Poppy, and Rollo would have to like it or lump it. At the top of the plank she gave the steward her ticket and he called a porter to take her suitcase, announcing in a French accent that "a lady should not carry 'er own luggage"!

On the way to her cabin, the porter pointed out the main attractions on board: the bar, the dining room, the games room, the library and a small shopping emporium. It consisted of a parfumier, a tobacconist, a barber's and hairdressing salon, a gentlemen's outfitters and a ladies' dress boutique.

Her cabin, although small, was luxurious. It seemed a bit of a waste, as the trip over would only take a few hours and she would have to transfer to the Blue Train for an overnight run to Paris. Thanks to *Bradshaw's Illustrated Travellers' Handbook* that she had borrowed from Grace and Dot's library, she knew that the ferry would be leaving Dover at ten o'clock and arriving in Calais at half-past midnight. A light supper would be provided, and for first-class passengers evening dress was required. This seemed a little silly to Poppy, as they would be transferring to a train in a few hours. Many of the toffs didn't bother getting changed again in Calais and Poppy had heard that some of the younger set started their party in the ferry bar and finished it in *Le Train Bleu* cocktail coach when it arrived in Paris at seven o'clock the following morning. Poppy intended to get some sleep on the train but did still want to be appropriately dressed for dinner on the ferry. So after tipping the porter she decided to do a bit of shopping.

The boutique, like everything else on the first-class deck, was small but luxurious. The shop assistant looked on her with pity in her fawn outfit, and brought out the cheaper dresses in their range. Even these were more than Poppy had hoped to pay, but it was too late to back out now. So Poppy told the assistant how much money she had to spend and the collection diminished yet again to a choice between two dresses: a simple turquoise faux silk shift that came to just above Poppy's knees and a drop-waisted yellow frock in cotton. Poppy chose the turquoise as most appropriate for evening. She was pleased to see that the dress had a matching bag decorated with Chinese-inspired embroidery.

With her purchases wrapped and placed in her satchel, she followed the stream of passengers up to the top deck as the *Fleur-de-lis* horn blasted its intention to set sail.

Midsummer in the south of England, the sun set well into the evening, so as the ferry pulled out of the harbour the town of Dover was silhouetted against an orange backdrop, and the famous white cliffs were bathed in pink and gold. It was the most beautiful sight Poppy had ever seen and it brought tears to her eyes – not of sadness, but awe.

"It gets you every time, doesn't it?" asked an elderly lady standing beside her. She was dressed in sensible tweed and Poppy noticed a *Bradshaw's* poking out of the pocket of her travelling cape.

"It's my first time," said Poppy softly.

"Ah," said the old lady. "Then don't get used to it. I've travelled the world, my dear, and nothing rivals this."

She then went on to enquire about the purpose of Poppy's voyage and with whom she was travelling. She was surprised to hear Poppy was on her own; she was with a party of continental travellers organized by Thomas Cook and Son.

"It really isn't safe for a young lady on her own. I'm surprised your parents let you come."

Poppy tried not to bristle and explained patiently to the lady – who had introduced herself as Miss Betty Swan – that she was a working lady and was going to Paris on business. Miss Swan appeared shocked and intrigued in equal measure and when she enquired as to the nature of Poppy's business, Poppy surprised herself by lying: the stationery business.

Later, as she prepared for dinner, she wondered why she had done it. And she realized it was because she just wanted to be left alone. Although she had worked at the newspaper for only a week (and two days of that had been spent in hospital) she had already discerned that the moment anyone heard you were connected with the press they were either on their guard, worried that you were going to splash their affairs across the front page, or the opposite, desperate that you would. After Poppy's recent ordeal and the shock of learning that Daniel was married, she did not have the emotional energy to deal with either. Lying just seemed easier. She would deal with the spiritual consequences later.

Supper was a shellfish bisque followed by a buffet of continental meats, cheese and fruit, topped off by a strawberry pavlova. Miss Swan invited her to sit with the Thomas Cook party and she made polite small talk about the stationery business, which everyone appeared to find fascinating. Poppy prayed that there wouldn't be a real stationery expert in the party, then repented for praying that God would endorse her lie.

As soon as she could, she headed for the bar – not that she was desperate for a drink, but at least there she didn't have to continue with her charade, as Miss Swan and her companions announced that they were going to take coffee on the deck. She balked at the price of pink champagne, which was the only drink she knew of, and took the advice of the barman to try a light chardonnay which, apparently, was cheaper but still suitable for a lady. For the second time that night Poppy wished Delilah was with her to help her navigate the complexities of high society.

Glass in hand, she looked for a place to sit. There were mixed groups of bright young people and separate groups of older gentlemen. The older men were obviously not an option, but she wasn't sure how to attach herself to a mixed group without actually knowing anyone. She lurked for a while, hoping to catch someone's eye and be invited into a group, but nothing happened. So instead she took her drink out onto the deck and leaned on the railing, watching the lights of Dover flickering dimly in the distance. She sipped her drink and found it less zingy than the champagne, but still pleasantly fruity.

"Why, if it isn't Miss Denby! You do get around."

Poppy nearly dropped her glass in shock. She turned to see Alfie Dorchester leaning on the railing with a whisky glass in hand.

"So they let you out of hospital. Did you get my flowers?"

"Yes and yes. Excuse me." Poppy turned to walk back into the bar, but Alfie blocked her path.

"Where are you going? Paris?"

"That's none of your business."

"That's rich from a girl who makes a habit of poking her nose into other people's business."

Poppy opened her mouth to retort and then decided against it. It was pointless getting into an argument with Alfie Dorchester. She tried to get past him again. He laughed coldly and took a step towards her. She took a step backwards and felt the railing press into the small of her back.

"Did you know that half a dozen people fall off ferries every year in the United Kingdom? A strange statistic that. It never seems to vary. You would think that some years it would be more and others less, but apparently not. It's as if the sea requires its quota." He leaned towards her. "I wonder how many have died this year?"

Poppy prepared herself to scream but was cut short by a bellow from the bar. "It's Alfie Dorchester! Alfie! Come join us! Viscount Dorchester won the Victoria Cross, you know …" This was met with a cheer and a round of "For he's a jolly good fellow".

Alfie straightened up and smiled. "If you'll excuse me, Miss Denby, my public awaits. I shall see you later." Then he raised his glass in mock salute before turning to embrace the applause.

Poppy felt sick. She poured the rest of her wine over the side and put the glass down on a nearby table. Then while Alfie's blond head bobbed above a throng of admirers, she hurried back to her cabin. She planned to stay there, behind locked doors, until they docked in Calais. However, when she opened the door she was greeted by an upturned room. Her suitcase had been emptied out onto the floor and its contents rifled. There was only one person who could have done this. She knew, however, that he was upstairs in the bar; but what if he had paid someone to do it? And what if that person was still in the room? She took a step backwards.

"Miss Denby! Are you all right?"

Poppy's heart leapt at the sensible voice of Miss Swan. She and two other ladies were walking towards her down the hall. As they reached her they poked their heads in to see what she was looking at.

"Good heavens! What's happened? Has there been a robbery? We must call the captain at once!"

Poppy imagined having to explain this to the captain with Miss Swan and her friends listening in. She would then have to admit she was a reporter on assignment and not a stationery rep. She might also have to tell them why she was heading to Paris, and she did not want to do that. Besides, she knew that the only thing of importance was still on her person. She slipped her hand into her turquoise evening bag and felt Sophie Blackburn's letter. No, another lie was needed.

"It's all right, Miss Swan. I picked the suitcase up without realizing it was unfastened. Silly me."

Miss Swan looked disappointed there was no crime to be solved and sighed. "Oh well, never mind. We're off for a game of rummy. I don't suppose you want to join us…"

"Actually, Miss Swan, a game of rummy is just what I feel like. If you'll give me a moment to tidy this up, I'll be with you in a tick."

Three rounds of rummy and an hour and a half later, Poppy disembarked the *Fleur-de-lis* as an honorary Thomas Cook adventurer. She glared at Alfie as she passed him and made sure he heard her tell the porter on the Blue Train that she was happy to trade in her single cabin for a bunk with Miss Swan and friends.

Alfie stubbed out his cigarette with a twist of his heel and headed straight for the cocktail carriage.

CHAPTER 21

Poppy felt well rested and, for now, safe when the Blue Train entered Gare du Nord at half past seven the next morning. Disembarking, she stuck closely to her new Thomas Cook companions and, although she could not see Alfie anywhere, decided to take them up on their offer to travel with them to their hotel. Bobby Smith in Dover had not booked a hotel for her ("Tell Rollo I'm not a bleedin' travel agent"), so she did not have any pre-booked accommodation. Miss Swan said they stayed at Hôtel du Congrès on the rue du Colisée every year. According to *Bradshaw's* it was "quiet, comfortable, clean and modestly priced". Just what she was looking for.

The hotel was situated just off the Champs-Élysées and although Poppy had never been there, she instantly recognized the world-famous Arc de Triomphe at one end of the boulevard and the Eiffel Tower on the skyline, south of the river. She enquired of her companions whether or not the tower was open for visitors on a Sunday and was informed that sadly it was not. The only thing to do in Paris on the sabbath was to walk down the boulevards or take a boat ride on the river. One couldn't even go to church, according to Miss Swan, because the whole place was "packed with Catholics".

So after breakfast Poppy decided to take a walk, declining the offer of another member of the Thomas Cook party to accompany her to the Arc de Triomphe to view the lighting of the eternal flame in memory of an unknown soldier. Poppy had

had her fill of war memorials and doubted the French version would be any different from the English.

Poppy followed the map in *Bradshaw's* and sauntered down the boulevard, hoping to find an avenue linking to the river. But before she got too far, bells pealed out from all directions, calling the faithful to Mass. Poppy automatically headed towards the nearest church, which turned out to be L'église de la Madeleine, a structure modelled on a classical Corinthian temple.

Poppy, who was now back in her sombre travelling clothes, took a large handkerchief from her pocket and tied it over her hair in imitation of the headscarves worn by the women heading towards the church. Although she received a few glances, no one questioned her when she entered the building and followed the lead of other worshippers, dabbing her finger into a water font and anointing her forehead. Poppy, like most non-conformist Christians she knew, had never been into a Roman Catholic church. And yet something was drawing her there.

She took a seat at the back and looked around at the white marble and gold gilt splendour, so different from the plain wooden Methodist chapel in Morpeth. And yet the expressions on the faces of the congregants were the same, ranging from piety to expectancy, boredom to indifference. Each person who knelt to pray had the same hopes, dreams and disappointments as the people she knew at home. How close each of them was to God, only they knew; it was as if each life was a stained-glass window with its own story to tell. Poppy looked up at the windows lining the chancel and she tried to identify the stories depicted. There were roses and lambs and crosses and men in robes. Angels or real people, Poppy had no idea. The iconography was lost on her, but the beauty of the images and colours was not. Did Catholics really pray to saints, as she had been taught? She had no idea.

Something was happening at the front of the church, in front of the richly embroidered altar: a procession of priests in vibrantly coloured robes carrying an assortment of brass and gold ornaments. One of them was swinging some kind of lantern on a long chain. With each swing a whiff of something sweet and pungent wafted her way. Was it incense?

Then one of the priests – the one in the most ornate robe – lit a large candle and muttered an incantation; or perhaps it was a prayer. It was then that Poppy noticed one corner of the church was filled with candles – some lit, some petered out – blending together in a sea of melted wax. Poppy had heard that Catholics lit candles to symbolize prayers of intercession for themselves or someone else, dead or alive. Each of the tiny flickering lights represented the desperate prayers of someone who had reached the end of their own ability to bring about change. A child they could not heal, a marriage they could not fix, a job that they could not secure, money that would not stretch to buy food to the end of the week, a husband, father, son or brother fighting in a foreign land… How many candles had been lit during the war, Poppy wondered? And if she were to light one, what would be her prayer?

And then the chanting began. In Latin or French Poppy could not tell, but each utterance was punctuated by a reply from the congregation. Poppy closed her eyes and imagined her father mounting the steps of the pulpit, offset from the central wooden cross, bare of the bloodied body of the Christ. And as the people around her began to chant their liturgy, she whispered to herself the only liturgy she knew: "Our Father, who art in heaven, hallowed be thy name. Thy kingdom come. Thy will be done on earth as it is in heaven. Give us this day our daily bread and forgive us our trespasses. Forgive us our trespasses. Forgive –"

Poppy caught her breath and opened her eyes. The service was continuing around her. She looked at the faces of the congregants, wondering if they too were at the point of confessing their sins. Would they be honest? Or would they just do it because it was what they had been taught to do? Would she? What were her sins? The lies? The deception? But weren't they for a good cause, the pursuit of ultimate truth and justice? Did God see it that way? Or was she mired with sin that needed to be confessed? She didn't know.

"What do you want from me?" she whispered, not expecting a reply. But then, as the priest intoned something at the front, she heard some words forming in her mind: "My peace I give to you, my peace I leave with you. I do not give to you as the world gives. Do not let your heart be troubled and do not be afraid."

Do not be afraid. That was what she needed to confess: her fears, her anxieties, her frustrations and her pain. So she did, whispering name after name after name: Christopher, Mam, Dad, Aunt Dot, Grace, Delilah, Gloria, Elizabeth, Bert, Rollo, Lionel... Daniel. She opened her eyes at Daniel's name and looked at the men in the congregation. Were any of them adulterers? And at the women. Were any of them contemplating having an affair? She asked God for the grace to forgive.

"Forgive us our trespasses as we forgive those who trespass against us. And lead us not into temptation... but deliver us from evil... deliver me from evil..." The faces of Alfie and Melvyn Dorchester flashed before her. And something else: a shadow whose face she could not see.

Poppy emerged from the church before the service was ended – as the Catholics were lining up to receive Holy Communion. She could not bring herself to go that far. It was a gloriously sunny day outside and the handiwork of the God she had just been talking to sparkled all around her. She continued her walk to the Seine, accompanied by choirs of birds and the incense of flowers in full summer bloom.

Finally, the cobbled street she was on led to a riverside pathway. So this was the Seine. As *Bradshaw's* had said, a mere canal compared to the Thames. It was similar in breadth to the River Wansbeck that ran through Morpeth. Along both sides of the river, wide grassy banks provided picnicking spots for the Parisians who were not bothered about going to church or had already been. Ladies held parasols to keep the sun off their faces, gentlemen wore boater hats and striped jackets; children took off their stockings and paddled ankle deep in the river or played with hoops, ropes and balls while their parents chatted or snoozed. Rowing boats glided past and peals of laughter rose and fell with the oars. It reminded Poppy of a painting she had seen in one of Dot and Grace's books on art. Renoir? Seurat? She couldn't remember.

She wondered if people could see any difference in her since she had just unburdened herself of her sins. She wondered if she could see any in herself. A family walked towards her: a father, a mother and two children, with a small white dog on a lead. The children were eating ice cream and the dog cocked its head expectantly, waiting for any drips that might fall its way. The parents talked quietly to themselves and, although not touching, shared an intimacy that Poppy could only dream of. She wondered what Daniel and his wife were doing that very moment. Or were Mrs Rokeby and the children at church while Daniel read the paper at home? "Forgive us our trespasses." A surge of bile rose in her throat. She swallowed it and forced herself to look away.

CHAPTER 22

The Radium Institute in Paris, built in 1914 by the University of Paris to house the groundbreaking work of Marie Curie into radioactive materials, now housed a team of two dozen scientists working under the direction of the Nobel laureate. Curie herself divided her time between supervising the research at the Institute and raising funds to keep it open. Radium was in short supply and exorbitantly expensive, but without it, and the funds to buy it, the lifesaving research of the Institute could not continue. This was as much as Poppy had found out about the Institute and its connection to Dorchester. The bottom line was: Curie needed money; Dorchester had it. The question was, how far was she prepared to go to get it?

However, Poppy and Rollo had both decided that that was not the purpose of today's visit. Today Poppy was not to interview Madame Curie – who would no doubt have turned down the interview request anyway – but to talk to Sophie Blackburn about the events surrounding the Chelsea Six in 1913. They had also agreed not to telephone or telegraph ahead so that Sophie would not have a chance to fly the coop. If Sophie wasn't at work that day, Poppy had been instructed to stay in Paris until she could speak to her, if necessary finding out where she lived and visiting her there. But Rollo and Poppy both agreed that it would be best to speak to her at work: if Sophie was the shadowy killer Elizabeth had witnessed, if indeed there had been a killer in the first place, it would be safer to have their first meeting in public.

Poppy entered the foyer of the Institute and approached the reception desk. A mutton-chopped gentleman in his fifties greeted her. In slow, broken French, she enquired as to whether Mademoiselle Sophie Blackburn was in. The man said she was and enquired who it was that wanted to see Mademoiselle Blackburn.

Poppy gave her proper name and then wondered whether or not she should have lied. Would the name Poppy Denby mean anything to Sophie? Would she connect it with Dot? And if so, would that cause her to be intrigued or apprehensive?

However, the receptionist said something that took her completely by surprise and she wondered if something had been lost in translation.

"Ah yes, Mademoiselle Denby. Mademoiselle Blackburn is expecting you."

"No, no, I don't think she's expecting me. I –"

"Come this way please." He rose and indicated a door on the right. But as he did, Poppy heard a familiar voice from the other side of the foyer. She looked up to see Alfie Dorchester coming down the stairs with a middle-aged woman whom Poppy recognized from press photographs: Marie Curie. Poppy froze. Alfie had got there before her. Alfie had warned them she was coming. Alfie, on the other hand, appeared engrossed in his conversation with Curie and had not yet noticed her.

Poppy murmured an apology and turned to leave while she still had a chance.

The receptionist grabbed her arm, forcefully, and pulled her towards the door, which he pushed open with his foot, dragged her through and then shut behind them.

"I must protest, sir!" Poppy said in English.

"I am sorry, mademoiselle, but I have my instructions," he replied in French.

"You no detain me!" Poppy tried again in French.

"I can and I must. Please, don't make this any more difficult than it already is. Take a seat." He gestured to a chair in front of a desk with neat piles of papers. The receptionist leaned against the door with his arms folded, blocking Poppy's only means of escape.

"What you want from me?" Poppy asked.

"That is not for me to say."

Poppy sighed and sank into the chair. "Can you tell –"

The receptionist raised his hand and said in broken English, "If you please, no questions. I know no answers."

From behind the door Poppy could hear a loud guffaw from Alfie. She looked fearfully at the receptionist. Neither his expression nor his position changed. Poppy could feel the armpits of her blue suit jacket dampen with sweat. She ran a tongue along her dry lips and flashed a quick look at the window. It was blocked by a bank of filing cabinets.

Alfie guffawed again.

"Please, monsieur!" Poppy pleaded.

"Shhhh!" He held his finger to his lips as he cocked his head, listening. Then, finally satisfied, he straightened up, opened the door a crack and said something rapidly in French to whoever was on the other side. It was too quick for Poppy to decipher, but she was sure she heard her name.

There was an incoherent reply in what appeared to be a female voice. The receptionist grunted a response. He shut the door and turned back to Poppy. In his hand he held a key.

"You must wait here. I will lock the door."

"But monsieur –"

He held up his hand again to silence her. Then he quickly let himself out and shut the door. Poppy's heart clenched in time with the key turning in the lock.

Poppy had given up trying to jimmy open the window, and, because it opened into an enclosed courtyard with no visible exit, she had decided against smashing it to make her escape. The noise would alert her captors and she doubted she would have long before they caught up with her. What was the worst that could happen to her? This was the Radium Institute, run by one of the world's most respected scientists. Surely the most she would get would be a good telling off.

But what if Madame Curie didn't know she was there? What if Sophie Blackburn and the receptionist were in cahoots with Alfie Dorchester? Surely not. Hadn't Sophie been the one to alert Bert Isaacs that something was amiss? On the other hand, she wouldn't want what had happened in 1913 to be brought to light... Poppy drummed her fingers against the desk, pondering her options and weighing up the potential reasons for the locked door.

And then it opened. The receptionist looked at her without emotion and stepped aside to make way for a woman in a white laboratory coat. She was in her mid-thirties with brown hair, worn unfashionably long, and pulled back into a tight bun. Poppy recognized her freckled face from the 1909 photograph in Aunt Dot's parlour. Sophie spoke to the receptionist in rapid French, too fast for Poppy to understand. The receptionist nodded and withdrew. He did not lock the door behind him.

Sophie, hands on hips, contemplated Poppy. "Well, Miss Denby, you've got us in a real fix. You really have."

"Why was Alfie Dorchester here?"

Sophie raised an eyebrow and gave Poppy a half-smile. "He had an appointment with Madame Curie. Which is more than you have."

"I am not here to see Madame Curie."

"So I hear. He warned her that you might come. He wasn't sure if you would try to see her, me or both of us."

"Oh?" Poppy swallowed to give herself time to think. This was not going how she had expected. She'd hoped to introduce herself pleasantly to Sophie as Dot Denby's niece who was just visiting Paris and decided to drop in to pass on her aunt's regards. She'd hoped to keep it casual and when she'd established a good rapport, then produce the letter to Bert. But there was no chance of a good rapport now.

"What else did Alfie say?"

"Just that we were to expect a visit from a yellow journalist hoping to dig up some dirt on Madame Curie and Lord Dorchester, and that you were the niece of my old friend Dot Denby. He warned us that you might try to use that personal connection to sweeten us up. So far, you haven't done a very good job."

Well, apart from the "yellow" bit, that was all true. Poppy needed to change tack. "Did he tell you he used his motorcar to run me down outside his sister's asylum?"

This was clearly news to Sophie. Her eyebrows crunched together and she sat down, leaning towards Poppy. "No, he did not. What were you doing outside Elizabeth's asylum? Did you see her? How is she?"

"I did. She's not well."

"Oh dear. Still? After all these years?"

"No, not like that. She's perfectly sane. Whatever condition she was in seven years ago, she's better now. And she should be released. But they won't let her out."

"They?"

"Her father and brother."

Sophie's lips set in a tight line. "What are you doing here, Miss Denby?"

Poppy drummed her fingers on the desk again, contemplating her options. A compromise was called for.

"I tell you what, Miss Blackburn, I will tell you why I am here – why I'm really here, not what Alfie thinks I'm doing here – if you tell me why you have had me forcibly detained. There's a law against that in England, and I'm sure there's one here too."

Sophie appeared to find this amusing. "My, you're a chip off the old block, aren't you? How is your aunt, by the way? We've lost touch."

"And why's that?"

Sophie shrugged. "I've never had a problem with Dot. But Grace is the jealous type. It's hard to keep up a correspondence with her in the way. Then of course there was the war, and…" Sophie spread her hands as if the rest was obvious.

"Speaking of correspondence…"

Sophie's eyes narrowed in suspicion. "What?"

Poppy held up her hand. "First you need to keep your side of the bargain. Why have you detained me and when are you going to let me go?"

Sophie leaned back in her chair and gestured towards the door. "You are free to go any time, Miss Denby. The door isn't locked."

"But it was."

"That was for your own protection."

Poppy gave a hollow laugh. "Oh really?"

"Yes. We didn't want Alfie Dorchester to see you. I told Marie I'd had some contact with the English press and we assumed you were here because of that. Is that why you are here, Miss Denby?"

Poppy shrugged. "All in good time, Miss Blackburn. I want to hear the end of your explanation about my detention."

Sophie appraised the younger woman, then nodded. "Fair enough. As soon as Alfie told Marie you might be coming to see us, she sent word to me. I was to arrange for you to be escorted out of sight if, by ill fortune, you decided to turn up while he was still here. And just like your aunt – whom I never much rated as an actress – your timing was atrocious." She spread out her hands again. "So here we are. Now, your turn. Why are you really here?"

There was a knock on the door. *"Entrez!"*

The receptionist came in carrying a tray of coffee.

"Merci, Henri."

He put it down and left.

"Coffee?" Sophie asked.

Poppy didn't answer.

"Oh, come now, enough of this cloak and dagger melodrama; it's not poisoned – although we could have slipped a lethal dose of radium into it." She laughed, then poured two cups without waiting for permission and pushed one across the table to Poppy. Poppy ignored it. Sophie shrugged and sipped hers thoughtfully.

"So, you work for *The Globe*. You must know Bert Isaacs then."

"I only met him briefly, unfortunately."

"Unfortunately?"

It suddenly dawned on Poppy that news of Bert's death must not yet have reached Sophie. And why would it? He had no family. No one to spread the news. And unless she subscribed to *The Globe*, which was doubtful, there was no way Sophie could have found out about his death. Unless Alfie had told her…

Poppy took a deep breath and said quickly, "I'm sorry, Miss Blackburn, but Bert is dead."

Sophie went pale, bringing her freckles into stark relief. She put down her coffee cup with shaking hands. "When?" It was barely a whisper.

"Last Monday. A week today. It was my first day at work. He fell from a balcony."

"Dear God." Sophie's shaking hand covered her mouth, her eyes widened and filled with tears. "Is that why you're here? To tell me?"

Poppy's voice softened in pity. "I'm sorry. But no. I hadn't realized you didn't know. But there's no reason you would. You weren't next of kin and –"

"I was the closest thing to kin he ever had!"

CHAPTER 23

The letter lay spread between them. While Sophie was staring out of the window, gathering her thoughts, Poppy read the incriminating text again: "'Dearest Bert, I'm sure it will come as a surprise that I am contacting you again after all these years ... Why did you write this, Sophie?"

Sophie swivelled her head back to look at Poppy. Her eyes were red and puffy and some wisps of hair had come loose from her bun. It softened her face and made her look younger.

"Just what it says. I wanted Bert to look into the deal between the Radium Institute and Melvyn Dorchester."

"You imply here that there is something underhand going on. Is there? My editor contacted Madame Curie and she said everything was above board."

"No, she didn't. She said she believed Dorchester had changed his views on women."

"Do you believe he has?"

"No. And neither does Marie."

"Then why did she take the money and give her endorsement to him receiving the X-ray contract?"

Sophie splayed her hands and flexed her fingers open and closed, as if examining their intricate workings. "Have you ever had an X-ray, Miss Denby?"

"Yes, I have. Although I was unconscious at the time. Just a few days ago, in fact, after my run-in with Alfie's motorcar."

"Then obviously it revealed that you had no broken bones."

"Thankfully not."

"But if you had – perhaps a hairline fracture that at first would not impair your mobility – and you had not had an X-ray, you could have been walking around with a time bomb in your body. The bone could have become infected; or a nearby nerve lacerated… X-rays save lives, Poppy, and" – she gestured towards the door – "so does the research into radioactive molecular science that we conduct here."

Poppy was intrigued and wished she could have come under different circumstances and received a tour of the laboratory. Perhaps when this was over she could come back and do a feature article on the work here…

"Has anyone close to you died of the Spanish flu?" Sophie continued.

"Some people from my home town, yes."

"Did you know that the latest estimates believe fifty million people have died around the world in only two years? That's far, far more than were killed in the war, but is about the same as deaths by cancer. The thing is, flu comes and goes, and with quarantine measures and improved hygiene can be contained, but nothing can contain cancer. The cause is not out there but in here" – she patted her chest – "and nothing can quarantine you from that."

Poppy cleared her throat and picked up the letter. "Miss Blackburn, if you don't mind, can we –"

Sophie's eyes flashed and she snatched the letter from Poppy. "I do mind! You asked me a question and I'm giving you an answer."

Chastened, Poppy nodded an apology. "Please, continue."

"The work we are doing here is saving lives. It will save millions of lives. Year after year after year. But we need money to keep it going. Melvyn Dorchester has money, and if turning a blind eye to his offensive views on women is the price we have to pay, then so be it. X-ray machines are soon going to be available in hospitals around the world. If he profits from it, that's a pity, but in our eyes the end justifies the means."

Poppy reached out and took hold of the letter. Sophie released it and allowed her to spread it out once again on the table before them.

"And yet you feel guilty about it."

Sophie did not answer.

"You say here that you want Bert to expose Dorchester. But what is there to expose if the deal was above board?"

"Financially, yes, at least from his side –"

"But not from Madame Curie's."

Sophie's eyes flashed again. "Marie is completely innocent in this. It was me. I am the one who – how shall we say? – *arranged* Dorchester's donation."

"And that could open you up to criminal prosecution."

Sophie sighed. "Yes, it could. But I was hoping that Bert exposing Dorchester's hypocrisy in his support for the sex disqualification bill would divert attention away from me. I've also written to Marjorie Reynolds, but I have yet to hear back from her."

Poppy felt they were just scratching the surface. Why would Sophie be open to criminal prosecution? What was her crime? Unless... unless her *arrangement* had taken the form of blackmail. Yes, that would make sense. She had threatened to reveal she was on Dorchester's payroll back when she was part of the Chelsea Six. Or perhaps it went further. Could it involve murder?

"They shouldn't have died."

They? Gloria and who else?

"We tried our best, we really did, but it was too late."

Poppy wanted to interject, to ask for clarification, but she bit her tongue and waited.

"There were thirteen of them. All young men. Most of them were already dead – shot to bits – but a few of them were still alive, impaled on the wire. They hadn't stood a chance. Anyone could see the Germans had the vantage point. We waved our white flags at their machine-gun nest on the knoll and they let us through with our van. But it was too late. Those that hadn't died in the charge had bled to death overnight. Apart from two of them. Incredibly, I knew them both. One of them was just a lad. The son of the window cleaner from King's Road. Is he still around? Thompson, I think his name is. Had a green wagon back then; don't know if he still does…"

Poppy nodded, stunned at the direction the conversation was going in, but not wanting to disrupt Sophie's flow.

"He was the only one still conscious. And he told me what had happened. His captain had told them to storm the nest. They'd told him they wouldn't stand a chance, but he'd been adamant, threatening to charge the lot of them with insubordination and cowardice in the face of the enemy. So they did what they were told, and, as predicted, they were mown down." Sophie's eyes were far away, as if viewing that Belgian battlefield again.

Poppy reached out her hand and touched the older woman's forearm. "I'm sorry. That must have been a terrible thing to see."

Sophie shrugged. "I was used to it by then. Death, that is. But not cowardice."

"What do you mean?"

"We found the thirteenth member of the group back in the trench. He had a bullet wound to his shoulder, but by the angle of it, and the evidence of the revolver lying beside him, Marie and I came to the conclusion that he had shot himself. If we had seen the bullet after it was extracted from him, we could have confirmed it. As it turned out, a friend of mine operated on him when we returned him to the field hospital. Unfortunately, my friend was killed a few weeks later, but before he died he gave something to me."

She got up and went to a filing cabinet, pulled out a drawer, and extracted a fat envelope. Returning to the desk she opened the envelope and slid out a wad of fabric, which, when unfolded, revealed a bullet. She placed it on top of the letter.

"Is that…?" asked Poppy, picking up the small metal object between thumb and forefinger.

Sophie nodded. "The bullet extracted from Alfie Dorchester. You'll find, under analysis, that it is British issue, not German, and that it matches Alfie's gun. The coward shot himself after he realized he'd sent his men to their death. Then he came up with the cock-and-bull story about trying to save them – and won himself the Victoria Cross."

"But surely witnesses could have come forward…"

"Who? All the troops died – including the Thompson lad. The Huns didn't care one way or the other, and as I said, the doctor who extracted the bullet was also killed soon after."

"But *you* knew…"

Sophie sighed and closed her eyes. When she opened them again they were filled with something Poppy could not quite decipher. Was it remorse? Guilt?

"It was just one of many, many death scenes we came across. And I only found out about the VC a couple of years ago. When I did, I thought of going forward, but" – she splayed her hands again – "I decided to use the information to my, to our, advantage."

"And you blackmailed him."

"Yes. I sent a letter to Melvyn Dorchester telling him what we knew about his son and that we would go to the press unless he contributed to the coffers of the Radium Institute. Don't look at me like that, Miss Denby. There was nothing I could do to save the lives of those poor young men, but there was a lot I – and Dorchester's money – could do to save the lives of others."

"But you're turning him in anyway."

"The money's spent. And Marie has made some contacts in America who are likely to open up a whole new funding stream." Sophie's shoulders sagged and she slumped further in her chair. "But I didn't expect it to cost Bert his life."

"What do you mean?"

"Come, Miss Denby, don't tell me you think Bert's death was an accident."

"No, I don't. I believe he was pushed because he was getting too close to the truth. But I'm afraid, Miss Blackburn, he wasn't looking in the direction you'd hoped. He was going back to 1913 to the secret the two of you shared… the secret witnessed by Elizabeth Dorchester."

"Whatever are you talking about? What has Elizabeth to do with this? Oh, surely you don't mean… She couldn't! She never knew anything about it. She was in Holloway at the time. It was just a few mad weeks and –"

Poppy shook her head. What was this woman talking about? She held up her hand. "Can we please just have some straight talk here? You said in your letter that you were deeply ashamed about something and that Bert knew about it and had kept your secret all these years. You also said it had something to do with Melvyn Dorchester."

"It has! Have you not been listening? It's this business about his son."

"And Bert knew about that?"

"No, no." She let out an exasperated sigh. "Bert and I were in love. We were hoping to get married, but he was just waiting for the right time to tell his mother. He was Jewish;

I'm not. His mother had wanted him to marry a Jewess. She died soon afterwards, actually. He was an only child and his father was already dead. If only I'd waited… But I didn't. I got impatient, insisting he just tell his mother to like it or lump it. He wouldn't. So weeks turned to months and I got frustrated. In the meantime, Frank and Grace were going through a rough patch and Frank confided in me. Before we knew it we were having an affair. I didn't love him and I don't think he loved me. We were just two lonely, frustrated people finding comfort where we could. But Bert found out, and… well, we broke up. Not that we were officially engaged in the first place, and no one even knew about us, other than Frank, but we ended it."

"And the secret?"

"My affair with Frank."

"Grace never knew?"

"She suspected, but no, she never had any proof."

"But she and Frank separated anyway."

"Yes, it was inevitable. Grace was obsessed with your aunt –"

Poppy was appalled at the insinuation and held up both hands. "I beg your pardon, Miss Blackburn. I hope you're not implying –"

"That Grace is in love with Dot? Yes, I am. Surely you can see that for yourself; you live with them, after all…"

"They are nothing but good friends!"

Sophie smiled pitifully. "Oh, Poppy dear, you are so very young."

Poppy smarted at the insult, but brought herself back under control. There was a lot more she needed to find out and getting distracted like this was not going to help. She took in a deep breath and continued her questioning.

"Have you ever heard it suggested that there was a mole in the Chelsea Six?"

It was now Sophie's turn to look surprised. "Why ever are you asking that?"

"Well, have you?"

"Well, if you must know, and I'm not sure why you need to –"

"Please answer the question, Miss Blackburn. If you want me to help you expose Melvyn and Alfie Dorchester while keeping yourself out of prison for blackmail, then you need to give me something in return."

Sophie straightened up and looked Poppy directly in the eye. "Hmm, a bit of backbone after all. Well, Poppy, for Bert's sake, and his only, I will tell you as much as I know. Yes, I had suspected there was a mole. Too often we planned things and the police were already there ahead of us."

"And were you the mole?"

If Poppy had expected Sophie to stand up in protest, she was disappointed.

"No, I wasn't. But I was approached."

"You were? By whom?"

"Richard Easling."

"He asked you to inform on your friends?"

"Not in so many words, but it was implied. So I implied what he could do with his offer."

"Do you think he approached someone else then? On Dorchester's behalf?"

"I do."

"And who was that?"

"Gloria Marconi."

Gloria Marconi? Poppy was stunned.

There was a knock on the door and Henri stuck his head around, asking if they wanted more coffee. Sophie looked at Poppy, who nodded wordlessly. She needed something with a kick after that bit of information. After Henri left, she resumed her questioning.

"What evidence do you have?"

"None really; it was just a suspicion. But why else would she suddenly be released from Holloway on the same day as Elizabeth? And why else would she be killed?"

Henri returned with a tray and placed it on the table. Sophie poured for both of them.

"So you also believe Gloria was murdered."

Sophie paused, milk jug in hand. "Also?"

"Yes, that's what Elizabeth believes too. She said she saw a shadow push Gloria under the train."

"A shadow? Nothing more specific than that?"

"No. And unfortunately, if you have no more evidence than a hunch, there *is* no more than that."

Sophie sipped her coffee thoughtfully. "So that's really why you're here. You thought the terrible secret I was keeping – and that Bert knew about – was that I had killed Gloria."

"Well, the thought had crossed my mind."

"If I was a killer, Miss Denby, your life would be in danger right now."

Poppy swallowed slowly, the fear that had dissipated now returning. "Indeed that would be correct, Miss Blackburn. However, my editor knows where I am and –"

Sophie raised her hand and laughed. "Oh Poppy, my dear little Poppy, I may be a blackmailer and an adulteress, but I am not a murderer. Frank will attest that he and I were... well, we were otherwise occupied at the time of Gloria's death. And your aunt, although she doesn't realize it, almost walked in on us." She laughed, coldly. "Well, not walked, of course. She'd just got back from the hairdresser's and we heard her in the hall and quickly got dressed. Just as well we did. Grace came back soon after."

"Came back?"

"From dropping Gloria at the train station."

Ah yes, this was familiar territory. This and the box. "Well, Miss Blackburn, you have certainly filled in a few gaps here. But there's just one more thing: did Gloria mention a box to you on the day she died?"

Sophie looked thoughtful, trying to remember. "No. I don't believe she did. But she could have. She wasn't well and I tried to get her to agree to go to the hospital. There was a lot of confusion and a lot was said, but I don't honestly remember a box. Why?"

She couldn't "honestly remember"? Poppy doubted that Sophie could be trusted to be completely honest about anything, but her story about being with Frank at the time of Gloria's death seemed completely plausible. As did her story about Alfie. And she did have the bullet…

"I can't tell you, I'm afraid. It was part of Bert's investigation. If something comes of it, you'll read all about it in the paper."

"And will I read all about my arrest for blackmail?"

Poppy smiled. "As you have pointed out, Miss Blackburn, I have a lot to learn, but I do know that journalists are supposed to protect the identity of their sources, and unlike you, I am a woman who sticks to her word. My editor Mr Rolandson will be in touch to discuss the finer details of our arrangement."

Feeling very much the grown-up career woman, Poppy retrieved the letter, stood up and walked to the door.

"Good day to you, Miss Blackburn, and thank you for your time. You have been most helpful."

Sophie appraised her, smiled, and then played her final card: "I do hope you get back to your hotel safely, Miss Denby. I believe the Hôtel du Congrès is rather full this time of year."

"How did you know –"

"I didn't. But Alfie Dorchester did. He also knew you were coming to see me *before* you left England. You don't think it was an accident he was on the ferry at exactly the same time as you, do you? Oh, Miss Denby, you *do* have a lot to learn."

Chapter 24

Poppy sat in the same pew of L'église de la Madeleine as she had done the previous day. A young priest nodded a greeting and pointed towards a pile of postcards near the door, then left her to her prayers or contemplation of the architecture; he did not know which and didn't seem to care.

She was too distracted to pray, but tried to focus on a window depicting the fall of man in Eden. Once she'd got to grips with the medieval style of depiction, she began to identify different elements: a woman, a serpent, a heart being crushed by the serpent... The door creaked. Poppy looked up anxiously. It was only an old lady in black. The woman dabbed her finger into the holy water, mumbled something, then shuffled off.

Poppy moved on to the second window. It seemed to depict the story of Cain and Abel: brother betraying brother; brother killing brother. Poppy had always felt sorry for Cain. No one had ever satisfactorily told her why Cain's offering of grain was not good enough. He kept crops, his brother kept livestock, they each gave what they had. Her father had said it was the blood that had pleased God. It was symbolic of Jesus as the Lamb of God. But how could Cain have known that? And what no one had ever explained to her was why God was so keen on blood in the first place. She looked over at the offering of candles and thought again of lighting one for Christopher. She was just about to get up, when the door creaked again. She looked up to see the man she had been expecting.

Henri came into the church without dabbing his finger into the font, without crossing himself and without bowing towards the altar. He slipped into the pew beside Poppy and placed a suitcase at her feet. He put out his hand. She placed a folded piece of paper into it, which he quickly perused then slipped into his inside pocket.

"Is it safe?" she asked in French.

"Oui. Dorchester a été envoyé dans la mauvaise direction."

Poppy nodded her thanks. She wasn't sure if she could believe this man, or Sophie Blackburn, but it was her only chance of getting out of Paris undetected.

With the revelation that Alfie knew where she was staying and that he had known about her visit to Paris before she had left London, Poppy had not felt safe going back to the hotel. But Sophie had had a suggestion. In return for a written declaration that neither Poppy nor *The Globe* would use her name in any story that may appear in connection with Dorchester, she would arrange to send false information to Alfie about where the English reporter was going next. Apparently she was going to be heading to Belgium to find her brother's grave. Poppy had no idea where her brother was buried, only that it was a mass grave somewhere in Flanders. There was something unpalatable about Alfie Dorchester seeing it before she did, but she doubted he would actually go to Belgium. He was more likely to stake out the train station. However, he would be waiting at another station to the one she would need to pass through to get the train back to Calais.

"And you saw him leave the hotel with that information from the manager?"

"Oui."

Poppy had no choice but to believe him. Sophie claimed that the manager of her hotel was a distant cousin of Henri's and that they would ask him to misdirect the Englishman if he came. They would also arrange for Poppy's suitcase to be collected from her room and the bill paid. Sophie had already extracted the money from Poppy at the Institute to pay for the bill; as Poppy handed over the francs she wondered if she was contributing to her own Judas purse. Poppy also had no idea whether or not Rollo would stick to the agreement, but she had written out a copy of the promise to show him anyway.

On the train from Paris to Calais Poppy took up her private berth and wondered if the Thomas Cook crowd had noted her absence and thought her rude not to say goodbye. When all this was over, she would write a letter of thanks and apology, care of the Thomas Cook office in London. But for now she just had to let them think what they wanted to think. She wondered if Alfie had found out yet that she wasn't on the train to Brussels. He definitely wasn't on this train – she had asked when she handed over her ticket, claiming Alfie was an old friend and she had hoped to meet up with him – but at each station the Blue Train stopped, she anxiously scanned the platform.

It was a very stressful six hours to Calais. Poppy had tried to occupy herself by making notes about what Sophie had told her, but her fountain pen kept blotching and she ended up with more ink on her hands than on the paper. But she did manage to get down a few pages. She slipped her notebook – along with the letter from Sophie to Bert, her ticket and her passport – into the inside pocket of her blue jacket. If she were somehow separated from her satchel on the journey she did not want the incriminating information to fall into the wrong hands. *The wrong hands?* She laughed at herself. That sounded as though she was in the middle of a mystery novel!

The rest of the journey from Paris to Calais, Calais to Dover, then Dover to London was uneventful. At nine o'clock the next morning she stood on the doorstep of 137 King's Road and noticed two days' worth of milk had not been brought in and two newspapers were sticking out of the letter box. She tried her key in the lock, but the door would not open – it was obviously bolted shut from the inside. What was going on? Both Grace and Dot were usually early risers. She rang the doorbell a few times, but again there was no answer. She looked up and the curtains of the upstairs rooms were still closed.

"There's been no sign of 'em for two days."

Poppy turned around to see Mr Thompson the window cleaner trundling past in his wagon.

"Oh, hello, Mr Thompson. I've been away for a few days. I've –" Poppy considered for a moment telling him about what she'd heard in France about his son, but this was not really the time and place. "Have you knocked?"

"I have. Due to do the windows yesterday, I was. No answer. Might be away."

"They might… but I think the door's bolted from inside and I'm a bit worried. Would you mind awfully if I borrowed your ladder?"

"My ladder?"

"Yes. That's Mrs Wilson's bedroom window up there. I think I need to take a look."

"You mean…"

"Oh, I'm sure there's nothing to worry about; it's just that… well… I'm worried."

Mr Thompson looked up at Grace's window, puffed out his cheeks and said, "Better safe than sorry, I suppose. Hold on."

He tied off Bess's reins and unhooked his extendable ladder from the back of his wagon. He put his foot on, ready to climb up.

"Could I go, Mr Thompson? I don't think either of the ladies would appreciate a gentleman looking in on them if they are simply having a lie-in."

Mr Thompson thought about this for a minute and nodded his agreement. "I'll hold the ladder for you then, miss. But you be careful."

"Oh, I will."

Poppy climbed the ladder carefully, hoping that Mr Thompson would have the decency not to look up her skirt. Grace's window was closed, but there was a small chink in the curtains. She peered through into the gloom beyond. She thought she saw some movement on the bed. She knocked on the window and called out, "Grace! Aunt Dot!"

To her relief there was a shuffle of bedclothes and Grace stumbled to the window, peering out blearily. Her eyes widened in surprise when she saw Poppy. She pulled the curtains and pushed up the window.

"Whatever are you doing, girl?"

"Are you all right, Grace? There was no answer at the door and –"

"We're both down with the flu. Haven't had the energy to go downstairs."

"But Dot –"

"Dot's all right. Well, she's got the flu too, but we're managing."

"If you open the door, Grace, I can come in and help you both. Cook you some breakfast."

"No, no, I don't think that's wise. No use you getting the flu when you've just come back from convalescing. How was Leamington Spa?"

"Leamington Spa? What? Oh yes, the spa. It was lovely, thanks. I'll be fine. Just open the door, please."

But Grace was adamant. "I don't think so, Poppy. Look, why don't you see if Delilah can take you in for a day or two? Give us time to get back on our feet."

Poppy suddenly remembered Sophie saying that Grace was the jealous type. Was Grace trying to keep her away from Dot? Was Dot all right? Had something happened to her and Grace was trying to cover it up?

But just as she was contemplating forcing her way in, she heard a croaky voice calling out, "What's going on, Grace?"

"It's Poppy. She wants to come in."

"But she'll get the flu! Tell her to go to Delilah's."

"I have. I've –" Grace broke off to hack out a series of coughs. She held up her hand to Poppy. "Please, pet. Come back in a couple of days."

"And tell her her father called from the Post Office. Did you hear that, Poppy?"

Poppy's stomach clenched. "I heard you, Aunt Dot. What did he say?"

"He wanted to know how you are. I told him you were in Leamington Spa and you'd be in touch when you got back. He was none too happy that I'd let you go on your own. So I said to him –" Dot's explanation was broken off by a hacking cough.

Poppy sighed. "All right, Grace. Tomorrow. I'll come back tomorrow. Do you want me to bring you anything?"

Grace gave her a thin smile. "I think by then we'll need some more bread. But we should be all right for today."

"Are you sure you're all right?"

"Right as rain. Now get down off that ladder before you do yourself an injury."

"Give my love to Aunt Dot. And if Dad calls again, tell him I'll arrange to speak to him from Delilah's. I'll telegraph him the number so he can book in the call."

"I will. Keep well, pet."

"And you get well. Both of you."

Grace waved, then pulled down the window and drew the curtains closed again.

"Everything all right there?" called Mr Thompson.

Poppy wasn't really sure.

"Hello, old thing! Whatever are you doing here?" Delilah stood in her doorway wearing a slinky black gown emblazoned with a red Chinese dragon.

Suddenly a man appeared behind her, gave her a kiss on her cheek and said, "I'll see you later at rehearsal."

"Adam, this is my friend Poppy. You know: the one I needed to borrow your motor to pick up from hospital?"

"Ah yes, the intrepid reporter. Are you all right now?"

"I am, thank you. But I need a place to stay. My aunt and Grace are down with the flu and have declared the whole house a quarantine zone. They suggested I come here, but…"

Delilah laughed. "Oh, Adam was just leaving, weren't you, darling? He… well, he just popped around for breakfast!"

Adam, one of the most dashingly handsome men Poppy had ever seen, flashed a smile and said, "And a scrummy breakfast it was too. Excuse me, ladies. I'll leave you to it."

Poppy stepped aside to let him pass. He doffed his boater and then headed off down the stairs and into the street, lighting a cigarette and whistling a jolly tune.

Delilah gave a dramatic sigh. "Didn't I tell you he was a dish?"

"Demetrius?"

"The very one. Come in, and I'll tell you all about it. Do you want some coffee?"

"I'd love some!"

CHAPTER 25

An hour and a half later, Poppy had been served a full English breakfast with a side serving of the highlights of Delilah's very complicated love life. In return she had given Delilah a blow-by-blow account of her trip to Paris. Delilah, smoking her third cigarette of the day, leaned back on her sofa and slowly exhaled. "Good heavens, Poppy. So what are you going to do now?"

Poppy curled up her feet under her and sipped another coffee. Although Delilah's flat was luxurious – she clearly had a source of income beyond her meagre pay from the theatre – it managed to be comfortable and homely at the same time. Poppy felt the stresses and strains of the last week start to drain from her.

"Well, what I'd like to do is sleep for the rest of the day. But what I should do is try to find Frank Wilson. He's the only living member of the Chelsea Six I haven't spoken to yet. He might be able to fill in some of the gaps."

"Frank Wilson. Golly, I haven't seen him since my mother's funeral."

"Have you any idea where he is?"

"Not really, no. But my dad might. Let me give him a ring."

Delilah uncurled from the sofa like a sleek black cat and padded her way across the parquet floor to a black lacquer and marble-topped sideboard. She picked up an ornate bronze telephone, styled like an Egyptian goddess, and dialled the number for the international operator. She asked to be connected to a number in Valetta, Malta, then waited to be put through.

Someone answered. Delilah launched into rapid Italian.

Delilah's branch of the Marconi family hailed from Malta, which had a large Italian community. Delilah was born there and received her British citizenship, then moved to England with her family when she was six. Her father, Victor Marconi, was the nephew of the Nobel laureate Guglielmo Marconi – known to the family as Uncle Elmo. Uncle Elmo was the son of an Italian father and an Irish protestant mother, but he too settled in England and launched his world-famous wireless and telecommunications company. Now the first Marquis of Marconi, Uncle Elmo had opened doors to the best social circles for his extended family, but Delilah was quick to point out that the family money was all their own – from a string of hotels her father owned back in Malta.

Delilah ended with an effusive "*Ciao Papa!*" and put down the phone. She returned to the sofa with an address written on some notepaper and presented it to Poppy. "Frank Wilson. Peckham."

"Is that far?"

"Not too bad. We can get the bus." She pouted. "Adam said he won't lend me his motor again until I've taken some lessons. Apparently I did something unforgiveable to his clutch." She threw back her head and laughed at her own joke then jumped up, pulling her friend with her. "Come on, let's get dressed."

Poppy and Delilah checked and double checked the address as they stood outside a slum tenement building in North Peckham. Barefoot children used rain-filled potholes as paddling pools in the summer heat and the stench of festering rubbish was overwhelming. Poppy and Delilah had to duck under a clothes line slung low with stained nappies and pick their way through piles of dog faeces to get to the door. A woman answered, holding a screaming baby on her hip while two toddlers clung to her filthy apron. The woman shouted over the baby's screams that Mr Wilson rented the room upstairs. She nodded to a narrow staircase set into the wall behind a coal shed that was almost empty. Poppy wondered if winter would bring any change. She handed over some coins to the woman for her trouble. If she'd expected any thanks, she didn't get it.

Poppy also wondered if Delilah, with her privileged upbringing, had ever been exposed to such conditions. The Italian girl was wide-eyed and pale, but didn't seem overwhelmed. Poppy had seen as much and worse during her time at the Methodist Mission in Morpeth and knew that the prosperity hoped for by so many now that the war was over would only ever reach a few. On the bus ride through Peckham she and Delilah had passed a dole office, where the queue, made up mainly of out-of-work ex-soldiers, stretched around the block. None of them would think kindly to womenfolk taking the few jobs available to them; and Poppy knew that the woman she had just met would never have the chance of starting a career – if she even aspired to one. She thanked God for her blessings.

When they got to the top of the stairs they saw a door that had been patched together more than once with odd planks of wood. It was loose on one hinge and leaned heavily on its latch. Poppy wondered if it would fall over if opened. She knocked gingerly, and waited for an answer.

None came. She knocked again. Eventually there was the sound of shuffling and muttering. The door opened a crack, its one good hinge creaking in protest. A gaunt, grey man with patchy facial hair and bloodshot eyes peered at them.

"Mr Wilson?"

"Who's asking?"

"My name is Poppy Denby and –"

The door slammed shut.

"Mr Wilson!"

"Get lost! And tell that bitch to leave me alone. She's taken enough from me."

"But Mr Wilson –"

Delilah put her hand on Poppy's arm. "Let me try."

"Mr Wilson… Frank… it's me: Delilah Marconi. Gloria's girl."

Silence.

"Can we come in, Frank? We need to talk to you. It's about my mother."

Silence.

"Please, Frank. I – I need your help." This time there was a tearful note in Delilah's voice. Poppy didn't think the young actress was faking it. Neither, it seemed, did Frank, as the door opened and he let them in.

Poppy and Delilah were instantly assailed with the stench of urine and a sound of scuttling that caused both women to look at one another in alarm. The room was piled ceiling to floor with crates, boxes and sacks filled with books, newspapers and household items. A narrow channel had been left open to allow access from the door to the living area, which consisted of a small table piled high with unwashed dishes, two chairs draped in clothes, a small wood-burning stove and cooking range. A line of crates filled with empty spirit bottles separated the "bedroom" – a thin mattress on the floor – from the kitchen. Poppy wasn't sure if the smell of alcohol in the air was a hangover from the night before or a fresh intake for breakfast.

Frank turned around and faced them. He was a tall, stooped man who might once have been described as dignified. But now his half-starved body in oversized clothes made him look like a scarecrow.

"What do you want?"

"Can we sit please, Mr Wilson?" Poppy asked.

"I was talking to her, not you." Frank's words dripped venom.

"This is Poppy, Frank; she's Dot's niece."

"I can see that."

"She has some questions. We – we both have some questions. About Gloria. Please, can we sit down?"

He shrugged. Delilah pulled out a chair; Poppy did the same. Frank stood for a moment chewing his lip, then overturned a crate with a clatter and sat down, arms folded across his thin chest.

"Look, Mr Wilson, I'm very sorry if anything happened between you and my aunt in the past," Poppy began. "I had nothing to do with that. But I do want to find out what happened."

"Why?"

"Well, I'm working for *The Globe* –"

That turned out to be the wrong thing to say. Frank stood up, sending his crate crashing into the wall. "Bert Isaacs! Bert bloody Isaacs! I knew he'd be behind this!" He pointed a bony finger at Poppy. "You can tell Isaacs to go to hell! Do you hear me? He can go to hell!"

Delilah stood up and put a soothing arm around his shoulders, making shushing noises as if calming a hysterical child. "It's all right, Frank; it's all right. Bert is dead."

Frank absorbed this for a moment then smiled, revealing the ravages of seven years of hard living. "Then justice has been served."

"Actually, Mr Wilson, justice has not been served. Not for Gloria or Elizabeth or..." – she almost said "Dot" but thought better of it – "or Delilah here, who deserves to know the truth about what really happened to her mother. And that's why we're here. Can you try to answer some questions please?"

Frank nodded. "All right. I'll tell you what I can. But be prepared: you will not like what I've got to say."

It was Poppy's turn to nod. "We'll take that chance, Mr Wilson."

After Frank had sat down again on his crate, Poppy took out her notebook and gave him an edited version of the events of the last week, including her trip to Paris to see Sophie. She did not tell him about Alfie Dorchester and the VC, and she tried to play down any mention of her aunt. She did tell him about Elizabeth being unjustly held in the asylum and their suspicion that Gloria might have been murdered. This did not shock him as much as she'd thought it would. So she asked him whether or not he remembered any mention of a box on the day Gloria came to see them. He said he didn't, but he did confirm Sophie's story that she and he were "occupied" and so neither of them could have been at Slough at the time of Gloria's death. Poppy noted to herself that they could both be lying, sticking to the same story they concocted seven years ago. Neither of them were paragons of virtue and she had no reason to assume they were telling the truth. But neither did she have evidence to the contrary.

"Were you aware of rumours of a mole in the Chelsea Six?" Poppy asked.

"You mean the seven."

"Yes, sorry, the seven. Do you think there was a mole, Mr Wilson?"

Frank thought about this as he picked at the dirt under his fingernails. "Yes, I do. We all did. Too many times Easling and his men were ahead of us. That's how Gloria and Elizabeth got arrested. They were waiting for them at Lord's."

"Do you have any idea who it was?"

Frank looked intently at Poppy and leered. "You look a lot like her, you know?"

"So I've been told."

"Do you also have *unnatural* inclinations?" He looked curiously from Poppy to Delilah.

"I do not. And whether or not my aunt does –"

"Whether or not? Well, I can tell you it's a definite 'whether'! That lesbian bitch ruined my life."

"Frank, please, there's no need for that," said Delilah, using her most soothing voice.

"I won't apologize."

"You don't have to," said Poppy. "You're entitled to your opinion, but I don't want your prejudice against her and your ex-wife –"

"We're not divorced. I wouldn't give her one."

"Your wife then. I don't want your prejudice against Dot and Grace to influence what you tell me about the mole."

"You mean you don't want me to tell you that your aunt *was* the mole."

"No, I don't. Not unless you have more than your jealousy to back it up."

Frank leered again. "Well, Miss-high-and-mighty Denby, what would you say if I said I had?"

"I'd say I didn't believe you."

"But if I did? Would you use it in your story or would you try to cover it up?"

"If there was any conflict of interest I would hand over all evidence to my editor."

"And I should believe you?"

Poppy flushed in anger. "I don't care if you believe me, Mr Wilson, because I don't believe you. I am sorry for your... your... *situation,* but all I see is a bitter man who has drunk himself into oblivion and is looking to blame anyone but himself. Marriages sometimes come to an end. It shouldn't happen, but it does. Whether my aunt was the cause of that, or whether it was you and your adultery with Sophie, I don't know, but you and your wife both had a choice in the matter. How you lived your life then and how you live now. What I'm interested in is the truth. The truth about what happened to Gloria and Elizabeth – and yes, what also happened to my aunt, whether you care about her or not. So if you've got nothing to contribute to that, then we will not waste any more of your time." She got up. "Come on, Delilah, let's go."

"Just hold your horses." Frank stood up and shifted a few piles of newspapers until he emerged with a rusted old cigar tin. He held it before him like a supplicant at an altar. "What would you say if I gave you proof about who the mole was?"

"Well, I'd look at it and then have the newspaper's legal team look at it too."

"Oh no, you won't take it anywhere. This is my insurance."

"Your insurance against what?"

"False accusations. I know people thought I was the mole, and that's why so many people turned against me: all my creditors, all my family; but they were wrong."

He opened the box, took out a letter and handed it over to Poppy. She opened it. It was dated 7th October 1910 and was addressed to Ms Dorothy Denby.

Ms Denby,

I cannot and shall not call you Dear. I could call you a lot of things, but there will be time for that later. So to business. This is to inform you that the transfer has been made to your bank account as per arrangement. In return, I expect full compliance, as we discussed.

Lord Melvyn Dorchester

Poppy showed the letter to Delilah and then turned her attention to Frank.

"What is this supposed to prove?"

"That your aunt was the mole, obviously."

"No, not obviously. This could mean anything."

Frank laughed mirthlessly. "You sound just like Grace."

"You showed this to Grace? When?"

"Soon after I found it. I came across it sometime in 1913 when I was sorting through Dot's receipts for the WSPU. She could never keep anything in order."

"And what did Grace say?"

"Just what you did. So I said I was going to confront Dot with it."

"And did you?"

"No. Grace went through the roof. Accused me of trying to discredit Dot."

"So what did you do then?"

"I kept quiet about it. I didn't want to rock the boat." He sighed and sat down on the crate, leaning his head back against the wall. "I still thought my marriage had a chance."

"Was this before or after the day Gloria died?"

"A few weeks before, I think."

"So 'saving your marriage' included having an affair with Sophie Blackburn while my mother was being murdered in a train yard?" It was Delilah, all pretence of soothing gone.

Frank snapped his head around to look at her. "Don't judge me, girl. I'm not proud of it. But I'm not a murderer and I'm not the mole. You'll have to look elsewhere for that."

"Can I take the letter?"

"No, you bleedin' well can't. If this ever comes to trial I'll produce it then. You have my word on that."

Poppy wondered if Frank Wilson's word was worth anything; she didn't have a choice but to comply. She did though ask his permission to transcribe the letter word for word into her notebook. He agreed and poured himself a large glass of foul-smelling alcohol and swilled it back. Then he looked at the dark-haired girl waiting for her friend to finish.

"It's been good seeing you, Delilah; you've grown into quite the young woman." He leaned towards her.

She sidestepped and grabbed Poppy's arm. "Are you done?"

"Yes," said Poppy and snapped her notebook shut.

CHAPTER 26

"You've done well, Poppy; very well. You have the instincts of a first-class newshound."

Poppy flushed with pride and took another sip of coffee so that Rollo would not see how ridiculously pleased she was.

"So, let me get this straight... ah – ah –" Rollo sneezed into his handkerchief with all the force of a transatlantic hurricane.

Poppy recoiled and put a hand over her coffee cup. "Bless you."

"Thank you. Righto, this is what we've got so far..." Rollo, who had been taking notes as Poppy recapped her latest adventures, turned around his book so that Poppy could see what he had written – or rather drawn. It was a timeline with arrows leading to boxes of text, which in turn led to other boxes and circles spreading across two pages. Poppy leaned in closer to see as Rollo guided her through his mindmap using a pencil as a pointer.

"Sometime between 1905 and 1909, Lady Maud Dorchester, a friend of Emmeline Pankhurst, gathered together a group of women – and one fella – that became a militant cell of the Women's Suffrage and Political Union, the WSPU. They were her daughter Elizabeth; Elizabeth's friend Sophie Blackburn, a nurse; Maud's friend Gloria Marconi, who was married to a relative of Elmo Marconi; and then your aunt, Dot Denby, a leading lady on the West End stage. After that, Dorchester's accountant Frank Wilson and his wife Grace also became involved. They eventually became known as the Chelsea

Six, despite there really being seven. And somewhere in this mix – although how many of them knew about it is still unclear – was our dearly departed Bert Isaacs, who was secretly engaged to Sophie Blackburn."

Poppy sipped her coffee and nodded in agreement.

"They – but not Bert, I'm assuming – were involved in a number of high-profile campaigns, including chaining themselves to the railings of Downing Street and the protest outside Westminster in November 1910 that became known as Black Friday. On that day your aunt and a number of other women were injured in clashes with armed police, and one of them later died. Of the injured women, your aunt was the most serious, being left crippled and in a wheelchair. Your aunt and her friends suspected that she was deliberately targeted by the then mounted PC Richard Easling at the behest of Maud's husband, Lord Melvyn Dorchester, an ardent anti-feminist at the time. How am I doing?"

"Spot on, so far."

"Good. Loads of angles we can use: scandal in high society, police corruption, and we haven't even got to Marie Curie, and Alfie lying to get his VC yet!" Rollo rubbed his hands in glee.

Poppy, with her personal connections, did not feel quite as gleeful. "We've still got to find proof of all this…"

"Well yes, otherwise this would all just go into a Jazz File, but hopefully that's where the ledger page will help. Shall I continue?"

"Please do," said Poppy and cleared a space on Rollo's desk to put her empty coffee cup.

"So, 1911 to 1912, despite Dot's devastating injuries, the WSPU and the Chelsea Six continued their campaign and were involved in a number of violent protests, including those following the death of Emily Wilding Davison under the king's horse at Epsom. Am I correct in saying she was a personal friend of your aunt?"

"Yes, you are. She was from Morpeth, my home town. I met her a few times when I was a girl."

"Good, good. So we're at June 1912 then. Oh, hold it, where does the *Titanic* come in?"

"That was April, wasn't it?"

"Yes, that's right. OK, hang on…" Rollo scrawled an arrow from a text box to the timeline, moving the *Titanic* back a few months. "Righto, here you are. Maud Dorchester dies on the *Titanic* in April 1912. Why was she on it, again?"

"Because Melvyn had become increasingly violent in response to what he considered her embarrassing association with the women's suffrage movement, which he publicly decried in the House of Lords on a number of occasions. Here's a list of his speeches – I asked Ivan to get them for me from the archive."

Rollo raised a shaggy red eyebrow and grinned. "Good girl. So, 1912. Maud leaves her abusive husband to join the sisters Stateside and dies in a freak shipping accident. Elizabeth increases her campaigning in memory of her mother and, a few months later, her friend Emily; she becomes increasingly militant."

"Yes, that's when Dorchester starts trying to have her committed to the asylum."

"But fails."

"Initially, yes."

"So now we're in 1913 and the Chelsea Six, who really are now only six, start planning the firebombing of the members' pavilion at Lord's."

"But when Gloria and Elizabeth do the job and try to leave, Richard Easling is waiting for them."

"They are arrested and jailed for six months at Holloway, where they go on hunger strike and are force-fed."

"However, they're unexpectedly released three months early. I'm not sure why…"

"Probably the Cat 'n Mouse Act," said Rollo. "Ask Ivan to give you the file on it."

Poppy made a note.

"Righto," continued Rollo. "So it's Guy Fawkes night, 1913, and Gloria and Elizabeth are on their way home from prison. But for some reason Elizabeth goes to the train yard at Slough instead. Why?"

Poppy chewed her lip thoughtfully, trying to piece everything together. "From what I can gather, she was going to go to America and asked Gloria to arrange to get a ticket for her from the Chelsea crowd. They were going to meet at Slough station."

"So where does the box come in?"

"That's the thing. We don't really know if there was a box. Only Elizabeth's word for it. And even though I think she's sane and doesn't deserve to be locked up, I won't discount that she might have imagined this – or simply lied outright to get us to help her."

"Assuming though there was a box, and it does contain the rest of the ledger that your torn page comes from, then she was going to hand the box over to Gloria in exchange for the train and shipping ticket. Is that right?"

"I think so, yes. But not one of the Chelsea Six remembers anything about a box. My aunt wasn't there when Gloria came home, but Grace, Frank and Sophie have all independently said that no box was mentioned. So Elizabeth could have imagined it."

"Or perhaps Gloria never told them for some reason."

"That's a possibility. I wonder why…"

"Didn't Frank say everyone thought there was a mole?"

"He did. And Sophie said they had suspected it for a while."

"Well then, maybe Gloria got wind of the mole and decided not to mention the box. If it did contain damning evidence, then if it got into the mole's hands it would be passed on to Dorchester."

Poppy jumped up and started pacing excitedly, much to Rollo's amusement. "Yes, that's it! It has to be. We need to get hold of that ledger – if it exists. What progress have you made with getting Elizabeth out?"

"Some. But I was out of the loop for a few days when I was in bed with flu. Last I heard the legal boys have looked into her initial sectioning and have determined that it wasn't a permanent thing. In other words it has to be reassessed every year. Thing is, no one but the hospital does the reassessing. And if they're in the pay of Dorchester…"

"Can't there be an independent psychiatrist on the panel? Could we arrange for that?"

"Yes, if Elizabeth becomes a client of our solicitors. They're trying to arrange that now. They say they've been struggling to get to see her. Last time they tried – yesterday – they told them she was being prepared to be transferred to Swansea."

"Swansea! But we'll never see her if she's there."

"I think that's the idea."

"So what can we do?"

"The legal guys say they're trying to get a court order to stop it, but as Elizabeth is not formally their client, they're not optimistic."

"When is she being moved?"

"Tomorrow morning."

"That doesn't leave us much time…"

"No, it doesn't."

Poppy sat down again, deflated.

"More coffee?"

"Please."

When Rollo returned with the coffee, Poppy was going over her notes from Paris. "I think we have two different stories here: the 1913 'murder' and cover-up of the 1910 bribery of Easling, and then the 1915 VC fraud and the Radium Institute blackmail leading to Dorchester's backing of the Sex Disqualification (Removal) Act and the award of the X-ray contract. Or are they four different stories?"

Poppy took the coffee from Rollo with thanks.

"And what about Bert's death and the attempt on your life outside the hospital? Are they a story or stories on their own?" asked Rollo.

"Probably not. We're not important enough."

Rollo laughed. "Sad but true. It's yours and Bert's connection to these other stories, and the possibility that Alfie and Melvyn Dorchester are trying to keep a lid on it all, that's the story there."

Rollo stepped on a stack of books that he used as a makeshift stool and clambered into his office chair. It was the first time since they'd met that Poppy fully apprehended his "difference". Most of the time his personality and brilliant journalistic flair outshone his lack of stature. But she knew – simply from her own "handicap" of being a woman in a man's world – that he would have had to work doubly hard to get where he was now. She registered a new level of respect for him.

He noticed her watching him. "What?"

"Nothing. Just thinking. This is all very confusing."

"Ah, but it's a confusion that will keep this paper in business for a few months yet. This is what's called a wave, Poppy, and we'll ride it for as long as we can. Big scandal stories are always like this. Stories within stories. And no doubt as we go we'll find more angles and more stories... and then, when the public are finally bored with the lot of it, we hope that another wave will come along."

"Or you make one."

Rollo raised his eyebrows over his coffee cup. "My, you're a bit young to be so cynical, aren't you?"

"I'm only in this to find the truth, Rollo."

Rollo smiled at her like an indulgent parent. "There are many interpretations of the 'truth', Poppy, and many ways to get them. You'll learn." He picked up his pencil and pointed to the mindmap. "Now, back to work."

Poppy left Rollo's office promising to check in with him later. She walked through the newsroom, slaloming between desks strewn with crumpled handkerchiefs. Didn't these journalists think to take them home to launder? If she got through the next few days without catching whatever was going around, it would be a miracle. She was happy to see Lionel's desk chair was empty. Rollo had told her that he had called in sick the day after their encounter and they hadn't seen him since. He said he was looking into the possibility that Lionel could be *The Globe*'s mole.

There was nothing for her to do in the newsroom, so she went downstairs to the archive, hoping to get some files from Ivan. It was locked.

"He's gone to lunch. Doesn't trust anyone in there without him."

Poppy turned to see Daniel coming up the stairs. Her heart lurched and then sank. She straightened up. "Good day, Mr Rokeby."

"Good day, Miss Denby." He smiled at her boyishly and leaned his shoulder on the wall. "So how was Leamington Spa?"

"Leamington… Oh yes, it was very… restful. Nice of Rollo to arrange it for me."

Daniel looked at her intently; Poppy turned away.

"You don't look very rested."

"Neither do you."

"Flu took it out of me. I'm fine though, if you were worried…"

"I wasn't worried. I telephoned your house to see how you were. You seemed to be doing all right."

Daniel straightened up. "Oh. I didn't know you'd called. Who did you speak to?"

"Two delightful children that I didn't know you had. And then –"

"Look, Poppy, I can explain. I was going to tell you at dinner, I really was. I –"

"Hello, you two… Is there something I can do for you?"

It was Ivan lumbering up the stairs like a great bear in a fedora hat.

Poppy sidestepped around Daniel to face the archivist. "Yes, there is, Mr Molanov. I need to look at some files."

Ivan put out his arm. "Please, Mees Denby, call me Ivan."

Poppy laughed and hooked her arm through is. "And you, sir, must call me Poppy."

Ivan unlocked the door and escorted Poppy into the archive. Neither of them gave Daniel a backward glance.

CHAPTER 27

Poppy arrived at The Old Vic at five o'clock, the time that Delilah had said she would be getting out of rehearsal. She was to wait for her in the foyer. She explained her presence to the man in the box office, who was selling tickets for that evening's show, and took a seat behind a large potted fern. Delilah had explained that there were three shows on the go at the theatre: the current run of a ballet, the rehearsals of *Midsummer*, which would replace the ballet at the end of its run, and auditions for the show after *Midsummer*. On the wall were posters for the three shows: *Coppélia* by the theatre's own ballet company, *A Midsummer Night's Dream,* directed by Robert Atkins, and Chekhov's *The Cherry Orchard,* directed by Constantin Stanislavski. The name rang a bell with Poppy and she made a note to do an article on it once this story had been wrapped up.

Golly, she thought, *I'm beginning to think like a journalist.* This story was her life, and that of her friends and family – not just a source of column inches. But she realized she would not always be this close to the stories she worked on. At least she hoped not, as she repositioned herself to ease the ache in her ribs.

Poppy watched theatre folk criss-crossing the foyer: paper-thin ballerinas sucking on their cigarettes as though their lives depended on it, a flustered Robert Atkins asking all and sundry if they'd seen Puck, a wardrobe mistress pushing a rail of costumes, a gentleman with a silver-tipped cane talking animatedly to an anxious young man in an accent similar to Ivan Molanov's. Could that be Stanislavski?

Through the glass panes of the outer doors, Poppy saw a silver Rolls-Royce pull up. A chauffeur wearing a top hat emerged and opened the door for his passenger. A pair of dazzling black shoes stepped onto the pavement carrying Lord Melvyn Dorchester. Poppy made herself as small as possible behind her fern.

Dorchester swept into the foyer as if he owned the place, heading straight for the box office. He too carried a cane and he slammed it down on the box office desk.

"My tickets."

"And may I enquire in whose name they are, sir?" asked the clerk.

Dorchester glared at him and rapped the cane in rapid staccato. "*Lord* Melvyn Dorchester."

The clerk flicked through a file and then flicked through it again. Then in a very timid voice said, "I'm sorry, sir, but there is no record of any tickets being bought in your name. Is it for *Coppélia*?"

"It is. And they were not bought. They are comps."

"Ah," said the clerk, "that explains it. Let me check." He opened another file and flicked through it. And then flicked through it again. Looking as though he wished the floor would open and swallow him, he said, "I'm sorry, sir, but there is nothing here either."

"Nothing here? Nothing here? Call Miss Baylis at once!"

"Yes, sir," said the clerk, and picked up the telephone on his desk and dialled an internal number.

As he did so something dawned on Poppy. *The telephone. That's it! That's how Alfie knew I was going to Paris. He somehow listened in to my telephone conversation with Rollo from King's Road. Is that possible? I'm sure it would be, if he'd bribed the operator to eavesdrop on that number… What else has Alfie heard? What else does he know?*

"Lord Dorchester. I believe you wish to see me."

A large lady in her fifties, with dark brown hair and round spectacles, walked calmly into the foyer. As she did, the hustle and bustle seemed to settle like autumn leaves.

Dorchester raised his cane and strode towards her. They met like two prize fighters in the middle of the floor. "Ah, Miss Baylis. I've come for my comps for the ballet."

Miss Baylis, in the quiet but authoritative tone of a school mistress, declared: "You have no complimentary tickets for the ballet."

Dorchester's nostrils flared and he pulled himself to his full height, reminding Poppy of the day she had interviewed him. He took a step closer to Lilian Baylis. Miss Baylis held her ground.

"As a... *patron* of this theatre, I expect a certain courtesy."

Miss Baylis smiled indulgently. "As an... *investor* in a specific show you will get your cut of the box office as we have agreed. But only of that show. However, if you would like to invest in other shows, I'm sure we can come to an arrangement, but that will be under a separate contract. For now, you are an investor in *The Cherry Orchard*, not *Coppélia*. We are only a small theatre and need to sell as many seats as we can. If we gave away free tickets to every Tom, Dick or Harry who invested in any show at any time we would have none left to sell to the public. And, I'm sure you'll agree, Lord Dorchester, that would not make good business sense."

Theatre folk had begun to gather around the edges of the foyer, watching their champion take on the challenger. Dorchester rapped his cane on the polished wood floor. "Miss Baylis, I am not a Tom, Dick or Harry. I am a peer in His Majesty's House of Lords."

"We have many peers who invest in us, Lord Dorchester, and they don't come begging for free tickets."

A collective gasp went up. Dorchester raised his cane and Poppy was convinced he would have struck Miss Baylis if they were not in such a public place. But with a herculean effort of self-control he lowered his cane and balanced his shaking hands on top of it. "Then, Miss Baylis, I shall be investing elsewhere. I have never been comfortable with your Bolshevik director anyway."

"Mr Stanislavski is not a Bolshevik."

"He is still based in Moscow, is he not?"

"He is."

"And he is on first-name terms with Lenin and Trotsky?"

"Many people are on first-name terms with Vladimir and Leon."

A titter spread through the foyer. Dorchester looked as if he was about to explode. But Miss Baylis stood firm. To Poppy's relief he sucked in his breath, turned on his heel and strode out of the foyer. However, as he did so, his eyes locked with hers. He stopped, mid-stride, and used his cane to part the fern.

"You! I thought you were –"

Poppy, like a trapped dog, snapped back. "Dead? No, Lord Dorchester, your son didn't manage to kill me when he ran me down."

Another collective gasp went up.

Dorchester's cane pointed between her eyes.

"I think it is time to leave, Melvyn, before someone gets hurt." It was Lilian Baylis. She pushed down Dorchester's cane with her hand. Behind her, the theatre folk gathered to see what was going on in the corner.

Dorchester, still managing to retain his poise, turned to face her. "Consider our contract terminated, Lily, and rest assured I will be having a word with the Lord Chamberlain's office about this theatre promoting revolutionary ideas."

"You do that," said Miss Baylis, and with a raised finger pointed him towards the door.

As Dorchester's Rolls pulled away, a cheer went up in the foyer. Lilian Baylis allowed herself a quick smile before barking out: "What are you all doing? We've got a show to put on!"

Poppy thought Lilian would stop to interrogate her, but she didn't, and she returned to wherever she had been before Dorchester tried to steal the show. But as soon as she was gone Delilah ran up to her. "Poppy! Did you see that? Wasn't Lily wonderful?"

"Indeed she was," said Poppy, still shaking from the encounter. "Are you off now? I really need your help."

"Yes, I am, but I need to be back first thing tomorrow, so no late night."

"Oh? You don't normally have early morning rehearsal. Have you been naughty again?"

Delilah laughed. "Quite the opposite. Robert has asked me to be understudy to the understudy for Titania! With all this flu going around, he's paranoid we won't have a leading fairy on opening night."

"Oh, that's wonderful news!"

"Isn't it just? And guess what else? Mr Stanislavski watched my rehearsal and asked me to audition for Anya."

"Anya?"

"*The Cherry Orchard.* It's a masterpiece. And Stanislavski is a genius. If it hadn't been for the revolution I was going to study at his academy in Moscow. But papa didn't think it safe. But now he's here. In London. Oh, Poppy, isn't it just spectacular!"

Poppy marvelled at her friend's ability to be crying over the possible murder of her mother one day and celebrating about her job the next. But, she supposed, that was how she survived. Didn't she do a similar thing with Christopher? And her aunt with her handicap? But it was time to focus on the job at hand, and she once again needed Delilah's help.

"Delilah, do you perhaps know where Mr Thompson the window cleaner lives?"

Delilah looked at her curiously. "No, I'm sorry, I don't. But I can ask Mrs Jones."

"Who's Mrs Jones?"

"My cleaning lady. She should be at the flat now. I usually pay her on a Tuesday."

She grasped Poppy's hand. "Come on. If we hurry we can still catch her."

Elizabeth Dorchester stared at the mould stain on the wall. It had definitely spread since last week. Then, there had been three blotches forming a motley cloud; now there were five. And was that the start of a new one? Elizabeth squinted in the fading evening light. She wasn't sure. She would check again in the morning. Or perhaps not.

The thought of facing one more night listening to the screams of other patients, one more morning forcing down watery porridge and waiting in line to use the bathroom, one more day reading and rereading the same old books and watching the mould spread on her wall...

She started to pray, but stopped, realizing they were the same prayers using the same words; that the same hope rose and fell ever so slightly, and the same comfort rested less than it had yesterday and less again than the day before. *Those that wait upon the Lord...* What was that verse? She couldn't be bothered to reach for her Bible on the windowsill. *Those that wait upon the Lord shall... shall... renew their strength... and... rise up on wings... like... like eagles.* Now that would be useful. Imagine if she had wings like an eagle and could fly out of her room, out of the asylum, over the walls and past the Battersea towers. What would she see? Families in the park? Wagon men lining up to cross Chelsea Bridge? The river winding its way to somewhere… She would follow the river and then… and then…

Yes, the mould had definitely spread.

CHAPTER 28

Mr Thompson was settling Bess down for the night. The hay was fresh, the water cool and the bucket of oats warm and filling – just the way the old horse liked it. He spoke quietly to Bess as she snuffled the oats, stroking her gently on her flank.

"The flu's 'bout again, Bess. Would you Adam and Eve it? Not as bad as the last time. Only a few've popped their cloggs – some old folk, some kiddies. Don't think I'd survive a second bout. What d'ya think, old girl?"

The mare lifted her head and snorted a reply before returning to her supper.

Mr Thompson straightened up, his spine creaking like an old winch. "That's what I thought."

He lifted the paraffin lamp off the hook and shut the stable door. Then he checked to see that the tarpaulin was tied securely on his wagon, which filled most of the small courtyard outside his East London house. The house itself was an end-of-terrace, two-up-two-down; he paid extra for use of the shed for Bess. The rent had been going up year on year, but Mr Thompson's income had not. If it hadn't been for the washing that his wife took in and strung across the courtyard when he and Bess were off during the day, the family would be struggling. Although the family was much smaller than it used to be. First it had been the twins: barely out of nappies when consumption took them. Then his boy in the war. Now there was just the girl, Vicky, named after the old queen. And if the fishmonger's son had his way, she would soon be moving out too.

Mr Thompson was just about to go into the house to join his wife and daughter, when the sound of a motorcar backfiring startled him. Bess stamped and snorted in the stable and he made soothing noises through the door. If she didn't settle, he'd have to go back in. The motor belched again... bleedin' modern contraptions!

The vehicle pulled up outside Mr Thompson's house and two young ladies, both wearing motoring goggles and scarves, alighted. The taller of the two approached the gate.

"Mr Thompson?"

"Who's asking?" He held up his lamp to see her more clearly.

"It's Poppy Denby, Dorothy Denby's niece. From 137 King's Road?" She pulled back her scarf and a shock of blonde curls caught the light.

It was the girl he'd helped up the ladder this morning. And the shorter one, on closer inspection, was the dark-haired Marconi girl from the posh apartments down the road.

"Evenin', ladies. You're a bit off your patch, aren'tcha?"

"We are," said the Marconi girl. "And we're sorry to bother you, but Mrs Jones told us where we could find you."

"She did, did she?" He'd need to have a word with his pal Jonesy to tell his missus to mind her own business. Nonetheless he was intrigued to hear why these two toffs were slummin' it in the East End.

"What can I do for you then?"

"Do you think we can come in?" asked the Denby girl. She looked over her shoulder, then leaned in and whispered, "It's of a rather... *private* nature. It's about... Well, it's about your son."

Mr Thompson felt the blood rise from his neck as he did anytime anyone mentioned his son. What did these girls know about it? What right did they have to scratch up old wounds?

"No. You'll not be coming in. I clean your windows and keep me nose clean. And I'd be much obliged if you did the same."

He spun around and caught his ankle on a loose cobble. He winced, but didn't falter.

"But Mr Thompson, I've just got back from Paris. I met someone who was there the day your son died. She – she said she held him until he was gone. And he told her the truth about what really happened that day. The truth about Alfie Dorchester."

Mr Thompson stopped in his tracks as the front door opened and his wife called out, "What's going on out there, Bill? Bleedin' hurry up, will ya? Supper's on the table."

Mr Thompson breathed in deeply and turned to face the young ladies on the other side of the gate. Then he called over his shoulder, "We've visitors, Doris. Put the kettle on."

Mrs Thompson lifted the heavy black kettle off the range, holding the handle with a thick wad of cloth. She had instructed seventeen-year-old Vicky to unpack the best china from the trunk that also kept the fine linen she'd been given the day she married Bill Thompson.

Delilah had said they oughtn't bother making such a fuss and that ordinary china would do, but Poppy had been on enough pastoral visits with her parents to know that people weren't putting on airs and graces for their guests but for themselves. She told Mrs Thompson that her great aunt Gertie in Morpeth had a set very similar. Mrs Thompson nodded in appreciation.

When the tea was poured in the front room, they sat with teacups and saucers perched on their laps while Mrs Thompson offered each of them a lump of sugar with a pair of silver tongs. Mr Thompson's stomach grumbled loudly, and he craned his neck to catch a glimpse of his supper growing cold on the kitchen table.

"We're very sorry to interrupt you at supper time. We won't keep you long," said Poppy.

"No bother at all," said Mrs Thompson, sipping her tea as delicately as Queen May. Vicky nodded enthusiastically beside her. Young Vicky appeared to be in awe of the visitors, and kept brushing her long hair self-consciously behind her ear as she took in their fashionable bobs. When Poppy explained that she worked for *The Globe* newspaper, Vicky nearly fainted in admiration.

"Oh, miss! What a treat. A lady working for a newspaper. Are they still hiring?"

Mrs Thompson shot her a warning look. "Now don't bother the ladies with your silly questions, Vicky."

"Oh, it's no bother at all," smiled Poppy. "What kind of job did you have in mind?"

"Well, I can read and write, and wouldn't mind doing a bit of office work. They had me in a factory in the war, but I reckon I could do better than that. I can –"

"That's enough, girl." Mr Thompson scowled at his daughter and she lowered her eyes. He grunted his approval and then turned to his unwelcome guests. "Let's get to it, then. What's this you've got to say about my boy?"

Mrs Thompson's hand went to her throat. "They're here about Billy Junior?"

"That they are. They've got some information for us. Haven't you?"

Poppy smiled sympathetically at Mrs Thompson. "We have. As I explained to your husband outside, I have just returned from Paris. When I was there I met a lady who had worked as a nurse in Flanders in 1915. The year I believe your son was killed."

"That's right. May Day, it was. In Ypres." She pronounced it Eeps.

"Well, this lady was working with Madame Curie. You've heard of her?"

"The famous lady scientist," contributed Vicky.

"That's right. She is a famous scientist. But during the war, she served on the front with her daughter and some other brave women – including Sophie Blackburn, the lady I met in Paris. They took around X-ray machines to field hospitals. They are these new-fangled machines that can take pictures of the inside of our bodies."

Poppy hoped she didn't sound too patronizing, but the Thompsons didn't seem to be offended, and if they were, they were too interested to hear how this all connected with Billy Junior to care. Poppy continued.

"They sometimes worked with the Red Cross. And it was on one of those occasions that Miss Blackburn came across your son and his unit after they had come under enemy fire."

Mrs Thompson was holding back her tears. "And – and was he still alive?"

"He was," said Poppy softly.

"How did she know who he was?" asked Mr Thompson, his gruffness disguising the catch in his voice.

"Sophie Blackburn was one of the Chelsea Six."

The Thompsons did not register any understanding.

"They were a group of women who were members of the Women's Social and Political Union."

"Ooooh, the suffragettes!" peeped Vicky.

"Yes, they were suffragettes. And they met at 137 King's Road, Chelsea, where I believe you, Mr Thompson, have cleaned the windows for the last few years."

"The last ten years," said Mr Thompson. "I always thought there was something funny going on at that house."

Poppy let that pass. "Well, this lady, Sophie Blackburn,

recognized your son. Or he recognized her; I'm not sure which. Either way, they realized that they knew each other, however tenuously, from back home. And I suppose when you're dying" – she looked apologetically at each member of the family – "it's a comfort to have some sort of connection." Poppy let them absorb this information before she continued.

"Tell them about Alfie," Delilah whispered. Poppy smiled tightly, hoping to communicate that she had not forgotten and was just allowing the family time to digest the information they already had. Again, she drew on her experience of visiting families with her parents, including bereaved families, and knew that these situations had to be handled very delicately. Finally, when she thought they were ready, she continued.

"I also mentioned to Mr Thompson that this had something to do with Viscount Alfie Dorchester. Do you know who that is?"

Mrs Thompson and Vicky nodded. Mr Thompson grunted. "Captain Dorchester was how we knew him. Didn't even come to see us after we got the news."

"That's because he was in hospital," said Mrs Thompson.

"He got out soon enough. Not like our Billy. Not like those other boys."

"That's right," said Poppy. "He had relatively minor injuries."

"He won the Victoria Cross, didn't he? He must have been very brave. Trying to save our Billy." Vicky's wide eyes were filling with tears.

"Well" – Poppy cleared her throat – "apparently not. Not according to your brother."

The Thompsons sat bolt upright as though they were one body. "What do you mean?" asked Mr Thompson, his voice barely louder than a whisper.

Poppy braced herself and said, "According to Billy, Alfie – Captain Dorchester – had told them to storm the machine-gun nest even though the men told him they didn't stand a chance. He... he threatened to shoot each of them for cowardice if they didn't. So they obeyed. And Alfie – Captain Dorchester – remained behind."

Mrs Thompson's hand went to her throat again. Poppy thought she might faint, but she didn't.

"So, are you telling us that Dorchester knowingly sent those boys to their death?"

"Well, I can't say for sure that it was 'knowingly' – perhaps he just didn't think it through properly – but whatever his understanding of the matter, the men knew it would be a suicide mission."

"And they went anyway." It was Delilah and she was openly crying. Poppy passed her a handkerchief, hoping she would pull herself together.

"Yes, they went anyway. They didn't have a choice. Alfie said he would shoot them if they didn't. Or at least have them up on charges of disobeying a direct order. They would have faced a firing squad."

"The bastard!" Mr Thompson's face was a mask of fury.

"B-but – he was shot too, wasn't he? He must have gone with them."

"Not according to your brother, Vicky, and not according to some evidence Sophie found."

"What evidence?" asked Mr Thompson.

"The bullet taken from Alfie's shoulder was British issue. From an officer's revolver. The same revolver Alfie used. Sophie believes he shot himself to pretend he had been in on the action too. That's what he told the VC committee. And that's what they believed."

"But he didn't. He watched while my little Billy was killed. Him and all those other poor boys."

"That's what we believe, Mrs Thompson, yes."

"We'll go to the police!"

"The police can't do anything, woman; it's a military matter," Mr Thompson said.

"Then we'll go to the army. There must be someone we can tell. Will you go with us, miss? Tell them what you know?"

Poppy nodded. "I will. Well, actually, my editor will – and his legal team. But first we have to get some more evidence."

"The bullet?"

"No, something else. Something relating to another part of the investigation. But they're connected and we can't go to print without it. And if we can't go to print we won't have any influence over the authorities to force them to do something about Alfie. So that's why we are here, apart from telling you about what we believe really happened to your son. We need your help, Mr Thompson. You see, this morning, when you lent me your ladder to climb up to Mrs Wilson's window, it gave me an idea. Do you know Willow Park asylum in Battersea?"

"I do. I clean their windows. In fact, I delivered a note from there to someone at your newspaper about ten days ago."

Poppy blinked rapidly as the enormity of the coincidence, or perhaps divine intervention, dawned on her.

"So you're the one she gave it to…"

"The lady? I don't know her name. But it was someone who used to be at 137 King's Road. I recognized her. Just like my Billy recognized that other lady. But I'm not sure if she realized who I was. We didn't speak, you see. She just gave me the note. Did you get it?"

"We did. Thank you." She thought for a moment of telling him about Bert and Sophie and how the whole investigation began, but decided against it. Rollo had used the phrase "need-to-know basis" in relation to good journalistic practice, so instead she asked: "Are you the regular window cleaner at Willow Park?"

"I am."

"Well, Mr Thompson, that could prove very useful. Very useful indeed."

CHAPTER 29

It was six o'clock the next morning and Delilah and Poppy sat in Adam's motorcar outside the south gate of Battersea Park. Delilah yawned.

"I'm going to look like hell for rehearsals. If I can get there in time. Do you think we'll be finished by eight?"

"I hope so," said Poppy and sipped at her coffee from the thermos flask mug. "It's a good job you got Adam to change his mind about the motor, though, or we wouldn't have made it on time. Was he furious about it last night?"

"Livid," Delilah grinned cheekily, "but I soon calmed him down."

"And he'll cover for you if you're late at the theatre?"

"That's what he said."

"The man's a gem."

Delilah threw up her hands in glee, nearly knocking Poppy's coffee all over her. "I know. And he's asked me to go to Monte Carlo with him. After the run."

"I thought you were going to be in *The Cherry Orchard* after that?"

"Hopefully. Mr Stanislavski hasn't put up the cast list yet. And Adam might be in it too. He's auditioning for Peter Trofimov."

Poppy looked puzzled.

"Anya's boyfriend. Oh, won't that be fun!"

"Not much time for Monte Carlo then."

"Oh, I'm sure we can squeeze in a bit of 'research time'. Stanislavski always encourages his actors to inhabit their roles, if you know what I mean." She winked shamelessly.

Poppy laughed. If only her relationship with Daniel was as simple. Not that they had a relationship, of course… but if they had… No, she was not going to think about it. She smiled at Delilah as the dark-haired girl pouted her lips and fluffed up her bob in the rearview mirror. She'd never met anyone as free-spirited as Delilah. But she wondered if the girl's laissez-faire approach to life was masking something deeper. Here she was, poised to spring the woman who had last seen her mother alive, and she was mooning over a boy and dreaming of Monte Carlo. Poppy hoped she would be able to count on Delilah if things got out of hand. What they were about to do was illegal and dangerous. There was no room for flippancy.

But then she remembered the raw Delilah she had glimpsed in the hospital room when she spoke about her mother. Yes, there was steel there. Just like Aunt Dot.

Aunt Dot. Poppy had lain awake most of the previous night thinking about her. Could she really be the Chelsea Six mole like Frank Wilson believed? It was so hard to countenance. Aunt Dot was fiercely loyal to her friends, family and the cause. And if she had been in Dorchester's pay in 1910 – as the letter Frank had shown her suggested – surely the events of Bloody Friday that year, which left her crippled, would have changed that. How could she have continued working for the man who was behind her accident and the death of her friend? That, of course, was assuming she was the mole in the first place. Why would she have done it? What could she have possibly hoped to gain?

Poppy thought of her aunt's character – so much like that of Delilah. They were both actresses, used to playing roles. Perhaps

Dot had just been playing at being a suffragist all along. But why? For fun? For the challenge? No, Poppy couldn't accept that. She remembered her aunt's fury the day she had been insulted at the Oxford Street stationer's. Dot believed in the rights of women. There had to be another explanation...

Perhaps, like the spy novels her brother had been so fond of reading, Aunt Dot had been a double agent, giving Dorchester false information... but the information hadn't been false. What had Frank said? Easling was waiting for Gloria and Elizabeth when they came out of Lord's. Why would Dot tell Dorchester that, even if she was playing a double agent? That information wasn't harmless. It had real, and ultimately fatal, consequences. But Dot couldn't have known that at the time... or could she? No, of course not.

Nonetheless, Poppy couldn't get the idea of role play out of her mind. She remembered something she had seen at the *Midsummer* rehearsal with Robert Atkins. As a warm-up exercise the director had got the cast to swap roles for a while. But not just any roles. Each actor had to swap roles with their direct antagonist – the person they were most in conflict with in the play. He said it was so that they could feel what their enemy felt. And that that would help them understand their own role better. Could this have been what Dot was doing? Could she have been "playing" the role of her enemy? To get inside his mind. To see how he thought. It was certainly possible. But she would only know when she had had a chance to speak to Aunt Dot personally. If it hadn't been for the flu she would have done so already.

There was a bang on Delilah's window. The girls jumped in fright. Looking at them in the dim morning light was a man wearing a bowler hat: Detective Chief Inspector Richard Easling. He motioned for Delilah to roll down her window.

"Morning, ladies. Miss Marconi. Miss Denby. Queer spot for breakfast."

"Morning, inspector. Just about to have a stroll in the park before work. Good for the constitution!" Delilah breezed.

"Walk in Battersea Park often, do you? No parks in Chelsea?"

"I work on this side of the river."

"There are parks in Waterloo."

"Ah, but none so lovely as this!" Delilah flashed him her most charming smile. He was unmoved.

"Get yourselves along then. There's a law against loitering."

This irked Poppy. How dare this corrupt copper lecture them about the law! "Actually, I was just showing my friend here the spot where I was recently run down. She couldn't believe that nothing had yet been done about it. Could you, Delilah?"

"No, Poppy, I couldn't. And I'm sure that's why the inspector himself is here – to do further investigations. Isn't that right, inspector?" She smiled again and this time added in some batting of eyelids. "I'm sure an officer of your calibre will not leave a stone unturned."

Flirtation won't work with this one, Poppy wanted to say to her.

But surprisingly Easling smiled back. "No harm done, ladies. But best you don't hang around here too long. There've been some muggings in the park – that's why I'm here."

Nothing to do with making sure no one gets near Elizabeth Dorchester before she is transferred to Wales this morning, then?

But before Poppy could formulate a more appropriate reply, a horse-drawn wagon trundled past. The driver looked curiously at the policeman and the two ladies in the motorcar.

Oh, please don't stop, Mr Thompson. Don't stop.

And to the girls' relief, he didn't. But where he was going they had no idea. The arrangement had been to meet at the south gate of the park. *Damn Easling!*

"I'll give you a hand with the engine then." Easling reached out his hand, clearly expecting to receive the crank lever.

Delilah smiled tightly, then reached behind her seat and gave it to him. As he bent down in front of the car she whispered to Poppy, "What are we going to do now?"

"Drive around the park. Follow Mr Thompson. We'll catch up with him."

A few cranks later and the engine roared into life. Delilah waved her thanks. Poppy glared. Easling doffed his hat.

A few minutes later, they were out of sight of the police officer and came across Mr Thompson and Bess waiting for them near a line of weeping willows.

"Better just slow down and let me out," said Poppy. "Don't stop the engine. This time of the morning, sound will travel across the pond. He might be listening to see if we've really gone."

"But how will I meet up with you again?"

"Go to your flat after rehearsal. I think it'll be better if I do this on my own. You at rehearsal will give us an alibi if Easling decides to check up on us."

"Are you sure, Poppy? It could be dangerous."

"It'll be no less dangerous with you with me. Besides, I've got Mr Thompson."

Delilah reluctantly agreed and slowed down enough for Poppy to jump out of the motorcar without risking injury. Then she pressed down on the accelerator and drove off. Hopefully if Easling had been listening – or if he had guards posted on Chelsea, Albert or Battersea Bridges – it would be noted that the black Model T Ford, driven by the pretty young lady, had indeed left the Battersea area as requested. And hopefully none of them would look too closely to see there was no passenger beside her. It was a flimsy cover, Poppy knew, but the best she could come up with on the hoof.

With Delilah roaring off into the distance, Poppy checked to see that there were no other surprises lurking in the bushes before approaching Mr Thompson. Bess snorted a greeting.

"I was worried you were going to stop there, Mr Thompson."

"I wasn't born yesterday, miss. That's Tricky Ricky Easling, ain't it? Bent as a butcher's hook, that one. Is Miss Marconi not joining us?"

"No, she's creating a diversion."

Mr Thompson raised an eyebrow but didn't comment. He got down from the wagon and pulled back the tarpaulin. "As we planned then?"

"Yes, Mr Thompson. As we planned."

Poppy took Mr Thompson's hand as he helped her climb into the back of the wagon. She lay down and made herself as comfortable as she could while he refastened the tarpaulin.

"You're here early, Bill."

"That I am, Georgie boy. Didn't get everything done the last time, if you remember."

"If you say so."

"So thought I'd drop by and finish them off early before me next job. Don't want Matron saying I'm not earning me keep now, do I?"

"That you don't, Bill; that you don't."

Poppy heard the wrought-iron gates to the Willow Park asylum opening with a creak and braced herself as the wagon lurched forward. She held her breath as Bess clopped up the gravel drive, fearing that at any moment the guard would see through Mr Thompson's feeble excuse for being there at half past six in the morning. But all she could hear was the closing of the gates and the laboured breathing of Bess and her owner.

Mr Thompson pulled back the tarpaulin and spoke quietly to Poppy without looking at her while he collected his usual equipment, supplemented by a bag of tools that he tied to his waist. If the guard decided to check up on what he was doing, he might legitimately ask why a window cleaner needed a crowbar and a bolt-cutter to do his job.

"If she hasn't been moved yet she'll be behind that window on the second floor. Fifth from the left."

If she hasn't been moved... That was their dilemma. Last night Poppy had gone to Mr Thompson's house hoping that he would accompany her to the asylum immediately. She told Mr Thompson that Elizabeth was due to be transferred in the morning. However, he had wisely pointed out that he would not be able to justify cleaning the windows there at night and the guard would not let him in. Unless she expected them to climb the wall carrying the ladder, it would need to wait until morning. They had all agreed that it was not likely they would be moving Elizabeth at the crack of dawn, and decided to meet at six o'clock and get as early a start as possible. But Easling had delayed them and they were already half an hour behind schedule.

It also worried Poppy that they didn't actually know what time the patients got up, had breakfast and so on, but there had not been time to find out. Oh, there were so many variables! And it was all out of Poppy's control. But it wasn't out of God's, and no matter what her current strained relationship with her creator was, she decided to ask for his help to save a woman who had been unjustly imprisoned for seven years.

So as Poppy prayed, Mr Thompson took his ladder and climbed up to the second floor. He decided to wash a few windows to the left of Elizabeth's room first in case anyone questioned why he had made a beeline for her window. The curtains were drawn on the first room and Mr Thompson assumed the patient was still asleep. The second room had a gap in the curtains and he saw someone moving around. The third window was Elizabeth's: the curtains were open, the bed was made, and all signs that Elizabeth Dorchester had ever been there were gone.

CHAPTER 30

Elizabeth was shaken awake. She squinted at the filtered light seeping through the curtains and realized that it was too early to get up. She hunched up and pulled the blankets back over her head.

"Get up! Get up!" The blanket was pulled off her. Above her stood a woman with short spiky black hair, just beginning to grow in again after being shaved. She was wearing a nightgown.

"Leave me alone," said Elizabeth and tugged again on the blanket.

"'Leave me alone! Leave me alone!' Lady La-de-dah wants me to leave her alone."

This was greeted with an alternating chorus of "Belt up, Bertha!" and "You tell her, Bertha!"

Elizabeth was encouraged that the Belt-up-Berthas seemed to be in the majority, so she tugged on the blanket more forcefully and wrenched it out of Bertha's grip. She held Bertha's eyes, trying to dominate her, but the stockier woman was not going down without a fight. Elizabeth did not enjoy fighting, but her years as a militant suffragist had equipped her to do so when necessary. She had had to fight on more than one occasion back in Holloway when she and Gloria had been put in with the ordinary prison population despite their demands to be treated as political prisoners. After a particularly bad scrap, she and Gloria had decided to go on hunger strike, as many of their sisters before them had. And although the force-feeding was hell, at least it got them into an isolation cell, away from the women who hated them simply for being "posh".

At Willow Park, she was grateful, if such a word could be used, that her father had paid for her to have a private room. But that was until yesterday. Yesterday, without warning, the matron and the young orderly who had been in the room the day the Denby girl had come to see her, had told her to pack her few things and go with them. They told her she was being moved. Transferred to Swansea. Elizabeth had demanded to see the head doctor. She did not want to move. No one had asked her. Surely she had rights! But her protests fell on deaf ears. And then, to add insult to injury, she was going to have to spend her last night in a general ward, with eleven other women. Apparently her room had already been allocated to someone else and the new patient was arriving first thing in the morning and they needed to clean it. As if she had somehow contaminated it.

Bertha was still looking at her. Weighing her up. Elizabeth braced herself for the assault, preparing to defend herself. But instead Bertha grinned, showing a line of crooked yellow teeth. Elizabeth grinned back and the two women laughed. Then the rest of the women joined in: some chortling, some shrieking. This brought a nurse in, who shouted at them all to "belt up" or they wouldn't get breakfast. The threat did the trick and the women all settled down.

But it was too late for Elizabeth to get back to sleep. She was awake now. And soon she would have to get ready to move to Swansea. She pulled a shawl over her shoulders and padded, barefoot, over to the window. This was going to be her last morning here. She opened the curtains a crack, to the half-hearted grumblings of the other patients, and looked out over the gardens, over the wall and to the Battersea gas towers in the distance. Her stomach clenched. It was over. Her hopes, dreams and prayers of being released had come to nothing. The Denby girl and her newspaper had not been able to get her out.

So Plan B it would have to be. It would have been far easier to do in her private room – she would not manage it in here. Perhaps she could do it in the bathroom. Yes, that was a possibility. There were pipes and things in there, strong enough to hold her, and she could use her shawl. Or tear a strip from her nightgown and fashion a noose…

Bertha and the other patients were settling back down for an extra half-hour lie-in. Now was her chance. She went over and knocked quietly on the door of the nurses' station. It opened. The nurse, red-eyed and weary after her night shift, growled at her. "What?"

"I need to use the toilet."

"Toilet time's not for half an hour still."

"I know. But I need to go. Desperately." Elizabeth crossed her legs and wriggled to demonstrate the urgency.

"All right." The woman nodded in the direction of the communal bathroom.

Elizabeth didn't move.

"What?"

"I'm moving to Swansea today. I've been here seven years. I –"

The nurse looked at her unsympathetically and started to shut the door. Elizabeth held it open. The nurse's red-rimmed eyes opened in surprise, then narrowed in suspicion.

"They told me you wouldn't be a bother."

"I'm not. I – I was just wondering if while I'm in the bathroom I could have a bath. It's my last day. These other women don't know me, but they don't like me. Please. I need a bit of privacy. Please… there'll be less chance of a commotion. If Bertha starts off again…"

The nurse considered this, then nodded. "All right. But make sure you're dressed and ready before that lot get up. You've" – she checked her watch – "just over twenty minutes."

"Thank you," said Elizabeth, with a catch in her throat. "You're very kind." And she meant it. This touch of humanity almost made her want to change her plans. Almost.

Mr Thompson came down the ladder and pulled back the tarpaulin, pretending to replenish his supplies. Without looking at Poppy he said, "She's not there."

"Maybe she's up already. Having breakfast. Or in the bathroom."

"No. Her bed's made and her things are gone. And I've checked some other rooms and the patients aren't properly up yet."

"So that means…"

"She's gone."

"We're too late."

"Looks that way. Swansea, is it?"

"Yes," said Poppy, desperately disappointed but immediately trying to reassess the situation. Perhaps Swansea was not out of reach. Perhaps Rollo's legal team could still get her out. But it would be delayed, and it would be out of her hands, and could Elizabeth take it? Poppy didn't know.

She needed to speak to Rollo. She couldn't risk a phone call – not with the possibility that Alfie was tapping in. She'd have to see him in person. She'd ask Mr Thompson to drop her off. But Mr Thompson was heading back to the ladder and starting to climb.

"Where are you going?" hissed Poppy.

Mr Thompson cleared his throat loudly and then made a mime of realizing he'd forgotten something. He came back to the wagon.

"I can't just leave after three windows. I need to do this whole wing, or the guard'll get suspicious."

"How long will it take?"

Mr Thompson shrugged. "Dunno. Half an hour?"

Poppy sighed and readjusted her cramped position.

Elizabeth collected her toiletry bag and padded quietly towards the bathroom, being careful to make as little noise as possible. She shut the door, then leaned her back against it and rolled her head from side to side, feeling the hardness of the wood against her skull. The communal bathroom had two bathtubs and a bank of showers, along with three toilets – not in separate stalls. Compared to Holloway it was the Ritz Hotel. Her father had at least considered her comfort in his choice of prison.

She had thought of writing a farewell letter – a suicide note. In it she would detail everything that had happened to her, making sure the blame fell squarely on the shoulders of her father. But she really couldn't be bothered. Nor did she have time if she was going to die before they moved her to Swansea. And besides, the folk at Willow Park were so deep into her father's pocket that she would expect any note to disappear before it ever saw the light of day. Her only hope of some kind of public vindication was the Denby girl. She wished now that she had told her where to find the box. She had chosen to keep that to herself to ensure she had some leverage: if the paper wanted the dirt on her father, they would need to get her out first. But now there was no way of exposing her father's crimes before she died.

Perhaps her suicide would prompt an investigation. Perhaps her brother would finally see their father for who he really was. The boy – because that's how she still thought of him – had been in his thrall since the day he was born. As he got older and the abuse of their mother became more frequent, she'd hoped his love for his mother would have caused him to side with her; but it didn't. He'd wept when he'd seen her black eyes and begged her to change her ways, but fully accepted that their father had no other choice – or was too scared to say otherwise.

Alfie was a coward. She'd heard he'd won the Victoria Cross for bravery in the war – how he'd managed that she had no idea. He'd brought it in for her to see on one of his visits. She had taken it from him, weighing the heavy iron in one hand and her Bible in the other like a pair of scales. "Mother would have been proud, Alfie," she'd said caustically. "Such a brave boy." And he'd slapped her so hard, there were welt marks on her cheek for two days.

She reached up and touched her cheek and was surprised to feel tears there. She wiped them away quickly, stood up straight and surveyed the bathroom for an appropriate place to hang her noose.

Poppy shifted her weight again. Her shoulder ached and her hip was pressing against something sharp. She rolled over and upset one of Mr Thompson's buckets, causing a clatter.

"You! Whatya doing?" A woman's voice.

She froze, holding her breath. Had someone heard her?

"Cleaning windows, Matron."

"I see that. But why are you doing it at ten to seven in the morning?"

"I didn't finish the last time I was here. Poured with rain, if you remember."

"Did it really?" The matron's voice dripped with sarcasm.

"Yeah, it did," said Mr Thompson. "I've got a job on this side of the river this morning and thought I'd squeeze you in. Don't want to leave a job half done. That wouldn't be right."

"Thought you'd be a peeping Tom more like it. That's the women's bathroom you're in front of. Get yourself down, you filthy scoundrel. And come into the office. I want a word with you."

Poppy heard Mr Thompson start to say something, but it was drowned by the clatter of a bucket hitting the wall. Then the tarpaulin was pulled back. She froze again, but was relieved to see it was just Mr Thompson putting his tool belt in the wagon.

"How long is this going to take?" he asked the matron.

"As long as it needs to," she said.

Elizabeth had been to the toilet, not wanting to soil herself in the throes of death. Then she ran the bath to mask the sound of what she would be doing next. She found a broken tile and used it to tear the hem of her nightdress, then made a fair approximation of a noose with the fabric. She looked around and spotted a sturdy-looking pipe running along the wall above the window. She stood on the side of the bath and hoisted herself onto the windowsill, steadying herself on the bars. There were no curtains over the window and the glass wasn't frosted. She took one last look at the world she was about to leave and noticed a horse and wagon below. It was the window cleaner. What was he doing here this time of the morning? Then she saw the matron, arms akimbo, giving someone a dressing down. A cowed Mr Thompson shuffled into frame, unhooked his tool belt and pulled back the tarpaulin on his wagon.

From her second-floor vantage point Elizabeth could see something the matron couldn't: a woman lying flat in the wagon. And if she was not mistaken, it looked very much like Dot Denby's niece.

Poppy raised her eyes to meet Mr Thompson's as he placed the tool belt beside her. He shrugged as if to say "can't be helped", then started fumbling with the tie to the tarpaulin.

"Leave that!"

He shrugged again and did as he was told, leaving one corner flap open as he followed the matron to her office.

Poppy readied herself to crawl further under the tarpaulin, away from prying eyes, when suddenly a movement at a second-floor window caught her eye.

Poppy looked up: there was a red-haired woman standing on a windowsill looking down on her. Dear God, it was Elizabeth Dorchester! There was no time to think things through properly. All she knew was she had to get up Mr Thompson's ladder before he and the matron returned. Poppy picked up the tool belt and vaulted out of the wagon.

CHAPTER 31

Elizabeth languished in the bath. *Lang-wish*. She wondered about the root of the word. *Wishful thinking about lounging? Longing to wish?* She scooped up some bubbles and held them on the palm of her hand before blowing them into a soapy mist. *Probably not. Probably something French.* She lay back and rested her head on the edge of the black marble tub and allowed both wrists to hang over the side. She noticed her fingernails: stubby and chewed. She bet the woman who usually *languished* in this bath would never allow her nails to get into such a state. Delilah Marconi. Gloria's daughter. How old would she be now? Twenty-one? Twenty-two? Did she realize the sacrifices her mother had made for her? Elizabeth remembered the last time she had seen Gloria, her black hair billowing in the snow and the wind, standing beside the railway track and then... and then...

There was a knock on the door.

"I've put out some clothes for you. They might not fit very well, but it's the best we can do at such short notice." It was the Denby girl.

"Thank you," called Elizabeth. "I'll be out in a minute."

The girl sounded far more provincial than her affected aunt. But Elizabeth didn't care two hoots about breeding. She and that cockney window cleaner had got her out of the asylum. She wasn't dreaming it; she wasn't. She was *free*!

Poppy lay the set of clothes on the back of a chair outside the bathroom door. Elizabeth was a tall, big-boned woman and nothing of Delilah's would fit properly. The loose kaftan and slacks was the best she could find, and a pair of men's deck shoes – Adam's? – finished off the outfit. It was a crime against fashion, but Poppy couldn't leave the woman in the torn, sodden nightgown she had found her in.

Back at the asylum, when she had got up the ladder she used Mr Thompson's crowbar to prise up the window, then the bolt cutters to break through the bars. Between them, Elizabeth and Poppy had created a big enough hole for the older woman to squeeze through. Only a few moments after she and Elizabeth had climbed into the wagon, Mr Thompson returned from his dressing down with the matron. He contained his surprise admirably when he noticed two women hiding under his tarpaulin instead of one and simply retrieved his ladder and headed back down the drive with Bess.

Once through the gates he geed the mare into a steady trot and headed as fast as he could to Chelsea Bridge. The whole way Elizabeth and Poppy wondered if anyone would apprehend them, but they didn't. When they got to King's Road, as per instruction Mr Thompson took them into the alley around the back of Delilah's apartment building.

As soon as she'd got Elizabeth up the fire escape and through the back door, as arranged with Delilah, Poppy came back out and thanked Mr Thompson, promising to be in touch with him as soon as possible to tell him what was going to happen next.

"I'll be out working all day, but leave a message with me missus or Vicky."

"I will, Mr Thompson. And I'm sorry you've lost your job at the asylum."

"So am I, miss, but it'll be worth it when Dorchester gets his come-uppance."

Poppy hoped she would not disappoint the grieving father. She was playing a dangerous game and she wasn't quite sure what her next move would be.

The art deco clock on Delilah's mantlepiece struck ten. Poppy and Elizabeth were sitting down to a full English breakfast, as per the older woman's request. Poppy watched her as she savoured every morsel of the egg, bacon, sausage, tomato and toast. Apparently all she got in the asylum was porridge, sometimes with prunes, and toast. Scrambled egg was a once-a-month treat.

"More coffee?"

"Thank you, yes. Another thing they denied us. Got us too worked up, they said."

Poppy smiled and poured the coffee.

"Delilah should be home soon. Later this morning, anyway. She said it was only a morning rehearsal."

"She's an actress?"

Poppy nodded.

"Just like her mother."

"And my aunt."

"Of course." Elizabeth blew on the coffee to cool it, then sipped tentatively. "So, what then? When Delilah gets back."

"I'm not sure. I need to see my editor. I can't phone him, because I think your brother is tapping the telephones."

"That sounds like him."

"So I will need to go in person. I'm just not sure it will be safe for you to come with me. You're a fugitive now. We need to find somewhere safe for you to hide."

"Why not here?"

"Because a police officer we know, Inspector Easling, spotted Delilah and me this morning, lurking in the vicinity of

Willow Park. I'm sure it won't be long before they start coming around asking questions."

Elizabeth stood up, her napkin falling to the floor. "Then we should go."

"Probably, but I want to wait for Delilah. She shouldn't be long." There was a knock on the door. "Ah, that will be her now."

She stood up and started towards the door, but Elizabeth caught her arm and whispered, "Why would Delilah be knocking on her own door?"

Poppy raised her eyebrows in alarm. Elizabeth was right. "Hide in the bathroom then," she whispered in return.

She walked slowly to the door, giving the older woman time to retreat, then put the security chain on before answering. And just as well she did, as Alfie Dorchester was waiting on the other side.

"Ah, Miss Denby. Your aunt and her friend told me you would be here. Is Delilah in?"

"No, she's at rehearsal. I'm staying here for a few days while my aunt and Mrs Wilson recover from the flu."

"Yes, that's what they said. Can I come in?"

"I'd rather you didn't."

"I'd like to see Delilah."

"I've told you, she isn't here."

He peered over her head and into the flat. "There are two plates on the table..."

"Delilah ate earlier. I haven't cleaned up yet."

"I thought the two of you breakfasted at Battersea Park..."

So Easling had run to his master.

"No, just an early morning walk. Then Delilah dropped me here before going to rehearsal. You can catch her at the theatre if you really want to see her. Goodbye."

She pushed the door to close it, but Alfie lodged his foot in the opening.

"Excuse me!"

"Come on, Poppy. Let's stop beating around the bush. I can't prove it – yet – but I know you've got something to do with it."

"With what?"

"My sister disappearing from the asylum. They think she was kidnapped by a window cleaner." Alfie threw back his head and laughed. "A window cleaner? Where did you get that idea?"

"I've no idea what you are talking about."

"It's just a matter of time before the police catch up with him. And then we'll find out where he's stashed my sister." He peered over her head again and called, "Oh Lizzy, darling. Where are you?"

"You've lost your marbles," said Poppy and tried ramming the door again. This time Alfie thrust out his arm and grabbed the front of her blouse, pulling her towards him. Her chin banged painfully against the door frame.

Poppy yelped.

"Is everything all right there?" A voice from across the hall.

"Ah yes, nothing to worry about," said Alfie soothingly and released his hold on Poppy.

"I'll be back," he hissed.

Poppy shut the door and leaned back against it, shaking.

"Are you all right?" It was Elizabeth.

"Yes. But we'd better get out of here. You heard him; he'll be back."

After scribbling a quick note for Delilah, Poppy and Elizabeth didn't waste any time scuttling down the fire escape and into the alley. Elizabeth took the lead, her years of experience in avoiding the police coming to the fore. She crouched behind bins, ducked into doorways and flattened herself against walls. Poppy followed suit. They gradually made their way to a bus stop a few streets away from King's Road – out of fear it was being watched – and jumped on the first bus that came along. Eventually they made their way to Fleet Street.

Poppy suggested that Elizabeth wait for her in St Bride's Church – also known as the Journalists' Church – while she went to see Rollo. The note they had left for Delilah had told her to meet them there as soon as she could. Hopefully, that wouldn't be too long.

As she was leaving, the older woman turned to her and said, "It's not just the flu that's keeping us from Dot and Grace's, is it?"

Poppy sighed and came and sat down beside her. "No, it isn't. Frank Wilson showed me a letter from your father to my aunt suggesting that back in 1910 he was paying her for something."

Elizabeth did not look surprised. "So your aunt's the mole."

"I don't know that. That's what the letter suggested, but it wasn't that clear what the money was actually for. Perhaps she was blackmailing him."

"About what?"

"I don't know," admitted Poppy. "I was hoping you would be able to shed some more light on it. You or whatever's in that box…"

"I can't tell you. Not yet." Elizabeth looked around her suspiciously, vetting the few lonely worshippers in case they were eavesdropping. "Look, Poppy, I'm grateful you got me out of the asylum, but let me be honest – you haven't filled me with the greatest confidence that you know what you're doing or that you will be able to get the information in the box into the right hands."

"Fair enough. But if I set up a meeting with my editor, will you give it to him?"

Elizabeth thought about this for a while, then nodded. "If I can get certain assurances from him in writing, yes."

"All right. But we don't have much time. Alfie already suspects I was involved in your kidnapping, and if the police think the same, there'll be a warrant out for my arrest. If they get me, I won't be able to help you. Believe me, Miss Dorchester, I want the truth just as much as you do. I want to expose whoever was responsible for my aunt's accident. I want to find out what really happened to Delilah's mother. And to my colleague, Bert Isaacs. This is not just a story, Miss Dorchester; it's my life."

Elizabeth gauged her, assessing her sincerity. "Those are noble ideals, Poppy, but noble ideals are what got me into trouble in the first place. That and trusting some people who should never have been trusted. So you'll forgive me if I want hard evidence that your newspaper will do what you say it will do. Agreed?"

"Agreed," said Poppy.

Poppy waited for a gap in the traffic and skipped across Fleet Street. It was half past eleven and the editorial staff would be gearing up for the noon briefing. She hoped to catch Rollo before he went in. Mavis Bradshaw was at the reception desk sorting through some mail.

"Poppy! Everyone's been looking for you."

"Who's everyone?"

"Rollo, Daniel…" She gave Poppy a maternal look. "What's happened with you two?"

"What do you mean?"

"He was so excited that you were coming back from Leamington Spa yesterday. He even asked my advice on which restaurant he should take you to. But then – well, I don't know – you tell me…"

"There's nothing to tell, Mavis. I'm not interested and that's that. I –"

Suddenly there was a wail of sirens. Mavis and Poppy looked up and saw a Black Mariah pull up outside the building and Richard Easling and a pair of uniformed officers get out. Poppy fell to the floor and crawled around behind the reception desk.

"Whatever are you doing, Poppy?"

"I think they're after me. Please, hide me. I'll explain later."

Poppy heard the door to the foyer being flung open and the clatter of boots on the mosaic floor. She crawled as far as she could under Mavis's desk and surreptitiously pulled down the receptionist's jacket from a chair to partially cover her.

"I'm looking for Poppy Denby!" shouted Easling. "And Rollo Rolandson. I have a warrant for their arrest."

"Whatever for?" asked Mavis, positioning herself over Poppy like a mother hen.

"Conspiracy to commit abduction and perverting the course of justice."

"I – well... they're both upstairs at an editorial meeting. I'll just ring up and let them know you're –"

"Don't bother. We're going up. Take the stairs – don't let them come down," he instructed his officers. "You're looking for a blonde girl and a dwarf."

The boots clattered off, then the lift bell clanged, suggesting Easling was covering the other avenue to the upper floors. After a minute or two, Mavis whispered to Poppy, "Get out of here, quickly! Go through the basement."

"What about Rollo?" asked Poppy as she scrambled to her feet.

"Don't worry. He can look after himself. Go!"

"All right. Tell him I've got Elizabeth Dorchester at St Bride's; but it won't be safe for us to stay there long. Tell him

I'm going to move her now. He needs to come and meet her. I'll send word of where and when. If he's not in prison…"

There was a shout and sounds of an altercation from above. Ivan's booming voice echoed around the atrium. "Vat do you vant here? Get out, you peegs!"

"Go!"

Poppy did not wait for further instructions. She ran as fast as she could down the stairs to the basement.

CHAPTER 32

Poppy ran through the basement without explanation for the second time in a week. The printers didn't blink an eyelid. Apparently journalists on the run from someone or other were par for the course at *The Globe*.

Outside she walked briskly down the alley and into Fleet Street, checking to see if there were any police officers in the Black Mariah. There *was* one, but he was busy picking something out of his teeth and didn't notice her as she slipped between parked cars and crossed the road. She slowed down her pace as she approached the walkway to St Bride's Church, hoping not to draw any attention in case the police decided to question the locals about the whereabouts of a blonde girl with a warrant out for her arrest.

Inside the church she was relieved to see the auburn hair of Elizabeth Dorchester and the black bob of Delilah Marconi.

"You made it," she said to her friend.

"Yes, I got your note. Good heavens, Poppy, I think the police might be after you. They came and questioned me at the theatre."

"What did you tell them?"

"That I hadn't seen you since I dropped you off at the flat after our 'breakfast walk' this morning."

"Good. That's what I told Alfie."

"Elizabeth told me he'd been round." Delilah used a string of expletives to describe her feelings for her former suitor, which raised a disapproving look from a nearby worshipper.

"Sorry," said Delilah, crossing herself in repentance, not realizing that wasn't the done thing in an Anglican church.

"Where's your editor?" asked Elizabeth.

"On the run from the police." Poppy explained what had happened in the *Globe* building. "But don't worry, he's resourceful. If they do take him in, his solicitors will get him out – freedom of the press, etcetera, etcetera. Besides, he honestly didn't 'conspire to kidnap' you. That was all my idea – he knew nothing about it."

"I hope you're right," said Elizabeth.

"What now?" asked Delilah.

"Now," said Poppy, rising to her feet, "we need to get somewhere safe until we can set up the meeting with Rollo and Miss Dorchester. This is too close to *The Globe* for comfort."

Poppy, Elizabeth and Delilah got off the bus in Wapping at the bottom of Mr Thompson's street. Adam apparently had been questioned about why his vehicle had been seen in the vicinity of the scene of a kidnapping and he had point-blank refused to give the keys to Delilah.

"Oh dear. Is it over between you two?" asked Poppy.

"Of course not. He'll get over it. But in the meantime, it's public transport for us."

Elizabeth, who had not been on the roads of London in over seven years, commented on how many motor vehicles there were compared to her day and how newfangled they all looked. But as they walked into Wapping, it was as if they were going back in time. Horses and carts and push barrows were the standard fare, and the roads were rutted and full of potholes. They walked to the end of the terrace and saw a group of women gathering up laundry strewn across the road. Mrs Thompson was in the midst of them. She started when she saw the three well-to-do women.

"Get away. You've caused enough trouble!" Her eye was swollen and her lip split and bloodied.

"Mrs Thompson! What happened?"

"Tricky Ricky Easling. He was round looking for our Bill. I told him he wasn't here. He didn't believe me and gave me this for me trouble. Then he trashed the place looking for – for her!" She pointed an accusing finger at Elizabeth. "It's her, isn't it? The one this is all about."

"Yes, this is Elizabeth Dorchester. But as I explained last night –"

"I don't care what you said. This has gone too far. Easling's after my Bill."

"Is he –"

"He's on the run, that's what he is. Him and his old horse. We didn't ask for this trouble. Now get out of 'ere before I tell them where to find ya."

"What have you told them?"

"I told them it was you and your editor's fault. I told them you was from *The Globe*."

So that's why there had been the raid on the *Globe* office… Staying here was no longer an option. She turned to Delilah. "Is there anyone in your family who can help us?"

"I'm not sure. Papa is in Malta. Uncle Elmo is in New York at a conference…"

"I know somewhere," said Elizabeth.

"Where?"

Elizabeth looked at Mrs Thompson's battered face and the curious gazes of the neighbours. "I'll tell you on the way."

The three women returned to the bus stop and waited for the next bus. Both Poppy and Delilah tried to ask Elizabeth where they were going, but the older woman looked around furtively, put her finger to her lips and said, "Walls have ears."

Poppy wondered if she was quite as sane as she thought. Years in an asylum must have rubbed off on her a bit.

They were getting curious stares from the locals: three middle- to upper-class ladies in a working-class neighbourhood waiting at a bus stop would always attract attention. Poppy wished the bus would hurry up.

Suddenly, a young woman ran around the corner and nearly hurtled into them. She pulled herself up, gasping an apology, and held a hand to her side. "Oh, I've caught you! Mum said you'd been."

"Vicky?" asked Poppy, not sure whether she'd correctly remembered the Thompson girl's name.

"That's right, miss. Miss Denby. Miss Marconi and – ah, you must be Captain Dorchester's sister."

Elizabeth's eyes narrowed. "How do you know that?"

"Because Miss Denby told us last night she was going to rescue you and that you would be able to put your brother away for what he'd done to our Billy."

Elizabeth looked at Poppy. "What's she talking about?"

Poppy realized she hadn't yet told Elizabeth about the Victoria Cross angle to the investigation.

When she'd finished, Elizabeth nodded. "Doesn't surprise me in the least. He was always a coward." Then to Vicky: "I'm very sorry about your brother. But I'm not sure what I can do…"

"Well, as soon as you give us the box and it turns out to provide the evidence we need against your father and Easling, then we will produce Sophie Blackburn's evidence about the VC and the true reason for Melvyn's support of the Radium Institute," offered Poppy.

"So that's your plan, is it?"

"It's my editor's plan, yes."

"I think I need to speak to your editor."

Poppy exhaled sharply. This was going round in circles. "I'm doing my best, Miss Dorchester. I can't produce him out of a hat. So if you just give me the box I will —"

Elizabeth raised her hand to silence Poppy. "I'll make you a deal. I will give your editor until six o'clock this evening to turn up. If he doesn't, I will give you the box, but then I'll disappear and you won't be able to use me as evidence. If I'm caught I will claim coercion. It will weaken your story, but it's the best I am prepared to offer."

"But we can't go back to *The Globe*. It'll be watched."

"I know that." Elizabeth turned to Vicky. "Did the policeman who hit your mother see you? Or any of the men who were with him?"

"No. I wasn't there when it happened. Me mum just told me now."

"Good. Poppy, do you have a notebook and pencil in that satchel?"

"I do."

"Excellent. Give it here."

Elizabeth wrote swiftly, filling one side of a page, then she folded it neatly and wrote *Att of: Rollo Rolandson and/or the* Globe *solicitors*. She then instructed Vicky to deliver it to Rollo in person. If he was not available then she was to ask to be directed to the *Globe* solicitors. Under no circumstances was she to give the note to anyone other than Rollo or a solicitor. If she was unable to do so, she was to destroy the note and come home and not say a word to anyone.

Vicky nodded vigorously as she received her instructions. "I won't let you down, miss. I promise!"

"Good girl," said Elizabeth, then instructed Vicky to go to another bus stop.

"And where are we going?" asked Poppy.

"That is on a need-to-know basis," said Elizabeth.

Poppy sighed.

When the bus came, Elizabeth asked the bus driver for three tickets to the nearest Tube station, which turned out to be Liverpool Street. At Liverpool Street Elizabeth asked for three tickets to Paddington station. It was only then that Poppy realized where they were going.

Chapter 33

5 November 1913

Elizabeth Dorchester ran. She ignored the cries of the engine driver behind her. She ignored the screams of the passengers who had got off the train to see why they had stopped so suddenly. She ignored the thought that she really should go and see if Gloria was still alive. And she ignored the snow that was turning to sleet and slicing at her face like a razor.

She didn't check to see if the shadow was still behind her as she ran into the maze of alleys between the locomotive sheds. It was only when Elizabeth's foot caught on some loose cable and she fell face first into a pile of coal that she stopped to look. There was no one there. She felt something warm run down her temple. She reached up and felt the wetness, then licked her fingers to confirm that it was blood. Funny, she felt no pain. None at all.

She could still hear the cries from the scene of the accident punctuated by the whizzes and bangs of the distant firework display. Each rocket that cascaded back to earth lit up the train yard. And while she was grateful for the light, she realized she too would be illuminated. People would start searching for her – if they weren't already. The train people, the shadow, her father…

Elizabeth picked herself up and retrieved her satchel from the coal stack. It felt lighter than it should, although she could still feel the shape of the cedarwood box through the canvas.

Something else was missing. She waited for the next fireworks to go off and used the light to search the black mound. Something shiny caught her eye – yes, thank God, it was the gilded pages of her Bible. She picked it up and held it tightly to her chest.

She prayed, as she had prayed every day since her incarceration. God had answered her prayers for freedom, but not in the way she had expected. He seemed to do that a lot. Give with one hand and take with another. How could he have let Gloria be killed? How could he? Her priest had once told her that God wept over each pain and heartache experienced by his children. Then why didn't he stop it? Why?

"Search the sheds!"

They were on to her. She checked to see that the page she had torn from her father's ledger was still in the lining of the Bible, stuffed it in her satchel and then removed the cedarwood box. She took the silk scarf from her neck and wrapped it tightly around the box. Then she tried a few shed doors. They were all locked. But then, just as she was about to put the box back in her satchel, she spotted a loose piece of corrugated iron around the back of one shed. She prised it open, not flinching as the rusty edge cut into her hands, and made a gap big enough to squeeze into. She pushed her satchel through first, then crawled after it. Inside were two locomotive engines, side by side like a pair of old pensioners. She made her way to the furthest corner of the shed and scuffed at the ground with her kid leather shoe. It was uncovered earth. She fell to her knees and started scratching a hole, tearing what was left of her fingernails. But it was slow going. Suddenly she heard the door of the shed rattle, then a gruff, male voice: "Locked."

She held her breath and waited to see if anyone would come in, but they didn't. After a few minutes she got up and went to the cab of one of the engines. Just as she'd hoped, there was a coal shovel hanging beside the cold furnace. She unhooked the shovel and went back to her corner. With the shovel to aid her, she made quick work of it and soon had a hole deep enough to bury the box. She took a few more minutes to cover the hole, pat it down and scatter some loose coal over the area. Then she returned the shovel to the engine and slipped back out through the gap in the corrugated panels.

She checked again to see that she had not been spotted, then headed as fast as she could to the fence at the back of the yard. She looked back and took her bearings. Two apple trees could be used as markers for when she returned to retrieve the box. Then, with her satchel slung over her shoulder, she climbed the fence and was off into the fields beyond, leaving the body of her dead friend to the mercy of strangers.

The next morning she was found lying in a ditch, nearly frozen to death, clutching her Bible to her chest. When she woke in hospital three days later she denied any knowledge of a stolen box and a dead woman called Gloria Marconi. When questioned further she started rocking backwards and forwards, giving furtive looks towards the window. When asked what she was afraid of, she answered, "The shadow, of course. Isn't everyone?"

14 JULY 1920

Melvyn Dorchester rapped his cane against his desk as his son stuttered through his report. The younger man stood in his father's study like a schoolboy before the headmaster. Alfie's feet ached after traipsing over half of London looking for the wretched Denby girl and his sister. He longed to sink into one of the soft leather armchairs facing his father's desk, but knew better than to do so without his permission.

"So the window cleaner hasn't been found then," stated his father in summary.

"No. But Easling's seen his wife and put the fear of God into her. She confirmed that the Denby girl and Rolandson put her man up to it."

"Any sign of Lizzy?"

"No, Father, I'm sorry. But Easling's now got grounds for a warrant for Denby and Rolandson."

"Good. The more we can keep this above board the easier it will be to clean up afterwards."

The telephone rang. "Lord Dorchester… yes, yes… he's just told me… And then?… Bloody Yankee dwarf! And the girl?… Ah! That's better. Keep on it."

He put the phone down and held his hands together down the centre line of his face, squinting his steel-grey eyes along his fingertips like the sights of a gun. "That was Easling. The dwarf's off the hook. Seems like he was in a meeting with his solicitor at the time Lizzy disappeared. Perfect alibi, so the warrant's been dropped."

"And Poppy?"

"She got away."

"Damn!" Alfie forgot himself in frustration and dropped into a chair, draping one long leg over the side.

Melvyn's eyes narrowed, but he didn't comment on his offspring's impudence. Instead, and to Alfie's immense surprise, he smiled.

"What is it?" asked Alfie, straightening up.

"Easling's managed to get a tail on the Denby girl. Seems like she, Lizzy and your Delilah went to see the window cleaner. Easling has an informant on the street. And he's following them now."

"Where are they going?"

"They've just arrived at Paddington station."

CHAPTER 34

Poppy, Elizabeth and Delilah emerged from the Tube tunnel into the hustle and bustle of Paddington station. Since arriving in London a month ago, Poppy had only travelled by Tube a few times, far preferring to be above ground in the warm summer air. Perhaps she might change her mind in winter and burrow underground like other Londoners, but for now she was grateful to be out of the tunnels. The train from Liverpool Street to Paddington had taken just under an hour. Poppy looked up at the station clock and noted that it was four o'clock in the afternoon – time for tea. She suggested this to the other women and they agreed.

"We should probably check first though when the next train to Slough is leaving," observed Poppy.

"Why do you think we're going to Slough?" asked Elizabeth.

"Well, aren't we?"

"You surprise me, Miss Denby."

"In a good way, I hope."

"Indeed."

Delilah didn't say a word. On the train journey from Liverpool Street to here she had been uncharacteristically quiet. As Elizabeth headed over to the ticket office Poppy lagged behind and put her arm around Delilah.

"Are you all right?"

"I'm fine. I suspected we were going to Slough, but I wasn't sure. I haven't been there since Mama died. Papa and I went together to see where it happened. I couldn't get out of the motor. Why do you think she wants to go? To retrieve the box?"

"Possibly. Or just to relive it. I'm not sure how stable she really is, Delilah. I think we need to be careful…"

"You mean she –"

"Shhhh," warned Poppy as Elizabeth rejoined them.

"We've got forty minutes before the next train. Time for a cup of tea." Elizabeth scanned the concourse back and forth, back and forth.

"There's a tea shop over there beside the Post Office," said Poppy.

"I know. Just checking that the coast's clear."

Poppy looked at the crowd of commuters criss-crossing the station, each of them intent on their own agenda. What was Elizabeth looking for? Would she be able to tell if someone was not what they seemed to be?

Suddenly a policeman strolled towards them. The three women froze. But he nodded politely and walked on by.

"Now," said Elizabeth when his back was turned, and strode briskly towards the tea shop. Delilah and Poppy had no choice but to follow.

There was a telephone booth outside the Post Office and Poppy considered calling *The Globe*. She wasn't sure how this phone tapping thing worked. Could Alfie have monitored every line into *The Globe* or was it just Aunt Dot and Grace's phone? That, after all, was where she had made the call to Rollo and they'd agreed that she was going to Paris. And it was to his house, not *The Globe*. Mavis had given her the number. So surely the "tap", if there was one, was linked to 137 King's Road. Would it be safe to call from here? She wasn't sure. But for now there was nothing she could do, as the booth was occupied by a man. He looked at the three women curiously as they walked past him into the tea shop. Oh dear. Had she been staring?

Inside the tea shop the women ordered a pot of Earl Grey and a selection of sandwiches. Poppy was famished – it seemed a long time since breakfast. But Delilah just picked at her crusts, while Elizabeth checked each sandwich from multiple angles before taking a bite.

As they ate, Poppy shared her musings about the phone tapping and asked her companions' opinion.

"Well, telephones weren't as common in my day as they are now, you know. And it was only the wealthiest households that had one. My father did, of course, but I don't think your aunt did, Poppy. Not back then. If she had, it might have made things much easier to contact her when Gloria and I got out of Holloway."

Delilah was pulling at a loose thread on the tablecloth. She looked up, and Poppy saw that she was near to tears.

"Are you sure you're all right, Delilah? Elizabeth and I can go without you, can't we?"

Elizabeth nodded.

"No. I need to go. I need to know what happened. Do you know what happened, Elizabeth?"

Elizabeth sighed, a flicker of sympathy for the younger woman registering on her face. "It's a bit of a blur, to be honest. I'm hoping that when I'm there – and I'm not starving or half frozen – I will be able to piece it together."

"So you're not really sure where the box is, then."

"No, on that I'm a bit clearer. I think I remember where it is."

"You think?" asked Poppy.

"It's the best I can do, all right?" Elizabeth snapped.

"Sorry."

The three women slipped into their own thoughts. Poppy noticed that the telephone booth was now vacant. Delilah had noticed too.

"My Uncle Elmo would know. About the telephone tapping. He's got some telephone exchanges as part of his business."

"Can you ring him?"

"Not sure exactly where he is. Somewhere in New York. But I could call his secretary. She might be able to help us. I doubt Alfie would have tapped her line. And if he had, they have engineers who can check that sort of thing."

"Sounds like a plan," said Poppy.

Elizabeth shrugged.

"Just don't tell her exactly where we are, or where we're going – just in case," advised Poppy

Poppy and Elizabeth remained at the table while Delilah went to the telephone booth. A few minutes later she returned, looking pale.

"What is it?"

"We need to buy a newspaper. Mrs Stemple says we've made the early evening edition. Apparently there's a manhunt for us all over London!"

"Did you ask her about the phone tapping?"

"I did. But she wasn't sure. She's going to get hold of Uncle Elmo and my father. And their solicitors. But in the meantime she suggests we keep a low profile."

"Did you tell her where we were going?"

"No. I wasn't sure about the tapping thing."

"Good."

"But if they *are* listening in," Delilah continued, "they'll know that Marconi Industries is putting its full might behind us. Dorchester isn't the only man with power in this town." Delilah set her pretty mouth in a grim line.

Elizabeth finished her last sandwich and folded her napkin neatly on her plate. "Better late than never, I suppose."

"What's that supposed to mean?" snapped Delilah.

"If Marconi Industries had done something to help us back in 1913 – or got me out of the asylum anytime since then – we wouldn't be in this position now."

"There was no way we could have known! Both my father and I believed my mother had committed suicide. And in fact, for all we know, she might have. We only have *your* word that she didn't – for what that's worth!"

"For what that's worth? Now let me tell you something, girl –"

"Shush! Stop it. We've got to stick together. If Delilah's uncle's secretary is right, then we don't have much time. I say we have two choices: one, we can make our way to Marconi Industries' offices, wherever they are –"

"The Strand."

"– or we can carry on on our own to Slough, where, Miss Dorchester, you will give us this box, if it exists –"

"I've told you, I will only give it to your editor."

"Oh, do belt up about that! He isn't here, all right?"

"I sent him a note with the Thompson girl. I told him where we were going and that he should meet us there."

"But we have no idea if he has got the note, do we?"

Elizabeth glared at her.

"No, we don't," Poppy finished for her. "So, if you are *not* going to give me the box, then I suggest we go back to central London and seek refuge with the Marconis."

"And if I am?"

"Well, then I suggest we carry on with our plan and go to Slough." Poppy looked out of the window across the station concourse. "I don't see any evidence of a mass manhunt yet. Do you?"

Elizabeth opened her mouth to say something, then appeared to change her mind. Poppy took this as compliance.

She turned to her friend. "What do you say, Delilah? Strand or Slough?"

The young woman again looked on the brink of tears, but she held them back and took both Elizabeth's and Poppy's hands. "I think it's time we faced the truth. Don't you? Whatever happens?"

Poppy and Elizabeth looked at each other across the table.

Elizabeth squeezed Delilah's hand. "I agree. What say you, Poppy?"

"So will you give me the box?"

"I will. And I'll tell you everything I know about it too."

"Then yes, I agree."

As the three women got up and paid their bill, they didn't notice a man in the corner lower his newspaper and watch them go. As they headed to catch their train he slipped into the phone booth and made a call to his paymaster.

CHAPTER 35

The train yard hadn't changed in the seven years since Elizabeth had last been there, though now it was a clear summer's evening instead of a snowy winter's night. The clock read quarter to six by the time the three women made their way from the commuter station to the train yard. They decided to walk down a nearby road rather than take the more direct route down the tracks, as inevitably – at this time of day – they would have been stopped by railway workers. As they approached the yard they made a point of turning their backs on the gates and looking out over the open fields. Poppy took out her notebook and began to sketch the scenery, as if they were three ladies on a walking jaunt.

At six o'clock they heard the gates behind them clatter shut and a group of men bade each other goodnight, raised their caps to the ladies and headed off in different directions. The women also pretended to move on.

When the coast was clear, Poppy called them into a huddle. "I think perhaps it's best if we don't go through the gate. There might be a night watchman. Do you agree?"

"Suppose so," said Elizabeth.

"Makes sense," said Delilah. "But how are we going to get in?"

Poppy reached into her satchel and pulled out some bolt cutters.

"Where on earth did you get those?" Delilah exclaimed.

"I forgot to give them back to Mr Thompson after we left the asylum."

"Oh, you clever girl! Do you know how to use them?"

"I had a bit of practice earlier," grinned Poppy, and made her way to a part of the railway yard fence that was partially obscured by a line of poplars. After a few aborted attempts she managed to cut a hole in the chain fence big enough for them all to crawl through.

Once inside, she turned to Elizabeth and asked: "Where now?"

Elizabeth looked around, trying to find her bearings. The locomotive sheds were to their left, the gatehouse to their right and – beyond an assortment of smaller sheds housing equipment, cables and tools – was the line from Paddington to Slough. They had passed through the yard on their journey from Paddington, and as they passed, Elizabeth had looked to see whether or not her markers were still there: a pair of crab-apple trees. Elizabeth thought she had glimpsed them from the train, but wasn't sure. She looked again from her vantage point near the fence and finally saw them, in full bloom, about a hundred yards to the left.

"Over there."

Delilah and Poppy followed her as she wove her way around cable bobbins and over piles of spare sleepers until she came to a large shed with twin single-gauge lines running under the double doors. Elizabeth told them to wait where they were and then slipped around the back of the shed. She returned quickly, shaking her head.

"There used to be a gap in the corrugated sheets. They've fixed it now. You'll have to use your cutters again, Poppy."

Poppy took them out of her satchel and set to work on the padlock and chain while the other women kept watch. It required a bit more muscle power than the chain fence, but not as much as the bars at the asylum, and it snapped with a satisfying *chink*.

Elizabeth took one more look around, then pushed the door open to reveal a pair of locomotive engines. Whether they were the same two that had witnessed her efforts to hide the box seven years ago, she didn't know.

"I don't suppose you have a shovel in that satchel, do you, Poppy?"

"Sorry, no."

"Never mind." Elizabeth climbed into the cab of one of the engines and emerged with a shovel, then pointed towards the back of the shed. Poppy and Delilah followed her lead.

Ten minutes of speculative digging passed. Each empty hole increased Poppy's nagging feeling that she had been wrong to place so much faith in Elizabeth's version of events. But then the sound of metal hitting wood and a gasp of triumph from the older woman told her that there may be something there after all.

Poppy and Delilah had been taking turns standing guard at the door. But as Elizabeth fell to her knees and started digging with her hands, Poppy called out, "Delilah! I think she's got something!"

The evening sun shone through a grease-smeared window and caught the red highlights of Elizabeth's hair, which had come loose from her plait. A few moments later the hunched figure straightened and with a look of immense relief Elizabeth presented Poppy with a rectangular-shaped object wrapped in filthy green fabric. Poppy took it from her, like a priest receiving an offering, and placed it in a pool of sunlight.

It was indeed a box. It was made of cedarwood and had the Dorchester family crest of the crow and the rose carved into the lid. She opened it to reveal three leather-bound ledgers. She took them out of the box and lay them side by side on the green scarf.

"So what am I going to find inside these, Elizabeth?"

"My father's financial records for the years 1908 to 1910. I wanted to get the records up to 1913, but they weren't in the safe when I broke in, and I didn't have time to look for them. But these were good enough. Inside you'll find records of payments made to a host of people in public office. A clever accountant and anyone with knowledge of government and public affairs for that period will easily be able to match the passing of bills and approval of business licences in favour of my father and his financial concerns."

"Bribes?" Poppy asked.

"Among other things. I tore the sheet I gave you from this one."

She opened the 1910 ledger and flicked through until she came to a jagged margin, evidence of a missing page.

Poppy had no doubt that the page came from these ledgers, and if what Elizabeth said was correct – and she had no reason any more to disbelieve her – the rest of the ledger would show a pattern of bribes to people, including Richard Easling. The date on the missing page, if she recalled correctly, was 3rd October 1910. The demonstration outside Westminster that had led to Black Friday and Aunt Dot's horrific injuries was 18th November. If there had been further payments to Easling or anyone else, Poppy was sure they were in these ledgers. Would she find evidence of the payment to her aunt? Frank's note had been dated sometime in 1910 too… Well, if it did, so be it. The truth had to come out. Even if it meant exposing her darling aunt as a traitor.

"Have you got enough to go ahead with the exposé?" asked Elizabeth.

"Yes, I think so. Rollo will know for sure."

"Good. Then let's get out of here. Delilah, do you think we can still go to Marconi House?"

"Yes, I think so, but it might be closed. We can ask the night watchman to take us in, though, and then I can call Mrs Stemple, and Poppy can call Rollo."

"Then let's do it." Poppy paused and looked at Delilah. "Is there anything else you want to do while you're here?"

"Like what?"

"I don't know. Perhaps you want Elizabeth to show you where it happened… to see if she can remember anything else…"

"I – I don't know. Should I? Can you?"

This last was to Elizabeth. But Elizabeth was not looking at her. Instead she was staring at the door, where a tall, shadowy figure stood, silhouetted by the evening sun.

Elizabeth's scream ricocheted off the corrugated metal walls like a pebble in a tin. She leapt up and backed into the corner as far as she could go.

The shadow walked towards them. Poppy grabbed the ledgers and put them back in the box, then stood, pushing the box behind her with her foot. Taking hold of Delilah's hand, the two younger women formed a protective wall between the terrified Elizabeth and the advancing shadow. The shadow soon took form and it was in the shape of a woman.

"Oh, Elizabeth! Is it really you?"

Grace Wilson held out her hands to the three cowering women. "Good heavens, girls! Whatever have you got yourselves into? Your aunt and I have been worried sick."

"What are you doing here, Grace?" Poppy tried to keep her voice calm while she frantically tried to put the pieces together. Was Grace the shadow? Was she here on behalf of her aunt? Was Dot outside? She tried to look over Grace's shoulder, but couldn't see past her tall frame. Instead she asked, "How did you know where we'd be?"

"I wasn't completely sure. We saw the early edition, you see, and couldn't believe it when we read that the three of you were the subject of a city-wide manhunt. I called your editor and he said he hadn't seen you but that the police were after you. Dot and I put our heads together to try and figure out where you could be. We concluded that the three together might be heading to where Gloria died. It was a lucky guess, but it was the best we had. So I jumped in the motor and –"

"Is Dot outside?"

"No. She stayed at home. In case we were wrong and you came there for help… but oh, thank God, I've found you!" She threw her arms around Poppy and drew her close. "We've been so worried." Then she opened up and looked at Delilah and Elizabeth. "About all of you. But come, I've got the motorcar. I'll take you home."

She reached down and picked up the box. "Whatever's this?"

Poppy snatched it from her. "It's evidence."

"Evidence of what?" asked Grace, taking hold of the other side of the box with both hands.

"Evidence of bribes. Please, Grace, I have to give it to *The Globe*'s solicitors. And we need to go quickly, before Dorchester and the police find us." Poppy pulled the box towards her. Grace did not let go.

"Of course you do. Here, let me take that and you help Elizabeth. She looks like she's seen a ghost. Oh, the poor mite is shaking like a leaf!"

Poppy turned to look at Elizabeth and momentarily loosened her grip on the box. Grace snatched it, turned and ran.

"Look after Elizabeth!" Poppy shouted to Delilah before taking off in pursuit.

Grace, in her early fifties, was more than twice Poppy's age. But she was fit and healthy and had been strengthened by years of lifting her paraplegic friend. She was also wearing culottes; Poppy was wearing a skirt.

The women wove their way through the yard, between sheds and around piles of debris. Grace seemed to be heading towards the gatehouse, but she was slowing down. The box was cumbersome and she had to keep hitching it up under her arm. As they rounded the shed closest to the gate, Poppy noticed it was still locked and Grace's car was parked not directly outside, but further down the lane. So she hadn't come in the official way either... Why was she coming back this way? Was she hoping someone would be here who wasn't? Poppy didn't have time to ponder before Grace double-backed suddenly and ran towards the railway line. Poppy spun around, but did not slow down. Hitching up her skirt and hurdling a pile of sleepers, she made up some ground on Grace, who was making a beeline for the tracks and... oh God, no... an oncoming train.

Grace had either not seen the train, or was going to try to outrun it and get to the other side before Poppy. Whatever the reason, Poppy could not let her reach the track.

"GRACE!" She accelerated and covered the ground between them, then launched herself at the legs of the older woman, like a rugby player in a tackle. Poppy hit the ground with a rib-crunching thunk, then felt a second jolt as Grace fell too, a split second before the train shot by. Poppy, though winded, got to her knees and threw her body on top of Grace, pinning her down.

Grace was rocking her head from side to side and sobbing. "I didn't mean it, I didn't!"

"Why, Grace? Why?"

By now Delilah and Elizabeth had caught up with them and stood clutching each other by the side of the track.

"I – I had to get the ledgers. Gloria told me about them when I dropped her off that day – yes, I lied about that. I did drop her off. I tried to get her to agree to give them to me after she got them from Elizabeth, but then she started getting defensive. I don't know, maybe I came across too strong... maybe she suspected something wasn't right."

"It wasn't, was it? You weren't going to use the ledgers to expose Dorchester, were you?"

Grace shook her head, sobbing.

"Then why did you want them?"

Grace fixed her eyes on Poppy. "I thought there might be something in them. Something that could have harmed us. I did it to protect us, Poppy, all of us, but most of all I did it to protect your aunt."

Grace heaved against Poppy's weight. The younger woman did not budge.

"The payment to her from Dorchester?" asked Poppy, already knowing the answer.

Grace stopped trying to shift her. "You know?" she whispered.

"Frank showed me the letter."

A haunted look came into Grace's eyes. "Then you'll know that if that got out – that Dot had been paid off – people would assume she was a traitor. But she wasn't. It wasn't like that."

Grace tried to raise her arms. Poppy tightened her grip. "Why did he pay her?"

Grace eased up. "She was blackmailing him. Trying to get money from him to use for the WSPU. You see, it was her sense of humour. You know what she's like. She thought that funny – getting a masochistic pig to fund the fight for women's suffrage. I told her it was stupid, I tried to make her stop, but you know what she's like. She's –"

Grace rocked her hips, trying to unbalance Poppy. Poppy planted her knees more firmly into the ground. "What did she use to blackmail him? What information did she have on him?"

"I – I – I'm not sure. I never found out."

"And you never asked her?"

"I – never thought to." Grace's voice was now reed-thin and Poppy had to lean in close to hear her, worried though that it might be a trick.

But it wasn't. The fight had gone out of Grace. Poppy allowed her to sit up, then pushed the box out of the older woman's reach with her foot.

Poppy stood up and looked down on Grace, who sat hugging her knees.

"Now that I find very strange, Grace. It's the first thing I would want to know. Wouldn't you?" Poppy looked at Delilah and Elizabeth for confirmation.

Delilah's eyes were wide with shock. Elizabeth's were vacant.

Poppy turned her attention back to Grace. "And why the big secret from the rest of the group? From Frank and Sophie and Gloria and Elizabeth? Surely she would have wanted to share the joke. She wouldn't be able to stop herself. We all know what she's like, don't we?" Again Poppy looked to her friends, awaiting an answer, but none came. She was on her own. She pressed on.

"You're right, Grace, I do know what she's like. I know for instance that she has absolutely no idea how to handle money – she doesn't even know her bank account number." Grace looked up at her, her eyes like a heifer's at an abattoir. Poppy knew she was on the right track. "And I know this because I asked her for it the other week so I could transfer my first pay cheque to repay the money she'd loaned me. And you know what? She didn't know it. She said she would have to ask you. Which has got me thinking. I don't think Dot was blackmailing Dorchester. You were, in her name."

"I – I – that's preposterous!" Grace released her knees and started to get up. So the fight was not entirely gone from the older woman yet. Poppy stepped closer, hoping to intimidate her, hoping she wouldn't try to run.

"Is it? You were his accountant for four years, weren't you? Up until he sacked you and Frank for your association with the WSPU in 1907."

"I was, but –"

"And if these ledgers are anything to go by" – she put her foot on the box – "you would have had a mint of material from those years to draw on."

Grace's eyes registered defeat.

Channelling Hercule Poirot, Poppy came in for the kill: "You were the blackmailer, Grace; you. And for whatever reason, you decided to use Dot: poor trusting Dotty, the woman you say you care for, to cover your tracks."

Grace pulled up onto her knees. Poppy jolted with fright, but the older woman didn't try to go any further. Instead she craned her neck and looked beseechingly into Poppy's face. "But I do care for her! I do. I would do anything to save her."

"Including killing my mother?"

Grace turned her head to look at Delilah, then reached out her arms like a child to a parent. "Oh, Delilah, I didn't mean to."

"You pushed her in front of a train!"

"I didn't, I didn't!" Grace lowered her arms and wrapped them around her thin chest, her shoulders heaving up and down. "I was trying to get her to listen to me. I was trying to tell her about the ledgers and how I needed to see them before she passed them on. But she wouldn't listen, she wouldn't. She ran.

I chased her. I kept calling her name. And then – and then – oh God!" She broke down into gut-wrenching sobs.

Poppy softened, reaching out a hand to comfort her aunt's old friend, but was stilled by a venomous look from Delilah.

When the older woman started to bring her breathing back under control Poppy took her firmly by the shoulders, looked into her eyes and asked, "Did you push Gloria in front of the train, Grace, like Elizabeth said?"

"No, I didn't. You might not believe me, but I didn't. Oh, Delilah, I would never hurt your mother, I wouldn't! She ran; she wasn't looking. It was my fault – yes, I don't deny that – but I didn't push her, I didn't!"

Delilah turned to Elizabeth, whose grey eyes were distant, staring back through time.

"Is she telling the truth, Elizabeth?"

"She's the shadow. She chased me."

"But did she kill my mother? Did you see her push Gloria under the train?"

Elizabeth's eyes came back into focus, then bored into Delilah's. "No. I don't think she did."

CHAPTER 36

The four women picked their way back to the hole in the fence. Poppy led the way, holding the box with one arm and Grace with the other. But Grace appeared defeated and Poppy doubted she would try to run. Behind them, Delilah and Elizabeth walked hand in hand, united by the memories they had just shared. Elizabeth had Poppy's satchel slung over one shoulder.

Poppy went through the fence first, pushing the box in front of her. Then she waited for the other women to climb through. From behind the line of poplars, she looked up and down the lane: apart from Grace's motorcar, twenty yards or so towards the gate, the road was empty. Poppy breathed a sigh of relief. They were almost on the home stretch.

Grace did not look in any state to drive. "Do you have the keys, Grace?"

She pulled them out of her pocket and passed them to Poppy.

"Delilah, do you think you can drive? If not, I'll give it a go."

"And kill us all? I think not, darling!" Delilah grinned at her and Poppy was relieved to see that the trauma of the last hours had not suppressed her spirit. Poppy handed the keys to her.

But about ten yards from the motorcar they heard the roar of an engine and looked up to see a silver racing Bentley speeding towards them. Poppy's first instinct was to run towards Grace's motor, but even if they made it there, they'd never get it cranked and started in time. And if, by a miracle, they did,

Grace's old engine would never outrun Alfie's sleek machine. The three other women must have had similar thoughts, so they stood together and waited for the Bentley to reach them. It didn't take long. Poppy thought for a split second that Alfie was going to run them down, but he didn't. The motor pulled up and he leaned out of the window and grinned.

"Hello, ladies. Fancy seeing you here."

"Let us go, Alfie. There are four of us, and you're on your own."

"That, Miss Denby, is where you are wrong." Melvyn Dorchester approached them on foot from the direction of the gatehouse. He was carrying a revolver.

"The night watchman won't be bothering us," he said to Alfie.

Alfie got out of the vehicle and leaned against it, his arms folded and his ankles crossed. "Well, well, well. You have given us quite the runaround, Lizzy."

Elizabeth glared at him, but didn't answer.

"I think you've got something of mine, Miss Denby," said Melvyn, pointing the revolver in her direction.

Poppy did not have a choice. She had to hand over the box. But just as she was about to, Grace stepped in front of her.

"You can take it, Dorchester, but there is more where that came from. Not of those years, perhaps, but from the years I worked for you. Remember when Dot Denby was blackmailing you —"

Melvyn's eyes narrowed and he pulled back the firing mechanism.

Grace sucked in her breath in alarm, but didn't back down. "Well, where do you think she got those tit-bits of information? That's right, from me. I have duplicate copies of your ledgers from 1903 to 1907, and believe me, they make for interesting reading.

The House of Lords, for instance, might be very interested to hear of your payments to Sinn Fein in November 1905... an English peer, providing funding for an Irish nationalist party in return for them not protesting the opening of one of your businesses in Dublin? Oh yes, that will go down very well."

"What do you want, Mrs Wilson?" Melvyn sneered.

"I want you to let my young friends go."

"And why would I do that?"

"Because I have given instructions that if I do not return safely with them by seven o'clock this evening, my duplicate ledgers will be delivered to the home of the editor of *The Daily Globe*."

"You're bluffing."

"Am I? Are you sure of that?"

"We can send Easling to Rolandson's house, Father."

Poppy, who wasn't sure whether or not Grace was bluffing but was grateful that the other woman was at least trying something, chipped in, "Well, unless you have a field radio unit in your motor, you won't be able to call him, will you, and" – she lifted Delilah's wrist and looked at her watch – "oh look, you only have ten minutes."

Alfie strode over to Poppy and slapped her across the face. The blow was so hard it knocked her to her knees.

"I've been wanting to do that since I first met you." Then he bent down and picked up the ledger box. Delilah launched herself at him; he parried with a punch to her solar plexus.

"Leave them alone!" Elizabeth sprung on her brother and knocked him over. The two siblings rolled around, each struggling to get the upper hand, until their father shot a round into the air. They stopped.

"Get up, both of you. Alfie, get the box. Lizzy, get in the Bentley. You three, line up beside that ditch."

"What are you going to do?" asked Grace, unable to hide the tremor in her voice.

"What I should have done years ago."

The women didn't move. Melvyn held the gun to Elizabeth's temple. Poppy, Delilah and Grace did as they were told.

"Now turn around."

Poppy reached out and took the hand of Grace on one side and Delilah on the other. Delilah was sobbing. Grace was shaking.

"Stop it, Father! Stop it! I'll do whatever you want. Send me back to the asylum, lock me up for the rest of my life, I don't care!"

"Take your sister away, Alfie."

"Noooooo!"

Suddenly there was a roar of an engine; a gunshot blasted; the women fell to their knees. But none of them had been shot. Poppy spun around to see a motorcycle and sidecar hurtling towards Melvyn Dorchester. Melvyn dived to take cover behind the Bentley while firing his revolver in the direction of the motorcycle; Alfie dragged Elizabeth along the ground by her hair.

A flash went off from the sidecar and Poppy saw a mop of red hair behind a camera. Rollo!

Daniel stopped the motorcycle and jumped off, throwing his whole weight against Poppy, Delilah and Grace, who tumbled like a set of skittles into the ditch.

"Put down the gun, Dorchester." It was Rollo. "You don't have enough bullets for all of us."

"You put down that camera, Rolandson, and I'll consider it."

"And miss the chance of having a front page pic of a peer of the realm shooting defenceless women? Oh, all right then."

Rollo put the camera down. "Now your turn."

Melvyn did not comply.

"How many shots has he fired?" whispered Daniel to Poppy.

"Er – I don't know. Two, I think. But he might have shot the night watchman, so that will be three."

"Then he should have three, possibly four, left. I'm going to draw his fire. Don't follow me."

Before Poppy could object, Daniel jumped up and sprinted across the road to the safety of the line of poplars, drawing two shots from Melvyn.

Now he's only got one or two bullets left, thought Poppy. Should she do the same as Daniel?

"Don't move! Any of you. Just killing one of you will be enough for me. Alfie, stop playing with your sister and get in the motor. And if anyone tries to follow, I'll put a bullet in Lizzy's head. Understand?"

"It's over, Dorchester," said Rollo. "There are too many witnesses this time. You'll never get away with it."

"I'll get away with it long enough to retire abroad, Yankee. Ah, what do you know, I have *two* bullets left. One for Lizzy and one for… now, who should it be…"

"Ahhhhhhhh!" Alfie screamed. Elizabeth was standing over him with Poppy's bolt cutters. He was rolling around holding his shoulder. She then turned and walked towards her father with the bolt cutters raised above her head like a club.

Melvyn trained the gun on her. "Stop, Lizzy, or I'll shoot. I don't want to. I love you, you're my daughter, but –" His words were cut short as the bolt cutters swung in an arc at his head, the gun went off, Elizabeth cried and fell to the ground. Alfie got up and reached for the gun that had fallen from his father's grip, but Poppy sprinted from the ditch, pushed him off balance and kicked the revolver out of his reach. She then fell to her knees beside Elizabeth. The older woman was holding her chest, her breathing laboured. Her father was lying three feet away with blood seeping from a wound on his head.

"Father!" Alfie struggled to his feet and stumbled to his parent. "You've killed him! You've killed him!"

"Unfortunately not," said Daniel, picking up the gun and training it on the two Dorchester men. "It's just a superficial wound. Didn't you learn anything in the army, captain?" Then he knelt beside Poppy, his gun still on Alfie and Melvyn. "How is she?"

Poppy had taken off her jacket and was staunching the wound in Elizabeth's chest. "It's missed her heart. But we need to get her to hospital."

"Can you and Delilah do that?"

Poppy nodded.

"Good. Rollo and I will finish up here."

"Give me the gun," said Rollo. "You take the camera, Dan. Poppy, get the keys for the Bentley."

Poppy stuck out her hand in front of Alfie. "So who's the slapper now?"

CHAPTER 37

26 JULY 1920

Poppy walked into the newsroom and took a seat at the back of the group of journalists. Rollo stopped mid-sentence and pointed his baton in Poppy's direction.

"Good of you to join us, Miz Denby."

"Sorry, I was showing Vicky Thompson the morgue and explaining about the Jazz Files."

"And where is our new editorial assistant now?"

"Ivan asked me to leave her there so he could show her the ropes."

There was a snigger of dirty laughter from the journalists. Rollo joined in.

Exasperated, Poppy snapped at them, "Mr Molanov is more of a gentleman than you lot put together."

They jeered back at her; Poppy retorted with a few choice put-downs.

Rollo raised his oversized hands to quieten them. "Now, now, children, we've got work to do. Poppy, I was just explaining to Mr Garfield here the background to today's lead about DCI Easling – aka Tricky Ricky – being charged with corruption and attempted murder. Ike, I don't believe you've met Miz Denby yet – this is the young woman behind the whole Dorchester exposé. Thanks to her it looks like Melvyn and Alfie Dorchester will be going away for a very long time. And Dorchester Junior will be stripped of his Victoria Cross."

There was a smattering of ironic applause.

A bespectacled, dark-skinned man stood up and reached out his hand. "Miss Denby, the pleasure is all mine. Ike Garfield." He spoke with a West Indian accent.

"Ike is joining our staff as a replacement for poor Bert."

Poppy's heart sank. She had been convinced that after all the work she had done on the Dorchester case – which had run as front page news in every newspaper from London to Paris for the last ten days – she would be rewarded with the vacant political editor position, particularly after Rollo had told her to find a replacement for herself for the editorial assistant job.

She had also finally had the courage to tell her parents what she'd been up to. They were, as predicted, furious with the deception and beside themselves with worry that she had been in such danger, but had surprised her by giving her their blessing.

"We've been praying for years that your aunt's attacker would be brought to justice, Poppy, but who would have thought the Lord would use you to do it?" said her father.

"Aye, he works in mysterious ways," commented her mother, before launching into a lecture on appropriate office attire for a young lady.

Poppy smoothed down her new red dress, fixed a smile on her face and tried to look happy to meet the West Indian journalist.

"Congratulations, Mr Garfield. I'm sure Bert would approve of the new appointment."

The diminutive editor nodded his approval. "Speaking of Bert, we've had some news." Everyone looked at Rollo. "The coroner's report has come in and it turns out Bert simply died of a heart attack."

Incredulous gasps filled the newsroom.

"So he wasn't pushed?" asked the sports reporter.

"It seems increasingly unlikely. Both Melvyn and Alfie say they didn't pay Lionel to do it. They could be lying, of course, but the coroner doesn't think so. Bert was a heart attack waiting to happen; we all knew that."

So it was just coincidence, then, thought Poppy, *Bert falling and sparking the investigation that led to the Dorchesters being exposed.* Or was it? What was it her mother had said? The Lord works in mysterious ways... She wished she knew what mysterious way he was working in now by not giving her the job she wanted. But no doubt she'd find out. Eventually...

"What's the latest on Mrs Wilson, Poppy?"

Poppy forced herself to stop thinking about her "lost job" and turned her attention back to Rollo.

"She's getting out on bail tomorrow," she answered. "Her court case is scheduled for the end of August. If she's convicted of perverting the course of justice, she's likely to get two years. They'll be looking at her covering up the truth of Gloria's death in 1913, as well as her attempts to do away with the ledger evidence now. But her efforts to save us from Alfie and Melvyn will hopefully go in her favour."

There were grunts of agreement around the room.

Ah, poor Grace. She had turned herself in to the police at the hospital when they came to see the reported gunshot victim. With a solicitor present from *The Globe* – sent by Rollo to make sure none of Easling's cronies were involved – she said she would confess everything. It turned out that she didn't have duplicates of Dorchester's earlier ledgers, but she did say she would tell them as much as she could remember of what was in them. The police took statements from Poppy and Delilah, in which both women stressed how Grace had tried to save them. The police said the statements would be presented to the Director of Public Prosecutions.

"We'll get Ike to cover it, shall we?" offered Rollo, smiling at the West Indian journalist. "You're probably a bit too close to it all, Poppy."

Poppy smarted. Another slap in the face. Of course, she knew Rollo was right: she *was* too close to it – at home and at the office. It had been left to her to tell Aunt Dot that the most important person in her life had been deceiving her all these years. Dot was devastated, but insisted on going to see Grace at the police station. She had come out, her eyes red with tears, and said, "Grace will be coming home with us when she's released, Poppy."

"Are you sure that's a good idea, Aunt Dot?"

Dot had taken Poppy's hand and said, "I've forgiven her, pet. I want you to do the same."

Poppy wasn't sure she could, but she would try.

Elizabeth was also staying with them. She had been released from hospital three days previously, a week after she had been shot. The bullet had missed all her major organs, but she had lost a lot of blood. Dot had said that if she didn't want to stay under the same roof as Grace, she would arrange for her to move to Delilah's. Elizabeth had said she would think about it and give them her decision that evening at the theatre.

Poppy smiled to herself. Ah well, perhaps she was not going to get her dream career, but Delilah was. Despite missing two days of rehearsal and being the subject of a city-wide manhunt, Delilah had been called upon to take the role of Titania after the lead and the understudy both came down with flu two days into the run. Poppy, Elizabeth and Dot were going to see her that night.

"And finally," said Rollo, "to entertainment. Firstly, I'm spitting nails about it, but I have to tell you that the police released Lionel Saunders without charge."

"What?" came the outraged chorus.

Rollo raised his hands. "Yes, yes, I know, and I'm getting the legal lads to appeal it, but the official line is that there's not enough evidence to charge him on anything criminal. They say it's an internal matter for *The Globe*. So naturally I've sacked him."

The journalists grunted their approval.

"Hang on, there's more. I've just heard *The Courier* have hired him as their new entertainment editor."

More howls of outrage.

"I know, I know. There's nothing we can do about it – for now. But we do have to replace him – internally."

Poppy looked around, wondering which of the journalists had applied for a transfer to the plum position that allowed flexible hours, late mornings and all-expenses-paid hobnobbing with the rich and famous.

"And I am happy to announce that *The Daily Globe*'s new arts and entertainment editor is… drum roll, please, gentlemen… Miz Poppy Denby!"

There was a round of applause and a few wolf whistles.

"Well, Poppy, what are you waiting for? Take a bow."

And Poppy did.

Poppy, Dot and Elizabeth emerged from the theatre to a wall of flash photography. Elizabeth tried to cover her face, but Dot wheeled herself to the front and greeted the photographers with her most dazzling smile.

"All right, boys. One at a time."

Poppy chuckled to herself and escorted Elizabeth to Grace's motorcar. Delilah had said she would drive them all to Oscar's after she had finished her "press duties". With Elizabeth safely in the back seat, Poppy went back to get her aunt, who was now sharing centre stage with Delilah.

"Oh, wasn't she a fabulous Titania! I'll let you in on a little secret, boys. Robert Atkins himself told me she is the best Titania he's seen since – well, since me!"

The journalists laughed and the photographers snapped away at the two actresses who had recently starred in a real-life drama that had brought down the great Lord Dorchester and shaken the entire House of Lords.

"I believe congratulations are in order." Daniel was at Poppy's shoulder.

She started, cross with herself that her heart still raced at his voice. She had hardly seen him since the evening outside the train yard. He had been sent straight to Paris to collect the evidence of Alfie's cowardice in Flanders and to cover the French fall-out of the Marie Curie Radium Institute revelations. On his return he had taken a few days' personal leave to deal with a "family issue". The few times he had been in the office he had tried to speak to Poppy, but each time she had conspired a way to escape.

"Yes, thank you. I've got Lionel's job; I'm just not working tonight."

"No, but you will be. And we'll be working together – a lot. So I think we need to clear the air."

"Look, Mr Rokeby, I have to help my aunt get in the motor…"

"Please, Poppy, we need to talk. If not now, then give me a time and a place and I'll be there."

Poppy felt her throat tighten and her eyes well up with tears. She turned away from him.

He reached out and took her hand. "Please, Poppy."

She spun around, not caring whether anyone was watching. "Don't 'please Poppy' me! You led me to believe you had feelings for me. You even asked me out to dinner!"

"I do have feelings for you. Which is exactly why I asked you to dinner. Look, it was stupid of me not to tell you about my children before. I'm sorry, but please give me another chance."

"Oh? Another chance? And what do you think your wife will think of that?"

"My... oh Poppy, no. Is that what this is all about?" He slapped his hand to his forehead. "Oh, how could I be so stupid? Of course it is."

He tried to take her hand again. She pulled away. So he took her by the shoulders and held her firmly. She thought of calling for help, but then she noticed the look in his eyes and didn't. She would hear him out, once and for all; she owed him that at least.

"All right, Daniel, I'm listening. But make it quick."

Daniel took in a deep breath and then exhaled. "My wife... my wife died two years ago of the Spanish flu. The woman you spoke to on the telephone is my sister. She lives with me to help look after the children. They are Amy and Arthur, three and five. I couldn't keep working without her. She's a godsend. But she does get a bit protective and I see that she allowed you to believe something that wasn't true. And I'm sorry. And if I'd handled this better I would have –"

He's not married. He's not married. He's not... Poppy reached up her finger and touched his lips.

"Shhhh! No, I'm sorry. She didn't lead me to believe anything. It's what I assumed. And I'm sorry I didn't give you a chance to explain – you or anyone. Mavis tried to and I... Oh Daniel, I'm sorry! Please forgive me."

Daniel looked at her with such immense relief that she almost laughed. "Well, is that dinner invitation still open?"

He grinned. "It certainly is! Do you have any preferences?"

"Oscar's," said Poppy. "I feel like dancing."

THE WORLD OF POPPY DENBY:
A HISTORICAL NOTE

The Jazz Files is set in the summer of 1920. It is less than two years since the armistice that ended the Great War, resulting in the death of seventeen million people, and only eighteen months since the height of the Spanish flu that wiped out a further seventy million. Poppy, who is just starting out on a career in journalism, is full of hope – but sorrow is never far away in *The Jazz Files*. While some characters are living the high life, others are in misery. And so it was with society as a whole. The 1920s – alternatively known as the Roaring Twenties, the Jazz Age and the decade of the Bright Young People – is characterized by a generation desperate to leave the horror of war behind them and to create a "bright new world". Little did they know, the world they were so blithely building would crash into economic darkness within nine years, and be at war, once again, by the time Poppy turns forty.

But in the summer of 1920 they did not know this and they danced to new jazzy music from America and wore skimpy dresses and cropped or "shingled" hair that scandalized their Edwardian mothers. Everything was new, daring and very self-consciously turning its back on the past. I have tried to stick as closely as possible to the fashion trends in clothing, music and dance of the period, but was frustrated at times that the more iconic styles that we now readily associate with the 1920s only came to the fore later in the decade. The Charleston, for instance, was first danced in London clubs in 1924, so even though readers might assume Delilah was dancing the Charleston with her twirling arms and legs, I do not actually call it this. Likewise, the jazz music associated with the period only became common in London clubs a few years later, but I have taken some liberties in assuming that Oscars' Jazz Club might have been ahead of its time. However, the specific jazz songs and tunes that are mentioned in the book had been released in America by 1920 and it might be assumed that they had made their way to British shores via phonographic recordings. I have no evidence however that they were played live in clubs in London so soon after their release.

Charlie Chaplin's film *The Kid* was only released in 1921, and that's when he actually visited London to promote it; but I have brought it forward a year to 1920, because Delilah told me she was desperate to meet him – and who can say no to Delilah? Generally though, I have not played fast and loose with the historical timeline and have only changed things when I felt the story would be poorer if I did not. This is after all a novel and not a social history text.

I originally conceived of Poppy as a suffragette reporter sleuth, but in the early planning stages, did not feel comfortable in the 1905–1913 period. So I decided to move the story forward to 1920 and have Poppy be the niece of a suffragette. As a result, the fabulous world of 1920s fashion, music and "jazz journalism" opened up to me. But more than that, I felt that I could now emotionally empathize with Poppy. I was born in the early 1970s and grew up with stories of the brave women of the 1960s and 1970s who made such strides forward for equal rights for women. So by the time I went to university in 1989 there were almost no courses or careers closed to me. I owe a great debt to these women, just as Poppy does to her aunt and the brave men and women who fought tirelessly for equality between the sexes. The Chelsea Six are a fictional group of people, but the Women's Suffrage and Political Union did actually exist. It was founded by Emmeline Pankhurst and her family. For more on the work of the WSPU please see some of the books I have listed below or visit www.poppydenby.com where you will find links to lots of online material.

The Sex Disqualification (Removal) Act Lord Dorchester so controversially supports was passed in 1919, not early 1920 as suggested in *The Jazz Files;* I changed the date so that Bert Isaacs could still be working on the story when Poppy first meets him. As there was no equivalent groundbreaking legislation in the summer of 1920, I felt this was a necessary anachronism. Marjorie Reynolds, the MP, is also a fictional character, and the Act was actually shepherded through parliament by the real-life MP Nancy Astor.

Marie Curie did visit New York in 1921 to raise money to finance her research at the Radium Institute in Paris, but the notion that she was so hard up before that as to justify being involved in a shady blackmail plot is pure conjecture on my part. Besides, Sophie Blackburn has already told you that it was she who did it, not Marie – and that's the story I'm sticking to!

In 1920, there was a real newspaper in London called *The London Globe*, but it merged with the *Pall Mall Gazette* in 1921. *The Daily Globe* is not based on this newspaper and is born purely of my imagination. I have though read many tabloid newspapers of the period in the archives of the British Library, including *The Daily Mail*, and have drawn my ideas for *The Globe* from all of them. *The Courier* that is the rival of *The Globe* in *The Jazz Files*, is also a fictional newspaper. Any similarities to tabloids still in print today is purely coincidental.

For further reading:

Visit www.poppydenby.com for more historical information on the period, gorgeous pictures of 1920s fashion and décor, audio and video links to 1920s music and news clips, a link to the author's website, as well as news about upcoming titles in the *Poppy Denby Investigates* series.

Housego, Molly and Neil R. Storey, *The Women's Suffrage Movement,* Shire Library, Shire Publications, Oxford, 2013.

Marr, Andrew, *My Trade: a short history of British Journalism,* Pan Macmillan, London, 2005.

Pankhurst, Christabel, *Unshackled,* Cresset Women's Voices, London, 1987.

Shepherd, Janet and John Shepherd, *1920s Britain,* Shire Living Histories, Shire Publications, Oxford, 2010.

Shrimpton, Jayne, *Fashion in the 1920s,* Shire Publications, Oxford, 2013.

Taylor, D.J., *Bright Young People: the rise and fall of a generation 1918–1940,* Vintage, Random House, London, 2008.

Waugh, Evelyn, *Vile Bodies,* Chapman and Hall, London, 1930.

Waugh, Evelyn, *Scoop,* (1938) Penguin Classics, Penguin, London, 2000.

For more information and fun photos about
Poppy and her world go to:
www.poppydenby.com